CONNECT WITH NATURE

One of the best things you can do for yourself, others and planet Earth

Les C. Higgins

Publisher: Inspiring Publishers,
P.O. Box 159, Calwell, ACT Australia 2905
Email: publishaspg@gmail.com
http://www.inspiringpublishers.com

A catalogue record for this book is available from the National Library of Australia

National Library of Australia The Prepublication Data Service

Author: Les C. Higgins
Title: Connect With Nature
Genre: Non-fiction
ISBN: 978-1-922618-76-4

We will never be truly healthy, satisfied, or fulfilled if we
live apart and alienated from the environment from which we
evolved.

Stephen R. Kellert, *Birthright: People
and Nature in the Modern World*

CONTENTS

PART 2 THE GOOD THINGS TO EXPECT WHEN YOU DO

1. INTRODUCTION

A connection with nature is one of the most desirable and valuable relationships we can have. It is a relationship that is good for us and good for nature. I know this from personal experience and from the evidence of thousands of studies. For us, it is a source of happiness, well-being and health. For nature, it is critical because nature connectedness motivates us to take care of the natural environment—and if ever there was a time when nature needed our care, it is now.

I am a deeply nature-connected person. That means I relate to nature as I would a friend. I respond to the inhabitants of nature and the environments they occupy with affection, interest, respect and concern for their well-being. Take my balcony plants, for example. I value their company, and I enjoy watching them grow, flower and occasionally play host to birds. I look after them conscientiously. I even feel regret when one of them dies. For their part, the plants give me pleasure, satisfaction, relaxation and pride in my gardening skills.

I enjoy almost everything about nature, especially being surrounded by it. The comedian and film maker, Woody Allen, once quipped: 'I am at two with nature'. But that's not me; I feel at one with the natural world. Nature is an important part of how I see myself and how the world sees me. I need regular doses of it just as I need love, nourishment, exercise, rest, happiness and a sense of purpose in life. Caring for the natural environment is hugely important to me.

I greatly value my friendship with nature—my *nature connectedness*. It has broadened and built me as a person, steered my life in unexpected and highly beneficial directions and furnished me with a host of precious memories. The friendship is one of the key strands of my life. Without it, my life would have been much less interesting, satisfying and fulfilling.

I am far from alone in appreciating the importance of nature connectedness. It is increasingly the focus of scientific attention. The University of Derby in the United Kingdom, for example, has set up the Nature Connectedness Research Group for the purpose of studying and promoting it. The Convention on Biological Diversity (CBD) has elevated it to prominence on the world stage. The CBD emerged from the Earth Summit organised by the United Nations in 1992. The purpose of the CBD is to unite the world's nations in preserving the diversity of the Earth's ecosystems and to ensure that the benefits of that biodiversity are available to everyone. The 196 countries that have signed up to the Convention meet and report regularly. The 2018 conference of the CBD issued this powerful and urgent call to action:

> The time is now. The evidence is clear. One of the most important things that any of us can do for ourselves, those we love, people throughout the world, and the living systems that support us all is to connect with nature[1].

This is certainly a big call, but it is backed by a wealth of scientific evidence from research in fields as diverse as environmental psychology and forestry; eco-psychology and horticulture; leisure studies and public health; architecture and neuroscience[2]. Much of this evidence tells us that we *need* nature connectedness just as we need food and close relationships with others[3]. It is an essential ingredient of life. Without water, death is inevitable. Without close and supportive social ties, physical and mental health are in jeopardy. Without nature connectedness, any chance of living our best life is missed. Living without the companionship of nature is rather like playing a piano but ignoring the black keys or having a sailing boat but never using the spinnaker.

Does the CBD's call strike a chord with you? Does it stir you to think about your relationship with nature? Does it move you to strengthen that relationship? Do you feel that the call is relevant to you in any way? If you answer, yes, to any of these questions, this book is for you because it will help you to connect with nature and derive enormous benefits from doing so.

Connecting with nature is easy, largely because we do not have to look far to find it. Some people mistakenly believe that nature is always outdoors, often remote and sometimes alien. For these people, such things as animals in the wild, national parks, ocean beaches, wilderness lakes and even some landscaped gardens are 'genuine' nature, but not the likes of street trees, household gardens, urban zoos, pets, and nature photographs. But nature comes in all these forms and more, making it accessible to everyone. Nature can be as close as the plants in your living room or on your balcony or patio.

My balcony plants are nature for me, not because I have been told they are, but because that is how I think and feel about them. I get a buzz from them as I do from trees, shrubs and flowers in the wild, a different buzz perhaps, but still a genuine one. I rely on my own intuition and feelings to tell me what nature is and is not. If my brain tells me that something is nature, then nature it is. The happy consequence is that I can find some form of nature virtually everywhere. You can look forward to doing the same, especially with the help of this book.

In saying this, I am aware that modern life throws up many impediments to having quality time in nature. The fact is that there is a growing disconnect between humanity and nature as people engage less, rather than more, with the natural world[4]. This is often put down to a lack of time and opportunity. The modern lifestyle is typically a crowded one. For city dwellers, it may also seem that there is little authentic or 'real' nature to access. Cities everywhere are becoming larger, denser and taller, almost inevitably at the expense of green space. Nature is being crowded out of our lives for another reason as well—the growing allure and convenience of electronic communication and entertainment. This trend is having a particularly concerning impact on the lives of children. Today's children have fewer opportunities to play in nature than did their parents and grandparents. This makes them vulnerable to what Richard Louv calls nature-deficit disorder, which is not a medical condition but a deficiency of intellectual, emotional and social experiences that are necessary for optimal growth and development[5].

This book describes an approach to connecting with nature that takes account of the personal barriers that may be in the way. It is a simple and direct approach that puts the action of connecting with nature ahead of thinking too much about doing so. This may appear that the cart (acting) is being put before the horse (justifying). Logically it is, but the logical way does not always work best psychologically. Countless times I have heard people say something like: 'I know that I should spend more time in nature, but...'. Such remarks are made even by people who know that nature is good for them and are aware of what they are missing. *Knowing* about nature's benefits does not necessarily motivate people to seek them. *Emotions* or feelings are usually required as well, and in many instances, feelings alone can do the job.

The story of my own journey to nature connectedness illustrates the point. The journey itself supplied all the motivation I needed. I was drawn on from activity to activity by the pleasures and rewards generated by the activities themselves. The story also exemplifies the 'good things' nature connectedness brings to individual and family life. I hope that there is something in the story that is interesting and encouraging for you. Its details make it my story alone, of course, but viewed broadly, it is the kind of life-transforming story that could easily be yours.

The story of my friendship with nature

I was not always a nature-connected person. My journey to nature connectedness began when I was in my thirties. Prior to then, nature did not figure much in my life. I appreciated natural scenery and enjoyed visiting natural places for recreation and socialising, but that was about it. The starting point of the journey was a family decision to take up bushwalking as a regular activity. My wife, Margaret, and I were heavily engaged professionally. We had other pressing commitments including caring for aged parents. It was a demanding and stressful time that occasionally put a dent in our emotional stamina and mental health. We both felt the need for a recreational activity that we could share with our two young daughters.

We linked up with experienced walkers from The National Parks Association of New South Wales (NPA), a conservation and bushwalking organisation. Saturday bushwalks became a regular family pastime. The girls were unfazed by having to walk in adult company; if anything, it made them feel grown-up. The bushwalking was also good for their self-esteem. They did not mind that their peers were not into bushwalking to the extent that they were. It helped them to accept that being your own person and doing your own thing are OK.

Not long after joining the NPA, I was lured into bush camping by the opportunity to take part in a bushcraft course where I could learn exotic but fun-to-do skills, such as fire-lighting without matches, making rope from grass, and building a shelter from natural materials. With hired gear and mentoring from the course leader, I found myself pitching a tent for the first time, cooking over a fire and sleeping in a down-filled bag on a bed of dry bracken covered by a ground sheet and a short piece of foam. Having to do this repeatedly and with the leader's expertise to call on, I gradually adapted to sleeping in a tent and living out of a pack.

At the same time, I became more aware of nature's sights, sounds, scents and textures. I also discovered the delights of a campfire, especially the soporific pleasure of 'fire gazing'—watching the dancing flames and glowing coals. Also, for the first time in my life, I was getting to know nature intimately. Although my mind remained centred on what I was doing—learning camping and bushcraft skills—my emotions were prompting me to experience nature for itself, not just as a setting for my activities. A new chapter in the story of my relationship with nature had opened.

I embraced backpacking enthusiastically. I added regular backpacking weekends to the Saturday family bushwalks. Now with my own state-of-the art gear, I became very focussed on becoming a competent backpacker. I was happiest after an outing if my boots, pack, tent and cooking gear had served me exactly as I wanted them to.

Although I was intent on honing backpacking and camping skills, my attention to nature was growing; it had to. Wilderness backpacking requires taking note of what is around you, especially for keeping track of where you are and where you need to go. Apart from that, the tempo and shape of a backpacking day expose you to the sensations and rhythms of the natural world—to the softening hues and growing stillness of twilight, for example, and the chorusing of birds at dawn.

I did virtually all my backpacking in national parks, mainly the World Heritage listed Blue Mountains National Park. Experiencing the magnificence, marvels and mystery of the Blue Mountains and places like it continued to deepen and reshape my relationship with nature. Being in nature gradually became as important to me as the activities I did there. I particularly valued the emotional 'highs' that nature's beauty, vastness and wonder evoked. The state of joy, contentment and bonhomie left by these highs—the 'bushwalker's glow' I call it—can last for hours and even days. As these highs are addictive, I found myself hooked on nature.

Meanwhile, my wife and daughters were becoming capable and enthusiastic day walkers. So much so, that they chose to accompany me on a trek in the Himalaya of Nepal organised by Ausventure, a well-regarded adventure holiday company. I was delighted and surprised as they had never camped, but here they were electing to do just that for 14 days. Granted it was to be a totally supported trek, effectively a succession of day walks, with all aspects of the camping looked after by a Sherpa team. Even so, a fair measure of adaptability and resolve was required, not to mention fitness and stamina. In preparation, we did a couple of practice campouts and many training walks, some on the steepest tracks in the Blue Mountains. Appropriate clothing, footwear and medical items were purchased, and strategies devised for coping with 14 days without showers or flushing toilets.

The trek was life changing for all four of us. We were captured by the majestic beauty of the mountains and the simplicity, routine, rhythm, fun and friendliness of camp life. The unwavering joy and kindness of the Sherpas won our hearts. Cultural contacts with the local people were limited but those we had were heartwarming, mind-broadening and sometimes deeply affecting. Coping successfully with the physical and emotional demands of the trek was especially good for the girls, boosting their confidence, self-esteem and resilience. Overall, the experience gave us new eyes through which to see ourselves and the world. Tears were shed at the end of the trek and for days after. We had fallen permanently in love with the Himalaya and the Nepalese people.

We returned to bushwalking in Australia with renewed zeal. Margaret and the girls ventured into full-pack walking and I introduced variety and challenge to my bushwalking by tackling other outdoor activities. These included 'off-track' exploring, rock climbing and canyoning (walking, wading, swimming, jumping and abseiling through deep, narrow and usually watery sandstone chasms). I also returned to Nepal, co-leading a four-week trek with high altitude components.

When an adult education organisation invited me to run an introductory bushwalking and camping course, I accepted with some trepidation but keen to share the delights of nature activities with others. I did not imagine that the course would run annually (sometimes bi-annually) for the next 25 years and out of it the

Yarrawood Bushwalking Club would emerge. My involvement in the course and Yarrawood greatly enriched my nature activities, especially by widening my circle of bushwalking friends. Soon after I began running the courses, the Ausventure team invited me to join them as an honorary trek leader. Many of my bushwalking friends joined me on my Ausventure Himalayan treks.

By any reckoning, I have had a long and extraordinarily rich association with nature. It was inevitable that I would become a deeply nature-connected person. I was certainly that by 2002, the year I retired from my job as a university teacher and researcher. I knew that I had a deep relationship with nature even though I did not use the terms 'nature-connected' and 'nature connectedness' to label it. At that time, these terms did not have the currency and meaning they have today. I was also aware that my experience was not special or unique. While teaching the course, walking with Yarrawood and leading treks, I had seen that nature does good things to and for all sorts of people. But I was still to discover just how astonishingly good it can be. Making that discovery was the next (and probably final) chapter in the story of my friendship with nature.

There I was in 2002, newly retired from my university teaching and research position and still passionately engaged (almost as a second career) in nature activities. I had recently co-written a natural history and bushwalking guidebook centred on the Sydney region. Selecting walks to feature in the book was challenging because there were so many to choose from. The task prompted me to reflect on my own bushwalking experiences—what they were, where I had them and how they had affected me. This stocktake made me more conscious of what nature had contributed to my life, its emotional impact especially. Memories of times and places associated with intense pleasure, awe, wonder and fulfilment flooded to the surface. I felt a responsibility to choose wisely so that users of the book would be stimulated by nature in the same way.

I had these bushwalking memories in my mind when I turned my thoughts to finding a retirement project. A merging of my academic and leisure interests gave me the idea of studying what science had to say about nature's effects on people. I had no notion initially just how vast, absorbing and rewarding the project would be. Nor did I anticipate how monumentally it would enlarge my understanding of what nature connectedness had done (and continues to do) for me and what it can do for everyone.

From the outset of the project, I was captivated by what I was learning. In no time, my understanding and appreciation of what had happened to me on my nature connectedness journey were transformed. Like someone finding more in a work of art after being helped to view it more deeply, I was viewing my nature experiences through new lenses. I found myself re-living and enjoying many of the experiences afresh.

Early in the project, I encountered an idea that supercharged my interest and radically changed my understanding of myself and of what it means to be human. This was Professor Edward O Wilson's proposition (or hypothesis as he called it) that we humans are born with a disposition to find nature interesting, attractive and inviting. Wilson labelled the disposition, 'biophilia' (meaning love of living things)[6]. Biophilia is in our make-up, Wilson says, because we are members of a species that has spent up to 300,000 years living in natural environments. Without biophilia, our species would not have survived because it underpins our ability and motivation to understand and negotiate natural environments. Although most present-day humans live in cities and towns, biophilia endures in us because our genes have not yet caught up with our change of address. Even committed city dwellers strive to have some form of nature, real, virtual or artificial, in their lives.

Encountering biophilia gave me an 'Ah ha!' moment. Here in a single concept was an explanation of why my nature activities were so rewarding. All the aesthetic pleasure (the 'beauty buzz'), awe, wonder, tranquillity, relaxation, restoration, rejuvenation, mental stimulation and curiosity nature had given me stemmed from biophilia, from the deep urge within me to make the natural world my kin. Biophilia directed and energised my nature connectedness journey. At the same time, the journey nurtured my biophilia. This was tremendously important. All of us are born with the seeds of biophilia, but not all experience biophilia to the full. If biophilia is ignored and not used, it can fade and atrophy.

Nature connectedness nurtures our biophilia by increasing our openness to nature and our capacity to benefit from nature experiences[7]. But even before we become nature connected, many of nature's rewards and benefits are available to us. Everyone can enjoy the calming pleasure and other benefits of even the simplest of nature contacts, a stroll through a garden, for example, or watching the waves swirl up and back across a beach. Most nature encounters provide an exciting foretaste of what a deeper relationship with nature has in store.

Other good news is that there are many ways of connecting with nature apart from being constantly or regularly immersed in it. I was intrigued to learn, for example, that photos of nature can affect us in similar ways to the real thing, evoking aesthetic pleasure, relaxation, awe and empathy[8]. I was also surprised to discover how little contact is needed for nature to be beneficial. This means that there are ways of connecting with nature for virtually everyone regardless of their circumstances—an encouraging thought for anyone who is still deciding whether a nature connectedness journey is for them.

A nature connectedness journey for you

This book asks you to consider starting (or resuming) your own nature connectedness journey with action rather than theory. It suggests you begin with an appealing and easy-to-do activity and then proceed at your own pace and on your own terms. Part 1 of the book, the 'how to' part, will help you do this. Part 1 is all about connecting with nature in ways that are suitable for you, beginning with a chapter that explains how common barriers to connecting with nature can be addressed. A chapter detailing a host of nature or 'green' activities follows. Among the activities described are many that can be done as part of everyday life. A full chapter is devoted to making connecting with nature a family affair. Parents, grandparents, relatives and carers can find guidelines in this chapter for fostering children's all-important free play and for providing activities suitable for children of different ages. Part 1 also includes a chapter on turning to nature in difficult times. This is not a chapter of therapeutic guidelines but one of stories about people who have found comfort, strength and healing in times of grief, mental distress and social difficulties. The final chapter in Part 1 turns the spotlight on caring for nature. Connecting with nature is all about caring—caring for yourself (and those near to you), all life and planet Earth itself.

Part 2 of the book is intended to serve you in the way my project served me. It offers new lenses through which you can view and reflect on your journey. This will enable you to enjoy many of your nature experiences afresh, to get to know them again for the first time, so to speak. There is a lot to be said for having nature experiences first and then reflecting on them. Words alone cannot capture the subjective or 'felt' features of most nature experiences. The emotional and spiritual content of aesthetic pleasure, awe or tranquillity, for example, is beyond the power of words to capture. It is only by experiencing such complex emotions that you can say 'I know them'.

Part 2 delivers the promise of the book to describe what you can expect from your nature connectedness journey. I am confident that you will be astonished by the extent and diversity of the things that are in store. The 'things' are so varied that it is difficult to find an apt label for them. 'Benefits' is probably as good as any. The benefits of nature connectedness described in Part 2 include aesthetic pleasure, awe, wonder, relaxation, restoration (from mental fatigue), tranquillity, camaraderie, enriched spirituality, strengthened resilience, reduced risk of disease, a conscience-driven concern for nature and, for your children, an 'advantaged childhood'.

How to use this book

I suggest you use this book as a companion and guide. Unlike a novel, the book is not meant to be read from beginning to end. It recognises that readers will have different needs and interests according to where they are on their nature connectedness journey. A person new to nature activities, for example, will find much of immediate relevance and interest in Chapter 2 and 3 ('Getting Started' and 'Do It Your Way'). A parent, however, might be drawn first to Chapter 4 ('Make It a Family Affair'). It is also possible, of course, that some readers may be attracted first to the chapters in Part 2.

The book's expanded table of contents and index are provided to make it easier to navigate the book in the way that most suits you. All chapters in the book can be read independently, although one or two chapters, the one on health, Chapter 10, for example, draw on the content of previous chapters to some extent, but even these chapters are largely free-standing.

Although solidly science-based, the book is written for the general reader. There are endnotes for anyone seeking more information about the science. Because discoveries about nature's effects on our brains, health and well-being are being reported almost every week, I will use my blog (www.ourgreengenes.wordpress.com) and the book's website (www.connectwithnatureguide.com) to keep the book's contents as up-to-date as possible. You are warmly invited to become a regular reader of my blog posts and visitor to the website.

PART 1

HOW TO CONNECT WITH NATURE

2. GETTING STARTED (For the first time or again)

Becoming nature-connected is a journey. Really, it is two journeys in one. The first is the physical or 'outer' journey comprising the succession of nature (or green) activities we undertake. The second is the 'inner' journey involving our minds and hearts. The two journeys are made together. In going outside to watch a sunset, for example, the 'going' and the 'watching' are steps on the outer journey; the emotions of pleasure and awe stirred by the spectacle are typical of the inner journey.

People who are fortunate enough to live or work in natural settings encounter nature as part of daily life. They are taking the outer journey without having to think about it. But that is not how it is for most of us. As urban dwellers, we need to be thoughtful and deliberate about the outer journey. Otherwise, nature and nature activities can easily fade into the background of our lives. Becoming nature connected does not simply happen for us; we must choose to take the journey by purposefully adding nature activities to our lives.

This chapter and the other four chapters in Part 1 will help you plan and sustain your personal nature connectedness journey. This must be a journey that progresses through activities that you want to do and believe you *can* do. Motivation to take the journey must come from within you. It should be motivation that is not driven in any way by negative feelings such as fear, guilt and shame, or by the pressure of other people's expectations.

I am confident that you can manage a successful nature connectedness journey for two reasons. First, there are literally hundreds of green activities for you to choose from. Second, because the activities are so varied, there are 'want to' and 'can do' activities for virtually everyone.

In fact, you may have already built green activities into your life and not be aware that you have. You can find out by taking a moment with this experiencing nature checklist[1]

1. Do I experience natural light that is constantly changing in direction and intensity?
2. Do I experience natural ventilation?
3. Do I experience open and moving water?
4. Do I experience plant and animal life along with nature's rhythms and cycles?
5. Do I experience the sights, sounds, textures, tastes and scents of nature?
6. Do I experience the natural world's diversity, complexity and order?
7. Do I experience the excitement of exploration, discovery, wonder and awe in nature?
8. Do I experience natural places where I feel calm, relaxed and restored?
9. Do I experience tranquillity in natural places?
10. Do I experience views of natural landscapes and other features from positions of safety and security?
11. Do I experience different forms of natural beauty?
12. Do I experience unspoiled nature and/or natural places where I feel remote from urban life?

Perhaps you have been encouraged to discover from your answers that you are more of a nature-connected person than you thought. Even if this is not the case, the checklist can be useful and supportive to you in other ways. First, it provides you with a snapshot of what connecting with nature 'feels' like; it tells you what experiences to expect: 'natural light that is constantly changing in direction and intensity'; 'natural ventilation'; 'plant and animal life'; 'nature's rhythms and cycles' and so on. Second, you can use the checklist in much the same way as you would a tour guide. But rather than places of interest to be visited, the checklist points you towards the kinds of nature experiences that are not-to-be-missed.

If you are contemplating the journey on behalf of children as well, you may be wondering whether the checklist can be applied to them. It can, but it needs to be supplemented by the more specific guidelines relating to children that you will find in Chapter 4.

Don't be hard on yourself or lose heart if the checklist revealed that your involvement with nature is rather 'lean'. Many aspects of modern urban life stand in the way of being a nature person: economic pressures, crowded lifestyles, the blurring of the boundaries between home and work and the prevalence of video-based and electronic entertainment, for example. If you are only just thinking about having more contact with nature, be encouraged. You are on the way. Thinking about or contemplating doing something is a step towards preparing to make a move, which in turn paves the way for finally taking action[2]. Regardless of the stage you are at, I am confident that there is material in the following sections of this chapter and in the next chapter that will help you to move forward (so read on).

Don't let mental barriers get in the way

While many of the obstacles to connecting with nature are genuine, others are mostly in our minds. Some people are put off spending time in natural settings by misconceptions about what nature is and what nature activities involve. The mistaken belief that nature exists only in rural regions, national parks and wilderness areas, for example, rules out many green activities that can be done at home, in urban neighbourhoods and by travelling short distances to parks, gardens, zoos and bushland reserves. Recall the point I made in Chapter 1: if it looks and feels like nature to you, then nature it is.

Another off-putting belief is that natural environments are typically inhospitable, uncomfortable, hazardous and inhabited by unfriendly creatures. If this were true, few people would visit them. But natural places tend to be hugely popular. There are effective and ample ways to be comfortable and safe in them, and to co-exist companionably with their inhabitants. Misadventures in nature do occur but they are usually not as serious or as dramatic as reported in (sometimes sensationalising) news stories. The truth is that green activities lie at every point along the spectrum from easy and virtually risk-free to arduous and hazardous. Even activities nearer the extreme end of the spectrum do not necessarily involve danger and hardship. Nowadays you can be safe, dry, warm, comfortable and well-fed in most outdoor conditions. But if you have feelings of unease and uncertainty about natural environments, 'wilder' ones especially, don't be deterred. Start your nature connectedness journey anyway. The best way to remedy feelings of alienation from nature is simply to venture into the natural world starting with ways that you know will be agreeable.

Another of the mental barriers to seeking happiness and well-being in nature stems from the culture of 'busyness' that tends to emerge in modern societies. Not only do we live crowded lifestyles, but we are coming to accept that this is as it should be, that being busy is normal and expected. My late friend, writer, inventor and artist Tory Hughes alerted me to how damaging this culture is for nature connectedness. I asked her why people were retreating from nature and missing out on so much pleasure, happiness, personal fulfilment and friendship as a result. According to Tory, it is because people have difficulty giving themselves permission to do otherwise. Real and perceived work, social and family obligations, she said, are getting in the way of doing things that really matter for oneself (and indirectly for those dear to us), including finding health and happiness in nature.

Tory's observation prompted me to compose my own connecting with nature permission statement. This is the result:

I give myself permission to:
- acknowledge my need for nature and to give priority to meeting that need

- work less and play more in natural environments (especially with my family and friends)
- find interest, emotional stimulation and inspiration in nature
- spend more leisure time with others in natural settings, and
- seek as much pleasure and happiness as possible in natural places and the things of nature

Why not do something similar for yourself? Remember that to have a friendship with nature is your birthright, part of your genetic inheritance and part of what being a human means. Make the promise to yourself, and act on it sooner rather than later. According to Bronnie Ware, a palliative care worker for many years, one of the five major regrets disclosed to her by people nearing the end of their lives is captured in the statement: 'I wish that I had let myself be happy'[3]. There is much happiness to be found in connecting with nature.

There are two important guidelines to follow on your nature connectedness journey. The first is: *start simply and proceed gradually*. This is the guideline to follow as you choose activities for the action or outer level of your journey. The second guideline, *stop, pause and engage (SPE)*, relates to the inner level. Following the SPE guideline transforms green activities into the mental, emotional and spiritual building blocks of nature connectedness.

Start simply and proceed gradually

My journey to nature connectedness proceeded gradually, especially in the first years. I began with an activity that I knew I could manage (day or shorter-length bushwalks with my family). I stepped from this activity to one that was more personally challenging (bush camping) only when I was ready. Once satisfied that I could stay warm, dry, well-fed and comfortable living in a tent and out of a pack, I graduated to full-pack walking (walking with a pack fully laden with camping gear and food for several days). Eventually, I was happy, keen even, to extend my full-pack walking from two to several days. While all this was going on, I introduced variety and challenge to my bushwalking by tackling other outdoor activities. These included 'off-track' exploring, rock climbing and canyoning (negotiating deep, narrow and usually watery sandstone chasms).

'Gradualism'—extending and varying nature activities gradually—served me well. I could have shortened the journey by taking more ambitious steps, but the way I chose preserved the all-important fun element, avoided setbacks and built my confidence. I have seen the gradualism approach work for many others as well. That is why I urge you to begin your nature connectedness journey with an activity that is right for you and then proceed gradually from there. Choose activities that are comfortable for you both mentally and physically. They can be challenging but not distressingly so. Avoid activities that you feel you should, ought or must do. The nature activities for you are ones that give you pleasure and keep you wanting more. You will have no trouble finding suitable activities among those catalogued in the next chapter. Many of the activities described are compatible with a busy urban way of life and there are plenty of others that can be adopted without having to make major lifestyle changes. There are even activities you can do without setting foot outside.

Stop, pause and engage (SPE)

Follow this guideline to get the most from your nature experiences. The Nature Connectedness Research Group at the University of Derby in the UK found that people connect with nature more rapidly when they interact with the natural world by stopping, pausing and engaging with it mindfully[4].

Stopping and pausing provides time for nature to be noticed. We can be surrounded by nature but pay it little attention. Under some circumstances that is understandable and appropriate. While catching up with a friend in a park, for example, chatting might be more important than communing with the surrounding flowers and greenery. Walking rhythmically along a bush track can induce a state of 'flow' that invites helpful inward reflection rather than outward observation. There will be times, too, when it is necessary and prudent to be focussed on the activity itself rather than the setting, crossing a stream on slippery rocks, for example. But for most of the time on your nature connectedness journey you need to be engaged with the natural world attentively, mindfully and caringly.

There are five practices or actions that create this kind of engagement. There may be more, but the five that stand out from the work of The Nature Connectedness Research Group are: stimulate your senses; 'seek and savour beauty'; 'notice your feelings'; 'discover what nature means to other people'; and 'care for nature in thought and action'[5].

Stimulate your senses

This practice is about making full use of your senses to absorb the sights, sounds, silence, scents, textures and tastes of the natural world. It is about getting to know the fabric of nature first-hand and intimately. It is about seeking pleasure through your senses by doing such things as walking barefoot across grass, watching the changing colours of a sunset, listening to the wind in the trees, smelling the fragrance of wildflowers and breathing in the aroma of damp earth (the petrichor).

We are programmed to pay attention to nature. Our attention is captured 'automatically' by the natural world—by its naturalness, aliveness, complexity and novelty. Nature is unequalled in its capacity to hold us in its spell or to fascinate us. But even nature's allure can lose out to distractions. It is especially vulnerable to conversation, troubling thoughts and intrusive sounds. We need to be aware of this vulnerability and do all we can not to fall victim to it. Try, for example, to have times free of chat and mobile phone intrusions during nature activities. Consider as well having a quiet time before an activity, a short breathing-focussed meditation perhaps, to get your mind in the right space.

It is also worth taking time to pay attention purposefully—by making a point of observing nature close-up, for example, or giving yourself mini-projects, such as looking for patterns on the bark of trees or noticing the different shapes and colours of leaves. You might also try selecting just one sound to listen to or a single object or landscape feature to explore with your senses. You could also try observing the natural world as if you are an artist, photographer, composer or poet. Consider following Rachel Carson's advice to attend to nature as if it were your last opportunity to do so.

Seek and savour beauty

This is the easiest and probably the most effective practice you can use on your nature connectedness journey. You possess an astonishing ability to find beauty in almost all forms of nature, including representations of it in pictures and photographs. Natural beauty (and beauty of every kind) is mainly experienced as aesthetic pleasure or the 'beauty buzz'. This feel-good and powerful emotion ranges from a warm glow to heady euphoria. Aesthetic pleasure heightens awareness, sparks curiosity, stimulates inquiry and inspires creativity. It can also trigger friendliness and kindness.

Aesthetic pleasure is a highly rewarding emotion. To experience it is to leave us wanting more. We are attracted to beauty and beautiful things for that reason. We are drawn to nature largely (but by no means exclusively) because it is full of beauty. One of the surest pathways to nature connectedness is to seek and savour natural beauty.

Beauty is everywhere in nature. Much of it cannot be missed; it 'hits you in the eye' so to speak. But there is much beauty that is easily overlooked in the natural world's complexity. Be prepared to look in and under, to watch and wait, to seek, explore and investigate. You may find that the simple undertaking of looking for 'three good things in nature' every day is a helpful way to start. Bear in mind that natural beauty is where you find it and not always where you expect it to be. As we tend to underestimate the pleasure of nature experiences, seek nature's beauty expectantly, with an open mind and with a readiness to be surprised.

Natural beauty is to be savoured by basking in aesthetic pleasure. This involves dwelling in the experience, discovering more about it and finally processing it. Dwelling is essentially increasing the impact of the experience by staying with it, ignoring distractions and noticing your feelings. Discovering more about the experience requires attending mindfully and purposefully. Aesthetic pleasure prompts us to do this. Processing the experience involves re-living it in some way. You might talk about it with a friend, for example, write about it in a diary or journal, capture it artistically or record it photographically.

I found this guide on a signboard in Mt Field National Park, a scenic gem in Australia's island state, Tasmania:

USING ALL YOUR SENSES
Take some deep breaths and relax for a while.
Have you noticed the wildlife in the forest? Have you heard the sound of the wind in the treetops or savoured the fresh air?
Our lives are not lived at the pace of the forest. In our culture, there is too little time for contemplation.
Why not take a seat? Or lie down and watch the clouds drift past the tops of the highest trees. Be silent.
Imagine yourself as a part of the forest.
Notice your feelings

Notice your feelings

Nature connectedness is something we feel; it is largely an emotional relationship. Learning and 'theorising' about the natural world will not deliver nature connectedness. Just as we can't intellectualise our way to love or friendship, we can't become nature-connected without the involvement of our hearts as well as our heads. This makes noticing your feelings an especially important way of engaging with nature. You do this by paying attention to your emotions, identifying them and registering how they are playing out in your body as well as your mind. It also involves thinking about the effects the emotions may be having on your happiness and moods.

The emotions that you can expect on your nature connectedness journey will mainly be positive ones such as pleasure, joy, happiness, awe, wonder, excitement, exhilaration, peacefulness and tranquillity. You are also likely to experience gratitude, empathy, love and humility. A few negative feelings, such as fear, anxiety and disgust, may find their way into the mix. But one great advantage of taking charge of your own nature connectedness journey is that you can largely avoid negative experiences or be prepared for them should they arise. In any case, a mature and resilient relationship with nature requires an appreciation of nature's 'darker' side. Just as our friends are friends, 'warts and all', we need to relate to nature on the same terms.

Rick Hanson, a neuropsychologist based at the University of California, has written extensively about the importance of milking all the goodness we can from the kind of positive or 'good' experiences nature provides[6]. These experiences should be enriched, he says, by spending time with them, by relishing and absorbing them, and by considering how their impact might benefit other areas of life. Hanson believes that processing good experiences in this way promotes happiness and a more positive world view. It does this, he believes, by countering our brain's bias towards remembering and recalling the bad rather than the good things that happen to us. Evolution shaped our brains to be biased in this way because avoiding harm must take precedence over everything else in the business of survival. As a result, we have a brain that works like Velcro as far as bad experiences are concerned, grabbing and holding onto such experiences tenaciously. But it works like Teflon when it comes to positives ones, letting these slip away rather than sticking. If negative experiences are not balanced by positive ones, Hanson says, our brain becomes wired to expect bad things as a matter of course. The threat-detecting centres in our brain, especially the amygdala, become over-vigilant, making us anxious, suspicious, defensive, angry and inward-looking. To prevent this happening, we need to make 'taking in goodness' a constant ingredient of life.

Discover what nature means to other people

No one can undertake our nature connectedness journey for us. Even so, our journeying can be enriched, guided and inspired by other people's nature experiences, especially those that are captured in photographs, paintings, poetry and other forms of writing. The practice of discovering what nature means to other people is a way of experiencing nature indirectly. While not as powerful as experiencing nature first-hand, this indirect way of accessing nature is beneficial in surprising ways. Viewing nature photographs, for example, can reduce stress and promote recovery from mental fatigue[7].

One of the most famous and iconic nature photographs ever taken in Australia was of a gorge on the Franklin River in Tasmania[8]. It is a very atmospheric and awesomely beautiful wilderness scene. The photo was used in an Australia-wide campaign conducted in the late 1970s to stop the proposed damming of the wild and magnificent Franklin River. The photo was the work of the late Peter Dombrovskis, the first Australian to be inducted into the International Photography Hall of Fame. Peter loved the Tasmanian wilderness with a passion and devoted much of his life to photographing its beauty on every scale, from the panoramic to close-up. The impact of the photo was extraordinary. It resonated with a large part of the Australian population. Somehow it gave people a sense of the magnificence, uniqueness and value of the river. More than that; it conveyed the broader message that the natural environment is precious and must be preserved.

To look at the photo is to view the scene through Peter Dombrovskis' eyes, to gain a sense of the meaning and significance the scene had for him and to feel something of his emotional relationship with the place. Looking at the photo is obviously a lesser experience than being present in the scene. But it is still an experience that can affect the viewer's understanding and emotional connection with the natural world.

Words can do much the same for a reader or listener. Mary Oliver was a Pulitzer Prize-winning author who drew on nature for much of her inspiration. An example is her poem, 'When I Am Amongst the Trees'[9]. The poem takes us into a forest scene, the different trees, the stirring leaves and the branches bathed in light. In it, Mary shares the joy and humility she feels in the presence of the trees and her gratitude for their call to slow down, to 'stay awhile' and be restored.

Jane, a bushwalking friend, contributed a post to my blog which also succeeds in sharing a powerful nature experience[10]. After marrying a keen and strongly nature-connected bushwalker, Jane found herself lured into attempting a 'longish' day walk in the stunningly beautiful Cradle Mountain area of Tasmania. 'Before that I thought walking was just a means of getting around the shops', Jane wrote in her post. Boots had to be purchased especially for the walk but her preference, she said, was for 'an Oroton handbag which was about the same price'. The walk was preceded by a bus trip to the remote starting point, Jane and her husband being the only passengers. This is Jane's lyrical account of what followed:

> We headed off on our own across the duckboards and through the yellow button grass plain.
>
> It was so very quiet.

And it was flat. Then we came to a hill. I plodded over the top and descended to Crater Lake where there was a small walkers' hut. We stopped there for morning tea.

It was so very quiet.

We left there along a well-marked trail that swept around the lake and then branched off over the hill to Wombat Pond. It was on the way down the hill we headed through the most perfect snow gum forest. We stopped.

It was no longer quiet.

Snow gums during autumn imperfectly shed their bark. Dead bark comes off in large, irregular strips before eventually tearing away from the trunk. The stripped bark reveals trunks of blonde wood. The bark after a little rain takes on a dark red colour. The gentle breeze off Wombat Pond was rising through these snow gums and causing the long bark strips to flap slowly like giant flags unfurling. The noise was like the clapping of many hands. The smell was bush, eucalypt, damp moss, mushrooms, truffles, wet socks, earthy.

We stood and listened. We didn't move and we didn't speak. We just stood there smiling like happy idiots. It was the most beautiful thing I had ever seen.

It was then I 'got it'. I understood why my husband and many others walk and love it. Places like this are unique. They can't be replicated by man. They can't be built. And they make you grin like a fool.

We just stood there for 10 minutes enjoying the show. We then walked in silence down to Wombat Pond where I took my first 'boot shot', a photo of my boots with background scenery to mark the occasion. I was hooked.

Jane has taken hundreds of 'boot shots' since. While she was still working, many of the shots decorated her office to remind her of 'better things' that lay outside. That encounter with nature at Wombat Pond did at least two things for Jane. It gave her an immediate experience of joy, awe and appreciation and it launched her on the pathway to nature connectedness. Jane and nature are no longer just acquaintances; they are friends. As she said herself, she was hooked. She wanted more of the same kind of experiences, more encounters with the natural world. She found these in urban bushland and the rural countryside as well as in wilderness areas. This is one of the most important ways nature connectedness works in us. It expands our desire and efforts to immerse ourselves physically in the natural world and to engage with it mentally emotionally and spiritually.

Entering the nature experiences of people like Jane, Peter Dombrovskis and Mary Oliver can enhance your nature connectedness journey in several ways. It can rekindle memories of your own experiences. It can set your sights on places and experiences you might not have considered. It can take you to places where you haven't been and perhaps cannot go, such as the depths of the Tasmanian wilderness. Most important of all perhaps, by placing you in the company of inspiring nature-connected people, it can strengthen your commitment to your journey.

Care for nature in thought and action

Chapter 6 is devoted entirely to this practice; such is its importance. The world is facing two unprecedented environmental crises: climate warming and loss of biodiversity. Unless these two crises are effectively addressed soon, human life as we know it will be unsustainable. Both crises are of humanity's making. They have arisen because human industrial, technological and commercial culture has spawned the ideology that humanity can ravage and change the natural environment with impunity. The inevitable consequences of this ideology are now playing out. The global climate is changing, the incidence of extreme weather events is increasing, droughts are longer, the oceans are warming, rain forests are vanishing, species are dying out in their millions and entire ecosystems are disappearing. The very resources essential for human survival are disappearing before our eyes.

There is hope that science and technology will save us. But this hope is doomed unless the real agency driving the crises is addressed. That agency is humanity's flawed mental, emotional and moral relationship with the natural world. A radical change of mindset is required—from one that values nature solely in terms of what it can do for us to one that also values what we can and must do for nature.

It is just this reformed and enlightened mind-set that the practice of caring for nature encourages us to foster in ourselves and others. Chapter 6 explains fully what this involves. In a nutshell, it calls for individual and collective actions that protect, preserve, repair and restore the natural environment. Be encouraged by the thought that as your connectedness with nature grows, so will your commitment to safeguarding it. You will become a nature person in attitude and values as well as in action.

3. DO IT YOUR WAY

Your nature connectedness journey will be enjoyable because you will choose nature or green activities that *you* want to do and are comfortable doing. It will also be enjoyable because you will diversify and extend your activities gradually; and it will be enjoyable because you know how to get the most from your activities by engaging deeply with the natural world. This chapter makes it easy for you to find suitable green activities. It describes over a hundred of them, ranging from those that can be part of your daily life to those that require exotic locations and special interests and skills.

You are encouraged to choose activities that you are confident you can manage and are appropriate for your level of fitness and state of health (If in doubt, check with your doctor). But don't be reluctant to extend yourself occasionally. There is much to be gained from being venturesome in nature, from being challenged, even doing things you might regard as risky. It is very tempting to stay within the boundaries of our mental comfort zone and to ignore valuable possibilities that lie just beyond. Keep your mind open to these possibilities and look forward to being pleasantly surprised by where your nature connectedness journey takes you. I have introduced hundreds of people to abseiling, which is more of a mental than a physical challenge. When people rise to the challenge, the buzz they get is wonderful to witness. I found special pleasure in the reactions of older women to their success. 'Wait until I tell my sons (or husband or the women at work) I did this', was the kind of remark I often heard. From this experience, I learnt the importance of not 'closing the shutters' on possibilities in life because of untested beliefs and assumptions about what you personally can or cannot do.

Many green activities occupy only a few minutes; some require much longer. So, you could find yourself choosing several short activities, a handful of longer ones or a combination of the two options. Is one of these options better than the other? There is no clear answer, even though it would be good to have one. The best guide we have comes from the findings of a United Kingdom study that investigated how much time spent in direct contact with nature is needed to produce health benefits[1]. Using data from 20,000 urban residents, the study found that an increase in health benefits was reported only by people who spent 90 to 120 minutes per week in nature. It did not seem to matter how the 120 minutes were accumulated. Activities of both shorter and longer duration served equally well to achieve the 120-minute 'threshold'. So, my advice is to use the 90 to 120 minutes as a broad guide, but only if you really feel you need one. Otherwise, do it your way, guided primarily by your own preferences and circumstances.

The 'Tree of Green Activities'

Green activities put us into contact with nature. Whether or not the activity literally takes place among natural greenery is immaterial. Swimming, scuba diving, surfing are green activities even though they take place on and in 'blue' water. Likewise, ski-touring across a treeless expanse of snowy whiteness can be a green activity no less than walking through a verdant rainforest.

Many green activities are simple, like taking a moment to smell a flower. Others are more involved—going on a bushwalk, having a picnic, spending time gardening or looking after a pet. Some can be done sitting in the comfort and convenience of our own home, watching a nature documentary on TV, for example, but others, like backpacking, white water canoeing and mountaineering, require a vastly different environment. The accompanying graphic shows many kinds of green activities. I did not set out to construct the chart in the form of a tree; it simply 'grew' that way. But it is an apt image, so I am happy to call the chart the 'Tree of Green Activities'.

TREE OF GREEN ACTIVITIES

As you investigate the 'Tree', notice how varied the green activities are, and the Tree does not paint the full picture by any means. For one thing, each activity on the Tree can take a variety of forms and be adapted to a wide range of abilities and needs. There are dozens of variations on the bushwalking theme alone. By choosing to walk shorter or longer distances on the same bush pathway, you can provide walks that are suitable for different people including young children and those with limited mobility.

Some activities are quite different from others, canoeing from gardening, for instance. Others are versions of the one basic activity such as those on the 'walking branch', which begins with an easy ramble that might take less than an hour and extends to trekking involving several days or even weeks of possibly arduous walking. The Tree also shows that nature activities can be indirect or 'virtual', looking at landscape photographs, for example, as well as direct and 'genuine'. Even among direct activities the extent or depth of connection with nature varies enormously. Tending a pot plant or balcony garden is a form of direct involvement, but one that is considerably less full-on than, say, multi-day backpacking, white-water rafting and recreational scuba diving.

Activities nearer the tops of the Tree's taller branches are ones that are usually associated with risk-taking or adventure such as snow-camping, trekking, caving, rock climbing, mountaineering and rough water canoeing. But these make up only a fraction of the green activities that are available to us. Connecting with nature does not necessarily involve arduous, adventurous or extreme activities. Most green activities can be enjoyed in simple and convenient pastimes such as having a picnic, visiting scenic spots, spending time in parks and gardens and taking part in community-based conservation projects.

To choose appropriately from the Tree you will need to find out about the nature that is in and around your locality. You could start with a search of maps of your district and then do some exploring by car, bicycle or on foot. Your local council is almost certain to have information about parks and gardens and community green activities, such as Landcare, that might appeal to you. If you find places close (within a kilometre) to home, so much the better, but don't disregard places that are further afield. You could consider visiting those weekly or monthly, maybe to add some 'green' spice and variety to your walking, jogging or cycling program. Visitor or tourist information centres in your town or city could also be helpful. If there are popular outdoor recreation areas available to you, information about these could be on the Internet or in walking guidebooks and local publications.

Green activities are usually best shared

Consider recruiting some buddies to accompany on your nature connectedness journey or parts of it. Apart from being emotionally and socially beneficial, sharing nature activities with others will help you stay motivated and committed to your journey.

If you are attracted to green activities that will take you into wild nature, such as bushwalking and backpacking, think seriously about finding your buddies in a walking or outdoor club. Although I co-authored a bushwalking guidebook intended for use on a self-help basis, I encourage everyone seeking to engage in any form of wilderness activity to join a club. There are considerable advantages in doing this. Apart from increased opportunities for friendship, clubs offer invaluable know-how and sometimes help with equipment. Bushwalking club members often have access to a wide range of activities apart from walking and backpacking, canoeing, canyoning, abseiling and kayaking, for example. And walking with clubs is generally going to be safer.

Bushwalking and other outdoor clubs are easy to locate on the Internet or through state- and national-level co-ordinating agencies like Bushwalking New South Wales, or the Ramblers Association in the UK and the Federated Mountain Clubs of New Zealand.

If you can, contact an outdoor club through someone who is already a member. This will make fitting in easier. But don't be reluctant to make an approach independently. When choosing your club, the features to look for are:

- a welcoming and informative 'shop-front', i.e., attractive helpful brochures or website
- a membership mix (in terms of age, gender, ability and experience) that is suitable for you (and, where appropriate, your family)

- an efficient system for handling enquiries about the club and for arranging membership
- good management and adequate channels of communication within the club
- affiliation with appropriate state or national organisations
- a program that caters for a range of individual needs and capabilities (apart from enabling the club to have a diverse membership, this is a gauge of the depth of experience within the club)
- social activities
- good support for beginners, preferably introductory activities and training courses
- a quality control approach to the recruitment of leaders (Self-elected outdoor leaders can be excellent, but they can also be unsuitable for the role.)
- assistance with equipment

Although I advocate doing green activities with a club, it is not entirely a matter of either-or. As a younger bushwalker I enjoyed the benefits of being with a club, but I also had great experiences with an informal group of three or four friends. Forming a green activities group with friends might be your preferred option. If it is, you will have to be self-sufficient as far as planning a program and organising activities are concerned. You will also need to be enterprising in finding appropriate resources.

Everyday green activities

Laden as the Tree is, it doesn't fully convey that opportunities for green activities are often close-at-hand. These are the 'everyday' green activities—activities that *bring nature to you* at your home or workplace, and/or activities that you can easily *make part of work and leisure life*. Even if there are activities on the Tree that immediately catch your eye, ones you are already doing perhaps or are ready to try, it is worthwhile to seek everyday green activities for yourself as well. You can do this readily by consulting the following lists and choosing suitable options. Alternatively, you can come up with actions and activities of your own, or you can do both. The objectives are to bring more nature to where you spend most of your time and to increase the number of 'nature moments' you have daily.

Bringing nature to you

Here are steps you can take to bring fresh air, natural light, natural sights and sounds and other natural (or biophilic) attributes into your home and possibly your work environment:

- Open windows and doors to achieve cross-ventilation.
- Place fans strategically (e.g., near an open window, in a space between rooms) to improve airflow.
- Use a room de-humidifier.
- Keep floors clean by vacuuming and mopping.
- Avoid practices that introduce toxic chemicals into indoor air (e.g., using cleaners containing formaldehyde and other toxic chemicals; burning wood or other fuels in open fireplaces; cooking on a stove without a hood; using an un-flued gas heater; allowing toxic chemicals to accumulate by not ventilating regularly).
- Adjust curtains, blinds, doors and shutters to admit as much natural light as possible.
- Soften domestic lighting in the hour before bedtime.
- Avoid using back-lit appliances leading up to bedtime.
- Have an outdoor fireplace, in a fire-pit or fire-bowl, for example, to increase exposure to the red end of the natural light spectrum while socialising, enjoying fireside activities (e.g., toasting marshmallows, campfire games) or cooking a meal[2].
- Have a house, patio and/or balcony garden with as many of the following 'natural' features as possible:
    - beauty
    - informal
    - more natural than built elements
    - graceful curvilinear shapes

- few architectural elements
- many native plant species following their normal habits of growth
- partly open rather than dense vegetation
- the absence of geometrical shapes and properties like axes and symmetry
- (ideally) natural-looking water features such as a fishpond or artificial stream[3].

- Decorate living and work areas with indoor plants such as peace lilies (*Spathiphyllum sp,*), dracaenas, spider plants (*Chlorophytum comosums*) and Boston fern (*Nephrolepsis exaltata v. bostontenis*), noting that some indoor plants are toxic to cats and dogs and that indoor plants cannot be relied on to clean indoor air of toxins[4].
- Install a fish tank.
- Place nature pictures or posters on your desk and walls.
- Choose nature images for your screen savers.
- Buy or borrow (and look regularly at) photographic books about nature.
- Watch TV nature documentaries or soothing videos (easy to find on the Internet, using such terms as 'relaxing sounds of nature' or 'videos of gently moving water').
- Listen to birdsong CDs and DVDs, e.g., 'A Morning in the Australian Bush', 'Favourite Australian Birdsong', 'Nature Walks – In the Forest'.

Adding simple green activities to work and leisure life

After being released from an Egyptian prison following his totally spurious conviction, Australian journalist Peter Greste was asked what he would most like to do. Among his answers was this: 'Watching a few sunsets. I haven't seen one of those at all for a very long time, watching the stars, feeling the sand under my toes, the little things'.

It is significant that the 'little things' Peter mentions are all centred on nature. Being deprived of them reminded him of how precious and important such little things are. I am grateful that he chose to share this reminder because it is easy to forget how deeply satisfying simple encounters with the natural world can be. They are calming and pleasurable, make us more sociable, and provide moments of timelessness.

The following list provides examples of activities that provide these encounters[5]. All the activities can be fitted readily into home and recreational life and many can be shared with others, including children.

- Look at the greenery outside the window for five minutes.
- Have flower arrangements inside your home.
- Go outside and feel the sun on your face for one minute.
- Look at clouds (perhaps with the help of resources from the Cloud Appreciation Society[6]).
- Watch a sunset and a sunrise.
- Look at the stars.
- Look at the full moon.
- Watch the birds in nearby trees.
- Count the birds (and perhaps try to identify them).
- Listen to bird songs and calls.
- Look for insects and watch their behaviour.
- Walk along a beach at dusk or early morning.
- Skim a rock across a pond or stream.
- Drop pebbles into a body of water and watch the ripples.
- Listen to natural running water for five minutes.
- Watch the reflection of the sun on water.
- Walk through a shallow stream.
- Visit a waterfall.
- Watch goldfish in an indoor aquarium or garden pond.
- Watch skinks and/or other lizards in your garden.
- Study the webs of spiders.
- Smell flowers.
- Crumple and smell the leaves of aromatic herbs and plants.
- Feel the bark of different trees.
- Notice how raindrops look on a flower or leaf.

- Go outside in the early morning and look at the dew on the grass.
- Have a meal in your garden or nearby park.
- Lie on grass for a short time.
- Walk on grass barefoot.
- Sit under a big tree and look up into the branches (perhaps climb into the lower limbs).
- Read or listen to music outside.
- Go for a short walk to look at neighbourhood gardens.
- Go for a walk in the rain (umbrellas permitted).
- Meet with friends out-of-doors (instead of, or as well as, in coffee shops).
- Take a short walk in the early morning sunlight (without sunglasses).
- Have a 'sunshine break' during the day (particularly important if you spend the day in artificial lighting and for maintaining your body's production of vitamin D).

Making a habit of green activities

You may find it helpful to schedule times for green activities in your diary or on your calendar, at least until they become part of your daily routine. But take care not to make doing the activities a source of pressure. Think of them as providing 'slow-down' or 'for-me' moments. This could be especially beneficial if you feel burdened by the busyness of work and family life. Moments of slowness distributed throughout the day may be just what you are needing.

Another strategy that might help you make a habit of doing green activities is to follow a program for a specified period. A 30-day program seems to be one that works for most people. The Wildlife Trusts in the United Kingdom, for example, have run the '30 Days Wild' campaign[7]. With the aim of promoting contact with nature, the campaign calls upon people to 'do something wild' every day for one month in summer. The campaign provides a range of resources including a list of suggested activities labelled

'Random Acts of Wildness'. Participants are encouraged to be self-directing and to design their own activities if they wish. They are also encouraged to share experiences and encourage wider participation in the campaign via social media. The campaign strongly emphasises seeking a deeper engagement with nature by using practices like those described in the previous chapter: 'stimulate your senses'; 'seek and savour beauty'; 'notice your feelings'; 'discover what nature means to other people'; and 'care for nature in thought and action'. Participation in the campaign was found to be associated with increased happiness, well-being and health[8].

For people who like to plan

In the previous chapter, I introduced you to my nature experiences checklist. The checklist comprises 12 questions, each beginning with 'Do I', e.g., 'Do I experience plant and animal life along with nature's rhythms and cycles?' 'Do I experience the sights, sounds, textures, tastes and scents of nature?' As I worked through the questions for myself, I realised that with a little 'tweak', they could form a tool of a different kind—a connecting with nature planning tool. The tweak involved substituting 'How can I' for 'Do I' as the stem of each question, resulting in the following:

1. How can I experience natural light that is constantly changing in direction and intensity?
2. How can I experience natural ventilation?
3. How can I experience open and moving water?
4. How can I experience plant and animal life along with nature's rhythms and cycles?
5. How can I experience the sights, sounds, textures, tastes and scents of nature?
6. How can I experience the natural world's diversity, complexity and order?
7. How can I experience the excitement of exploration, discovery, wonder and awe in nature?

8. How can I experience natural places where I feel calm, relaxed and restored?
9. How can I experience tranquillity in natural places?
10. How can I experience views of natural landscapes and other features from positions of safety and security?
11. How can I experience different forms of natural beauty?
12. How can I experience unspoiled nature and/or natural places where I feel remote from urban life?

These questions are intended to be practical as well as personal. They invite answers that indicate enjoyable, practical and feasible courses of action. My answers to question 3, for example, are: 'Continue rowing regularly'; 'Make a point of looking at (and listening to) the water feature near my apartment'; 'Include a waterfall visit in as many of my monthly nature walks as I can'. Clearly, these are answers that reflect my own circumstances, lifestyle and preferences. They all point to actions that are, for me, appropriate and realistic.

You can find your answers to the questions by consulting the 'Tree of Green Activities' and the two lists in the 'Everyday green activities' section above. In response to the first question, 'How can I experience natural light that is constantly changing in direction and intensity?', for example, you might select the following activities:

- Go on an overnight walk and camp.
- Adjust the curtains, blinds, doors and shutters in your house to admit as much natural light as possible.
- Soften domestic lighting in the hour before bedtime.
- Install a fire-bowl on your patio and use it occasionally to have a family campfire.

Alternatively, you can answer the questions without reference to either the Tree or the lists. The source of your answers does not matter providing the activities you come up with are appealing to you and 'do-able'.

4. MAKE IT A FAMILY AFFAIR

This chapter is especially for parents, grandparents, great grandparents, uncles and aunties, teachers and anyone else involved in the care of children or adolescents. Our youngsters depend on us in all sorts of ways, not the least of which is helping them to have an advantaged childhood. This is the childhood that is likely to follow from regular exposure to nature (See Chapter 11). Children and adolescents who have such a childhood avoid the risk of 'nature deficit disorder'[1] and enjoy a host of academic, intellectual, emotional and social benefits, many enduring throughout life. They are also highly likely to form a strong connection with nature.

As early as eight years of age, and certainly by the time they are 11, children can be strongly nature connected[2]. A study comparing nature connectedness across the lifespan found that the average nature connectedness of children can be comparable in strength to that of the most nature-connected of adults. Like adults, children can enjoy nature, feel empathy for living things, sense oneness with the natural world, and possess a sense of responsibility towards the environment. But, also like adults, children differ widely in how strongly nature connected they are. A study of 775 children aged 10 – 11 from 15 schools in central England found that only a small minority (18%) scored 'high' on a measure of nature connectedness with the majority (46%) scoring in the 'low' range[3]. But on a more positive note, the children who scored high were more likely than the others to report environment-friendly attitudes and actions.

Another way to enjoy your children

There is still much to learn about the development of nature connectedness through childhood. But it seems likely that it occurs in three broad stages[4]. The stages flow together, with each successive stage building on the preceding one until there is a full flowering of nature connectedness in middle to late childhood (8 – 12 years of age). I call the stages the 'Three Ls'.

The first 'L' is the 'liking and enjoying nature' stage, which emerges during infancy and toddlerhood. In this stage, the child becomes:

- at ease and secure in natural places
- comfortable with the sensations and elements of nature, such as dirt, water, sand, mud, rain, sun and vegetation and
- curious about the natural world.

The second 'L' is the 'learning about nature' stage, which mainly develops between the ages of two and five. In this stage, the child:

- learns where and how to play in natural spaces
- displays increasing knowledge about the natural environment
- forms attachments to a natural place or places
- builds memories about nature experiences.

The third 'L' is the 'looking after nature' stage, the appearance of which roughly coincides with the elementary or primary school years. In this stage, the child:

- relates to nature with empathy and concern
- feels a sense of oneness with nature
- values nature and wants to take care of the environment.

My great granddaughter, Zoe, is making her way through these stages. Zoe is growing up with nature in her life. She has always lived close to parks and bushland and with nature-loving siblings, parents and other adults. She attended a pre-school that had regular nature talks and excursions. She frequently bushwalks, plays by a lake, watches the bird and lizard visitors to her home and goes boating and fishing. Occasionally, she watches episodes of *Planet Earth* curled up with her father and siblings.

Although a child of the electronic age—she has her own iPad, for example—she is very much at home in the outdoors. Even when she could barely manage a crayon, she insisted on 'doing colouring' outside on the lawn, an early sign of being at ease and secure in natural places. Earlier in her life when she was still a babe in arms, I took her to look at my back garden. As I entered a fernery, I was conscious of her stillness and intensity of gaze. She was looking at a large and striking spider plant (*Chlorophytum* sp) and continued to do so for several minutes. This was an indication, I believe, of a burgeoning curiosity about nature. A year later she acquired a pet rabbit. I still have a mental image of her squatting near the creature, alternately looking at it and gently stroking its back. She did this for over five minutes. It is easy to overlook the significance of such an otherwise ordinary event. Here was a toddler literally reaching out to nature. In doing so, she was adding a small but valuable increment to her liking and enjoyment of the natural world.

Fast forward four years and we have the five-year-old Zoe standing by a lake holding a Murray River turtle which her father had caught accidentally. 'I held a real turtle', she excitedly reported to her mother. The turtle was returned to its lake, but a week or two later, Zoe surprised her mother with the remark, 'I wonder where the turtle is now'. The encounter with the turtle was both exciting and memorable for Zoe, indicating that the natural world is becoming significant and valuable to her. 'How big are fish's stomachs?' is another unexpected question she posed. In an interesting blending of her outdoor and indoor worlds, Zoe consulted 'Mister Google' to find the answer. It is not only animals that stimulate her interests and enthusiasms. Spotting differently coloured and patterned lichens is another source of pleasure and wonder.

She is also interested in insects, especially ladybirds. When she expressed a desire to keep a ladybird in a jar as a pet, her mother prompted her to think about the proposal from the ladybird's point of view. Zoe willingly abandoned her plan, accepting apparently that the ladybird's interest should take precedence over her own—a tiny but real venture into a way of thinking that lies at the heart of environmentalism.

On a bushland walk with her grandmother, Zoe was picking up sticks and stones. One stick became a magic wand, and a particularly flat stone was placed against her ear as a pretend smartphone (another blending of her indoor and outdoor worlds). On another of her walks, Zoe wanted to find areas among the trees that could be the rooms of a house. More than just cute and charming, such bushland excursions into make-believe point to Zoe's developing ability to play imaginatively and independently in natural places.

I have shared these incidents from Zoe's life to illustrate how simple, informative and rewarding it is to observe children through the lens of nature connectedness. All that is involved is paying attention to what children say and do as they experience nature and matching what is observed to the 10 nature connectedness features comprising the Three Ls. It is simply a matter of looking and listening closely and knowing what to look and listen for. Monitoring children's progress towards nature connectedness in this way is interesting and enjoyable. It also secures information that adults can use to support and guide children on that important journey.

Families have a vital role to play in introducing young people to nature and in supporting them as they forge their nature connection. This is reason enough for making connecting with nature a family affair wherever possible. In building a friendship with nature, as with so many other aspects of behaviour, children look to parents, older siblings and other family members as models. If, as parents, we have also incorporated nature into our lives, our children stand to benefit greatly as well. That's why sharing nature experiences with our children is so important.

It's about play

Connecting with nature as a family affair is really all about play, for the adults involved as much as for the younger ones. Humans are one of the very few species that play throughout life. For adults, play is mainly about socialising, having fun and competing. For children, in addition to being fun, it is a primary and powerful way of learning and meeting basic physical mental, emotional and social needs. Free play is particularly valuable. This is play chosen, managed and owned by children themselves without any *apparent* adult intervention. Adults can influence free play, especially by encouraging and facilitating it, but such influence does not undermine the autonomy of the players. When playing freely, children can match activities to their own desires, needs and interests. Under these conditions, learning and development proceed in optimal ways and rates, reducing the risk of several physical and mental health problems in later life including obesity, anxiety and depression.

But that said, children also benefit from adult-initiated and adult-guided play. There would be no formal early childhood education without it. Among other things, adult participation can extend the scope and diversity of play through direct instruction, guidance and modelling. It can also facilitate the acquisition and development of physical, mental, language and social skills. Many of the activities suggested in this chapter benefit from adult involvement for that reason. But despite their value, structured play activities must not be permitted to exclude free play. It is a matter of striking the right balance, and that can only be determined by 'tuning into' each child individually. The obvious way to do this is to follow the child's lead when it is practical and safe to do so.

It is also helpful to keep in mind that play takes several forms:

- active (e.g., running, climbing, balancing, swinging and throwing)
- object (e.g., building cubbies, using natural materials as 'tools', making a fire and fishing)

- imaginative (e.g., pretending to be an animal)
- creative (e.g., making leaf paintings, building sand sculptures) and
- social (e.g., 'hide-and-seek', chasings)

Green activities cater for all these forms of play. That is why we do our children a great service by giving them opportunities to make natural environments their playgrounds.

Finding and creating natural playgrounds

The nature that can serve as children's playgrounds may be near at hand, around the home or in the immediate neighbourhood, as well as more distant. It is easy to miss the play potential of a green space unless we look at it with children's play in mind. Features to look for are:

- flat, open spaces
- sloping grassed surfaces (for rolling, sliding and riding down)
- climbable rocks and trees
- fixed objects (for jumping over, jumping on to and down from, and balancing on)
- non-rigid fixed objects (for climbing up, and swinging and hanging from)
- detached or graspable objects such as sticks, stones, twigs, leaves, bark, pinecones and seeds (for collecting, building, using as tools and for creative activities)
- mouldable materials such as soil, mud, sand and clay (for shaping, modelling and building)
- water (for swimming, fishing and water play)
- enclosed spaces in rocks and vegetation (for cubbies, make-believe play, and secret children's business).

Start your search in your own backyard if you are fortunate enough to have one. Assess what it offers, first as it is and then as it could be with modifications such as:

- installing a sand or soil pit or mound
- building a swing (A tyre attached to the limb of a tree could prove surprisingly popular.)
- allocating a space for a child-sized garden
- planting bird-attracting shrubs
- installing low stumps and rocks as stepping-stones
- designating a sheltered or hidden garden nook as a 'cubby corner' or quiet spot.

It is easy to find additional suggestions by searching the Internet using the terms, 'backyard' and 'nature' as starters[5]. Other ideas can be found in Jennifer Ward's books, *I Love Dirt* and *Let's Go Outside*. Although these books are pitched to North American audiences, readers from elsewhere will find them helpful.

When it comes to broadening your search for natural playgrounds beyond the home, make sure you investigate your neighbourhood and district as well as any obvious areas of rural and wild nature accessible to you. Use your local area maps to locate parks and other nearby green spaces. Obtain maps and other information from your local government office. Ask friends and neighbours for suggestions. Check the availability of natural history field books that have something to say about the plants, insects and wildlife in your locality. You may also find that local associations of bird watchers and other nature enthusiasts have helpful resources available. A thought worth keeping in mind as you undertake your inquiries is that urban nature is genuine nature. There can be nearly as much natural diversity in an overgrown urban allotment as in an Amazonian rainforest.

Make checking-out local green spaces a family fun activity. Provide time in each visit for thorough exploration. Assess the play potential of each space using the list of features already provided but be guided as well by the responses of your child or children; they are the ultimate judges after all. Schedule regular visits to places that appeal to your family. Look forward to some of them becoming favourite green playgrounds.

Helping children get the most from playing in nature

I live in a country that loves and values sport. To become a champion sportsperson is the dream of many children and an enormous amount of money is spent on children's organized sporting activities. At least one Australian state government gives parents a grant to offset the costs of sports uniforms and participation fees. This largesse is said to be justified by the urgent need to counter falling physical activity levels in childhood and adolescence and the associated rise in the prevalence of childhood obesity and in the risks of cardiovascular and other diseases. In addition to its contribution to physical health, participation in sport is fun and, under the right conditions, can build self-esteem, resilience, confidence and social skills.

But the conditions may not always be 'right'. Some people thrive on competition; others are threatened and even damaged by it. In his book, *No Contest*, Alfie Kohn argues that there is no such thing as *healthy* competition, because competition always means that one person can succeed only if others fail[6]. This may be an excessively critical view of competition and competitiveness, but it sounds a valid warning. Kohn is certainly not against children learning discipline and tenacity and experiencing success and failure. His point is that this learning does not require competition, winning and losing, and having to beat other children and worry about being beaten.

A great advantage of nature play over sport is that it calls for co-operation rather than competition. It is the form of play that Fred O Donaldson calls original play[7]. The capacity for original play resides in humans as a means of communicating love, trust and belonging. Even at its best, sport is competitive and potentially divisive—them and us, home team and opposition, winners and losers. Original play is completely different. It is the opposite of 'them and us'. Original play involves just 'us'—us together, not competing but co-operating, us sharing equally in the rewards of an experience and us accepting one another unconditionally and not for what we can contribute to winning.

Play in nature, whether it is the free play of children or the more structured nature activities that adults prefer, is very largely original play. No competitiveness is needed when collecting firewood with your mates or looking for an easy route through a cliff line or cooling your feet in a creek. The people with you are simply companions in an enterprise that requires nothing more than the willingness and an ability to join in for the sake of the activity itself.

Another great advantage of original play is that it comes naturally to children. Be prepared, however, for the possibility that your children may initially resist the idea of nature play. If they have had limited exposure to nature, they may not immediately see natural settings as playgrounds. This makes your attitude towards green activities all that more important. If your children sense that your feelings about nature are genuine and positive, you are off to a good start. Take heart from the fact that children soon find being in natural settings enjoyable. If they are helped to overcome any initial reservation and uncertainty, children quickly discover that nature is made for play. You can assist them to make this discovery by:

- guiding them towards activities that provide the opportunity for at least one, but preferably several, of the following:
    - free play, activities chosen by the children themselves
    - supervised (controlled) risk-taking, activities which have a low level of risk and can be supervised effectively from a distance, but which children perceive as challenging such as wading a creek, scrambling up a sloping rock, making a camp-fire, climbing a tree, investigating a cave or overhang
    - co-operative interaction with others, preferably children of the same age, but bear in mind that children welcome the participation of adults in many green activities

- potential to stimulate interests in landscape features: cliffs, caves, overhangs, creeks, waterfalls, outlooks, fossils; in features of the forest, especially hiding places; in native fauna/flora, in evidence of an indigenous presence, in navigational/ way-finding 'challenges'; in the use of a map and/or compass; in completing fauna/flora identification tasks; in collecting shells, rocks, feathers, etc.

- accepting that a green activity suitable for adults may not be suitable for children and that many activities may need to be customised for young people (See the next section for more about this)
- accepting that children will often find pleasure and satisfaction in the little things of nature and in simple green activities and encouraging them to do so
- responding positively to children's discoveries and delighting in nature
- proceeding gradually from activities that are within the child's perceived comfort zone to ones that are novel and more challenging (remember the gradualism principle)
- avoiding experiences that fatigue excessively, hurt or induce fear
- encouraging children to be aware of nature rather than to be apprehensive (Instead of telling them all the time 'to be careful', teach them 'to pay attention'.)
- involving children (and especially teenagers) in the planning of activities
- making children aware that they can take responsibility for their own safety by discussing with them possible hazards and risks associated with an activity and letting them (as far as is possible and reasonable) take preventive measures and plan what to do if something does go wrong
- giving children the physical and psychological space to enjoy green activities in their own way; intervene only when necessary, in the interests of safety and well-being
- ensuring as far as possible that, whatever the nature of the activity, it is fun.

As you seek the most from nature for yourself and your family, you might find helpful guidance in the notion of *frituftsliv*. Frituftsliv or 'free-air life' is a philosophy that permeates life in Scandinavian countries. The central message of frituftsliv is that it is everyone's birthright to experience the natural world freely, directly and unconditionally. A conspicuous expression of this philosophy is the convention of *allemansrätten* (the right of public access), which entitles anyone in Scandinavia to visit the land of another for the purpose of engaging with nature. Experiencing nature in the spirit of frituftsliv, is never a means to an end but always and only an end in itself. A nature activity undertaken purposefully or with a particular goal in mind, to get fit, to gain knowledge or to have an adventure, for example, misses the essence of frituftsliv. To be an authentic frituftsliv experience, nature play requires no purpose or justification beyond the 'doing' of the activity itself. So, why not follow the Scandinavian lead and enjoy nature with your family unconditionally, with no strings attached?

Green activities for the young and the young in spirit

The activity suggestions in this section are organised into age categories, but only as a rough guide. Children develop at varying rates so that an activity embraced enthusiastically by one four-year-old, for example, may be rejected by another. In any case, the most reliable way of matching children with outdoor activity is to let the children themselves do the choosing. Some of the activities are adaptations of options mentioned in the previous chapter, but most are new. While dozens of ideas are presented here, others can be found in the resources listed in the appendices at the end of this chapter. Besides, you will almost certainly come up with ideas of your own.

Many of the suggested activities, especially those for infants and young children, require the assistance and often the participation of adults. But we can help all young people get the most from their nature activities by following these general guidelines:

- Model positive attitudes, feelings and actions towards nature.
- Be enthusiastic about nature activities.
- Mentor play by suggesting, supporting and guiding activities (gently without being bossy).
- Model consideration, co-operation, taking turns and empathy (towards wildlife as all well as other people).
- Encourage conversation about nature experiences by, for example, naming objects and features, giving labels to sensory experiences, asking open-ended questions, joining in 'chats' about activities, indulging in fantasy talk.

Birth – 18 months

Infants are busy taking in the world through their senses. From early in life, they are highly attentive to the human face and voice. Within weeks they display an awareness of 'aliveness' and a marked interest in living things. Well before the end of their first year, they have worked out that objects do not cease to exist when they disappear, the basis of their enjoyment of 'peek-a-boo' and other hiding games. As their mobility increases, they become active investigators of their surroundings; becoming sensory-motor scientists, as nature play guru, Robin Moore, says.

Investigating (finding out about the surrounding environment)

- Make lawn/balcony/patio the 'nursery' for short periods throughout the week.
- Put plants, insects and other animals in the way of the child's senses (touch as well as vision and hearing).
- Let the child experience a variety of natural places (e.g., park, garden, beach, lakeside).
- Give the child access to a sand pit with suitable sand-play tools.
- Let the child look at blue sky, the sky at sunrise and sunset and at night.

Walking (either on the legs of others or the child's own)

- Carry or push your child on green walks (talking about nature on the way).
- Go to places where your child can walk on different surfaces (e.g., sand, rock, grass and up and down gentle slopes.

Hiding and seeking (of objects, self and others)

- Play simple hiding games out-of-doors using natural materials.
- Hide feet, legs under leaves or sand.

Reading (being read to as well as 'reading' for oneself)

- Include books with nature images and themes among the books you read to the child (See Appendix A at the end of the chapter for suggested titles).

Reporting and recording

- Share with your child simple songs and rhymes with nature themes.

18 – 36 months

This, the age of toddlerhood, is marked by rapid progress in the basic movement skills of walking and running. Toddlers can walk backwards, for example, and negotiate stairs (initially with a little help). They can express themselves verbally, using language to name things, to communicate and to influence others. They have a growing sense of personal autonomy and a desire for independence (which is sometimes out-of-step with their capabilities). Their strength lies in doing rather than making and in investigating their immediate environments: house, yard and secure play spaces beyond. They enjoy the company of adults and love helping with household tasks, including gardening. They enjoy collecting, transporting and mixing things and will do so repeatedly. Sharing is not one of their talents; they play happily alongside rather than with others.

Investigating

- When visiting natural places, give your child freedom and time to discover and explore (model being enthusiastic and excited about discovering things yourself).
- Make opportunities for play in and with water (especially in puddles, streams, ponds).
- Give your child access to a sand pit with suitable sand-play tools.
- Look at the sky under different light and weather conditions.

Walking, running, balancing, climbing and other motor activities

- Go to natural places where your child can practise walking on different surfaces and through, over and around obstacles.
- Spend time in places where your child can climb and balance on low objects.
- Play chasings and simple games involving throwing catching, kicking and jumping.
- Take advantage of soft surfaces (e.g., grass, leaves and sand) to encourage rolling and gentle 'rough-and-tumble' play.

Collecting

- Provide opportunities for collecting natural objects (consider equipping your child or yourself with a suitable container for transporting the collected 'treasures').
- Make displays of collected objects in the house or garden.

Creating

- Paint or decorate natural objects.
- Make pictures, designs, craft objects and constructions using natural objects.

Imagining and pretending

- Play at being other living things (you may have to give a lead).

Hiding and seeking

- Play hide-and-seek.
- Make a den or cubby for your child in the backyard.

Reading

- Include books with nature images and themes among the books you read to the child (See Appendix B at the end of the chapter for suggested titles).

Reporting and recording

- Make a photographic and/or video record of your child's nature play and use the record to stimulate parent-child chats.

Socialising

- Have meals in your garden occasionally.
- Go on picnics.

4 – 6 years

Children at this age are usually highly active. Their gross motor skills have expanded to include skipping, hopping, jumping from low heights and climbing. They enjoy painting, drawing and modelling with malleable materials. Their vocabulary is expanding rapidly, and they are becoming proficient in making their desires and feelings known and in interacting socially. They are getting better at playing co-operatively and in appreciating the viewpoint of others (including animals). They are rapidly become masters of free play and enjoy discovering and collecting, and their love of stories is boundless.

Investigating

- Spend time in gardens and plant nurseries.
- Visit zoos, aquaria, wildlife sanctuaries, museums.
- Have farm, seaside and snow country holidays.
- Make games of looking, listening and touching in nature (e.g., Take a 'listening walk'. Play 'I spy'. Play nature bingo using images of natural objects in the squares to be filled).
- Spend time looking at nature through a magnifying glass.
- Let your child help you in the garden.
- Help your child make a small garden (Select quick-growing plants and vegetables your child will enjoy eating).
- Use a sifter to investigate life in a pond (A sifter can be made by stretching tulle across a hoop and securing firmly).
- Keep a terrarium and/or aquarium.
- Create a 'bug village' by leaving a board on bare soil for a couple of days and then removing to observe the creatures that are underneath.
- Make a bug 'B & B' that you can visit by placing pieces of fruit in a hole and cover with an ice-cream tub weighted down with a brick or stone.
- Do a 'worm call' by inserting a stick about 10 cm into moist loose soil and tapping the stick with another and watch the worms emerge.
- Add star gazing to your sky-watching activities.

- Watch age-appropriate TV and video nature documentaries and nature-themed children's programs.

Walking, running, balancing, climbing and other motor activities

- Visit natural places where your child can use and improve all the motor skills she has developed especially in the context of free play.
- Provide your child with opportunities to scramble up sloping rocks and to climb into, and swing from, the low branches of trees.
- Go bushwalking. Select walks that are 1–1.5 km in length, on constructed tracks free of deep steps, free of overhanging vegetation and having interesting features such as a creek, a pond or lake, rocks to explore, a cave or overhang, a variety of vegetation types and a twisting track inviting exploration (See Appendix B at the end of this chapter for notes on how to keep children interested on a bushwalk).
- Go tri-cycling and scooting in parks.

Collecting

- Provide opportunities for collecting natural objects (Consider equipping your child or yourself with a suitable container for transporting the collected treasures).
- Make display of collected objects in the house or garden.
- Engage in sorting activities (If these do not produce logical groups at first, don't be concerned; formal classification skills will come).

Creating

- Paint or decorate natural objects.
- Make pictures, designs and constructions using natural objects.

- Make craft creations using natural and other materials (for ideas, consult the resources listed in Appendix C).

Imagining and pretending

- Play at being other living things.
- Use a den or cubby as a setting for make-believe.
- Create a fairy house or garden.

Hiding and seeking

- Play hide-and-seek outdoors.
- Find hide-outs and 'secret places' among vegetation or rock.

Reading

- Include books with nature images and themes among those you read to your child (See Appendix C at the end of the chapter for suggested titles).

Reporting and recording

- Make a photographic and/or video record of your child's nature play and use the record to stimulate parent-child chats.

Socialising

- Have meals in your garden occasionally.
- Go on picnics.
- Use green spaces to play more complicated games such as 'Drop-the-hanky', 'What's the time, Mr. Wolf?' 'Simon says', and 'Tag'.
- Make and play in a den or cubby
- Sit around a backyard campfire playing games such as 'Whispers' and toasting marshmallows (s'mores in the

USA). The fire could be in a purpose-built pit or bowl or in a large terracotta pot lined with foil[8].

- Institute a family weekly 'green hour' (half-day or full day).

7 – 12 years

David Sobel, another children's play guru, calls this the hunter-gatherer age. Children in the middle to later years of childhood are physically and mentally capable of venturing beyond home territories (even though they are often constrained by parents from doing so). Intellectually, they are equipped to understand the concrete world more objectively rather than intuitively (as it really is rather than as it may appear). They are also stronger at fitting the world into categories and in appreciating and applying rules. This means that they are better equipped to see the world from the perspectives of others and to engage in social interactions requiring give-and-take. They enjoy playing according to rules but still have a need for free play. Friendships are important to them especially with those of the same sex. The family also continues to provide an especially important base, but they benefit from being able to push boundaries and to venture into the wider world with a measure of independence. Many of the activities suggested for 4 – 6-year-olds are suitable for older children and so can be considered for the hunter-gatherers. Some of the activities need to be adapted and extended to preserve their suitability. These are some suggestions.

- Bushwalks can be longer and more demanding (logs across the track, creek crossings, ascents and descents). More sophisticated awareness activities can be added ('plant spotting' using a field guide and looking out for different types of rocks and forms of weathering, for example, but take care not to make a bushwalk a 'classroom on legs'). Appendix B contains further suggestions for tailoring a bushwalk to the need and interests of older children.

- Gardening can be adapted by letting your child assume more responsibilities including planning, watering and fertilising, and pest and weed management.
- Similarly, your child can be the terrarium, aquarium or fishpond 'manager' with responsibilities requiring her to become more aware of the underlying science.
- Backyard nature observation activities, such as creating a bug village or a bug B&B, can be used to stimulate the reading of nature books and the exploration of nature websites.
- Cubby or den creating can be made more sophisticated by (a) making a wider range of construction materials available to your child and/or (b) giving them access to settings where there are genuine hiding places (e.g., caves, copses of trees, tree hollows, fallen rocks, overhangs).
- As well as having nature-related books read to them, older children can read such books for themselves. Stories set in nature or with nature woven into the plot are also appropriate to put in the way of hunter-gatherers. Check your bookseller, the Internet (search 'children's books set in nature', for example), your local library and Appendix A for suitable titles.
- Campfire fun can be extended to include the learning of fire-lighting and bush cooking skills in actual bush settings as well as in the backyard.

Along with these adapted activities, there are additional ones for you to consider. These are activities that cater to the older child's need for adventure, desire to do things with friends and growing social conscience. Among the popular options are:

- torchlight bushwalk, which can incorporate animal spotting and stargazing
- camping. Start perhaps with a backyard camp (see Appendix D) and try car camping before attempting a genuine bush or wild camp. A good deal of 'know-how' is needed for bush-camping. While there are books and

websites providing camping guidelines, novices are strongly advised to seek the assistance of people with backpacking and camping experience
- scavenger and treasure hunts in green spaces
- geocaching (a treasure hunt using GPS devices including mobile phones). Hidden at a great many locations across several countries are caches, usually plastic or metal boxes containing a logbook and possibly novelties of one kind and another including small toys. Some of the caches are in hard terrain and difficult to locate while others are much more accessible and easier to find. To learn all you need to know about geocaching and how to take part visit the website of the geocaching organisation in your country
- taking part in organised conservation activities.

13 – 18 years

These, the years of puberty and adolescence, span the child's journey from childhood to early adulthood. They can be turbulent years as the young person strives to accommodate the changes that are occurring in their bodies and the powerful need to form a strong and comfortable sense of self. The maturing of their minds enables them to contemplate possible worlds as well as the world that is. This disposes them to be questioning, rebellious, idealistic and needing social affiliations and psychological support beyond the family. They seek strong and influential attachments with their peers and may take up causes with great zeal. Their dependence on electronic communication is unremitting and the 'fear of missing out' (FOMO) on social information keeps them glued to their mobile phones for hours on end. Even adolescents, who were ardently involved with nature as children, may step back from green activities and their nature connectedness may drop sharply. Connecting with nature may no longer be the family affair it once was. But once we have made a friend of nature, the relationship is not easily set aside permanently. If your adolescent is at all open to your guidance concerning green activities, here are some options you could suggest:

- 'green' outings (picnics, beach visits, boating excursions) with friends
- backpacking or simply camping without days of hiking involved
- nature journaling, photography, sketching and poetry writing
- using electronic technology to produce nature films or a photographic portfolio
- posting accounts of nature activities on a blog or social media platforms
- rock climbing, canyoning, snorkeling, canoeing or other adventurous activities
- participating in conservation projects
- taking on leadership roles in the Scouts or other organisations that provide nature experiences for older children and adolescents.

APPENDIX A
Children's nature books

Websites to visit for suggestions

Children Nature and You. http://www.childrennatureandyou.org
Start with a Book; Nature: Our Green World http://www.startwithabook.org/booklists/nature-our-green-world
We Are Teachers: 17 of Our Favorite Picture Books about Nature. https://www.weareteachers.com/picture-books-about-nature/
M.G. Leonard recommends the best Nature Books for Kids. https://fivebooks.com/best-books/mg-leonard-nature-books-kids/
P.J. Delhomme, *The 16 Best Fiction Adventure Books Every Outdoor Kid Should Read.* https://www.outdoorlife.com/photos/gallery/2016/03/16-best-fiction-adventure-books-every-outdoor-kid-should-read

Fiction and non-fiction books

With hundreds of children's nature books to choose from and more appearing all the time, the following list covers a fraction of what is available. But it does give an indication of how amazingly varied children's nature books are. Included in the list are some 'classics' and more recent quality books that you might look out for as you browse libraries and bookshops and online book retailers.

Fiction

Mem Fox & Julie Vivas, 1983, *Possum Magic*, Sydney, Scholastic.
Matt Shanks (Illustrator), 2019, *Der Glump Went the Little Green Frog*, Sydney, Scholastic.
Martin Waddell & Patrick Benson, 1992/2017, *Owl Babies*, London, Walker Books.
Peter Brown, 2009, *The Curious Garden*, New York, Balzar & Bray.
Max Jackson, 2018, *123 Anteater Stuck Up a Tree*, London, Michael O. Mara Books.
Nina Lawrence & Bronwyn Bancroft, 2018, *Clever Crow*, Broome WA, Magabala Books.
Hanako Clulow, 2017, *The River: An Epic Journey to the Sea.* London, Caterpillar Books.
Paul Stickland & Henrietta Stickland, 1994/2016, *Dinosaur Roar!*, London, Macmillan's Children's Books.
Megan Wagner Lloyd & Abigail Halpin, 2016, *Finding Wild*, New York, Alfred A Knopf.
Rudyard Kipling, *The Jungle Book* Various editions.

Non-fiction

Jeannie Baker, 1987, *Where the Forest Meets the Sea,* London, Walker Books.
H. Joseph Hopkins & Jill McElmurry, 2013, *The Tree Lady: The Story of How One Tree-loving Woman Changed a City Forever,* New York, Simon & Schuster.
Frané Lessac, 2017, *A is for Australian Animals: A Fantastic Tour*, Newtown NSW, Walker Books.
Ben Hoare, 2018, *An Anthology of Intriguing Animals*, London, Penguin Random House.

Piotr Socha & Wojciech Graykowski, 2018, *The Book of Trees*, London, Thames & Hudson.
Oliver Jeffers, 2017, *Here We Are: Notes for Living on Planet Earth*, London, Harper Collins Children's Books.
Charlotte Milner, 2018, *The Bee Book*, Melbourne, Penguin Random House.
Jenny Broom & Kristjana S Williams, 2015, *The Wonder Garden: Wander through 5 Habitats to Discover 80 Amazing Animals*, London, Quarto.
Diane Hutts Aston & Sylvia Long, 2014, *An Egg is Quiet*, San Francisco, Chronicle Books.
Lynn Peppas, 2012, *What Are Cumulus Clouds?*, St Catharines Ontario Canada, Crabtree Publishing Co.

APPENDIX B
Nature walking with children

Bushland can be relied on to arouse children's interest and desire to play. For most children, the bush will work its magic spontaneously. Some, however, may need guidance, encouragement and time to discover that the bush is a special kind of playground. The best way of delivering this guidance and encouragement is by example. Children are responsive to the attitudes and behaviour of the adults in their lives. If parents genuinely delight in being in the bush, then their children are much more likely to have the same response. Care is needed, however, not to push a reluctant child too far or too fast. 'Gradualism' is the order of the day.

Another mistake to avoid is to make a bushwalk into a classroom on legs. A nature walk is a wonderful learning opportunity, but it is better to let the learning take place incidentally. Guide children's attention to objects and events of interest but don't make a walk into an extended nature study lesson. Our goal is to have children see the bushland as a playground. Some will not do this without some prompting and help. Children who are new to the bush, for example, may need coaching in rock scrambling, paddling, stone skipping and the like. Give them all the support they require.

Because we want children to enjoy the bushland in their own way, it is best to draw judiciously on the following guidelines. Reserve your intervention mainly for moments when interest appears to be flagging or when children are going to miss a nature experience that they are likely to enjoy.

Sharing responsibility

- Involve children in reading the map and in simple wayfinding.
- Make them responsible for carrying the compass and or binoculars.
- Ask them to locate track signposts and track junctions.
- Have them identify good resting, eating and hiding spots.
- Let them be, or walk with (holding hands perhaps), the leader.
- Ask them to be a helper for younger children.
- Get them to find a stick suitable for use as a walking pole.

Walking with awareness

- Engage in 'plant spotting'. Make a game (e.g., 'Lotto') of identifying common or iconic native plants.
- Do some 'rock watching': looking for distinctive rock types, shapes and forms of weathering, e.g., arch, overhang, honeycombs, tessellated pavements.
- Initiate 'let's look for' activities:
    - insects, spiders and webs
    - seed pods
    - wildflowers
    - native fruits
    - signs of animals (tracks, droppings) and birds (calls, droppings feathers)
    - lizards
    - fish, frogs and tadpoles.
- Play 'I-spy'.
- Try counting (e.g., of signposts, steps, particular kinds of flowers, etc.) games.

- Have some stop-look-listen moments, including lying down to watch the clouds.
- Conduct sensory quizzes, e.g.:
    - What do you hear?
    - How many different green colours can you see?
    - How many different bird calls can we hear?
- Conduct a search for the rainbow challenge, i.e., find as many colours as you can.
- Do an alphabet walk, i.e., find something with a name beginning with 'a', then something with a name beginning with 'b' and so on.
- Hug some trees to feel differences in bark texture.
- Carry and use a magnifying glass.
- Carry and use binoculars specially to watch birds.
- Spend time pond/creek watching for birds and pond-life.

Record keeping

- Let the children take or suggest subjects for photos.
- Make sketches (remember to pack pad and pencils).
- Add the location of interesting natural features to the map of the walk.
- Permit the collection of leaves, seed pods, rocks, shells, feathers and the like but only on a restrained basis and taking nothing that is alive or serving as a habitat.
- Encourage the keeping of a nature journal (the Gould League's inexpensive and good starter kit for keeping a nature journal, the *Bargain Book Bag -010*, can be ordered from http://www.gould.org.au/shop/).

Stimulating the creative juices

- Give a theme to the walk, e.g., colours, bark textures, leaf shapes.
- Collect seed pods and leaves for making prints and collages at home.
- Look for markings (in the bark of trees, for example) that suggest interesting paintings or designs.

- Use clay or mud to make figures and shapes.
- Make pebble pictures with creek stones (remember to return the pebbles when finished)
- Immerse stones in water and watch the colours change.
- Find a stone to be painted at home.
- Draw pictures (Remember to pack a pad, coloured pencils, crayons or pastels).
- Make word pictures (using three or four words only to capture the experience).

Adventuring

- Find small trees suitable for climbing.
- Allow older children to go ahead occasionally but with clear directions regarding stopping and waiting at frequent intervals.
- Permit scrambling through and over rocks.
- Encourage hide-and-seek games in suitable locations.
- Do some wading in shallow creeks and ponds (but not in bare feet; remember to pack spare shoes).
- Try skipping flat stones across a pond.
- Float stick and leaf 'boats' down a waterfall or cascade.
- Go on a treasure hunt.

APPENDIX C
Things to make with natural materials

Websites

Alanna Okun, *32 Awesome Things to Make with Nature.* https://www.buzzfeed.com/alannaokun/nature-crafts-rock

Rhythms of Play: Nature Crafts and Nature Art Activities that use Natural Materials.

https://rhythmsofplay.com/arts-crafts/nature-crafts-and-art-projects-that-use-natural-materials/

APPENDIX D
Where to find more ideas for children's nature activities

Books

Joseph Bharat Cornell, 1998, *Sharing Nature with Children 2nd ed.*, Nevada, Dawn Publications.

Angela J. Hanscom, 2016, *Balanced and Barefoot: How Unrestricted Outdoor Play Makes for Strong, Confident and Capable Children.* Oakland, Calif., New Harbinger Publications.

Richard Louv, 2008, *Last Child in the Woods: Saving Our Children from Nature-deficit Disorder,* rev. ed., Chapel Hill, Algonquin Books of Chapel Hill. (In the Field Guide at the end of the book).

Richard Louv, 2016, *Vitamin N: The Essential Guide to a Nature-rich Life (500 Ways to Enrich the Health & Happiness of Your Family and Community),* Chapel Hill, Algonquin Books of Chapel Hill.

Scott D Sampson. 2016, *How to Raise a Wild Child: The Art and Science of Falling in Love with Nature.* New York, Mariner Books. (Mainly background material that indicates the kinds of nature activities that are suitable for young people)

Caroline Webster, 2016, *Helping Kids Find Wonder in the Everyday: Easy Outdoor and Indoor Activities to Inspire Kids of All Ages,* Binda, NSW, Sally Milner Publishing.

For general parenting guidelines about sharing nature with children, see

Jessica Joelle Alexander & Iben Issing Sandahl, 2014 & 2016, *The Danish Way of Parenting: What the Happiest People in the World Know About Raising Confident, Capable Kids,* New York, TarcherPerigee.

Websites

General

Jimmie's Collage: 100 Things to Do Before, During, or After a Nature Walk.
https://jimmiescollage.com/100-nature-walk/

Nature Play at Home: A Guide for Boosting Your Children's Health, Development and Creativity. https://natureplayandlearningplaces. org/wp-content/uploads/2014/09/NaturePLayatHome_ WEB_0_508.pdf
Children and Nature Network. http://www.childrenandnature.org
Sharing Nature Worldwide. http://www.sharingnature.com
Nature Play WA. https://www.natureplaywa.org.au/
Nature Play Queensland. https://www.natureplayqld.org.au/
Nature Play S.A. https://natureplaysa.org.au/

Backyard camping

Mallory McInnis, *28 Genius Backyard Camping Ideas You Need to Try This Summer.*
https://www.buzzfeed.com/mallorymcinnis/a-backyard-camping-we-will-go

5. TURNING TO NATURE IN DIFFICULT TIMES

When news of the terrorist attack on the World Trade Centre in New York saturated the American media on September 11, 2001, Richard Louv bundled his then 13-year-old son into their Volkswagen van and travelled to a favourite nature haunt on the beautiful Owens River which runs through the Sierra Mountains of California.

> We fled from the great pain that would lead to greater pain, and drove the six hours from San Diego to the Owens, and parked next to the current that washed out all the sound and all the fury. That night, inside the van, we flipped down the table and ate granola bars and drank hot chocolate and watched the window screens grow opaque with a late hatch of insects.
>
> And all the next day and the day after that, we cut the electrical cord to the outside world and found a sense of equilibrium[1].

As people often do at a time of emotional darkness and turmoil, Richard Louv and his son turned to nature for solace and restoration. The place they chose had happy associations for them as well as being one that comforted them directly through its naturalness, beauty and serenity. Reading this touching father and son story prompted me to bring together other accounts of burdened people using green activities to cope with difficult times. This chapter is the result.

The purpose of the chapter is not to offer self-help guidelines for mental health and interpersonal relationship problems. The chapter presents the simple message that nature is not just a fair-weather friend but is there for us in difficult times as well. It is possible that the stories told in the chapter contain guidelines you can apply to your own life. But it is important to remember that, because of differences in our personalities and circumstances, what one kind of green activity does for one person it will not necessarily do for another. And the stories are certainly not presented as a source of guidance to replace professional counselling and therapy.

The stories describe a variety of green activities that helped people cope with different forms of physical and emotional distress arising from devastating life events, impaired mental health or self-image issues. Six different kinds of green activities are represented in the stories. The activity undertaken by Richard Louv and his son is an instance of 'finding refuge', for example. It is unlikely that we can take Richard Louv's path exactly. But we can still profit from his example by seeking alternative refuge-seeking green activities for ourselves, should the need arise. The other five kinds of green activities discussed in the chapter are: nurturing, dwelling, extending, creating and meditating.

Finding refuge

Finding refuge in green activities is both an escape *from* and an escape *to*. For Richard Louv and his son, the trip to the Owens Valley was an escape from the overwhelming shock and horror of 9/11 and an escape to the beauty and serenity of a much-loved stretch of a wild mountain river. This is also how it was for Australian journalist Jeff McMullen. His was an escape from the psychologically traumatic images of witnessing and reporting horrifically violent events, including the civil war in Rwanda and its unspeakably confronting aftermath. His escape was to the untainted and incomparable beauty of Antarctica and to the naturalness and diversity of the Galapagos Islands. 'If you see a lot of horror, and you want to stay balanced, you've really got to seek out the beauty', he said.

As McMullen acknowledges, he went to great extremes to seek out the therapeutic beauty of nature. By contrast, Rob Cowen found the escape he needed a mile from his house in Harrogate, England[2]. Admittedly, Cowen was not escaping the kind of traumatising horror that McMullen had to combat. But the way Cowen found the wildness he needed in an 'ordinary' corner of the English countryside is both inspiring and instructive. After a decade of living and working as a freelance journalist in London, Cowen and his wife moved to Harrogate. The move took them from a 'shoebox flat' to a house. But with his wife working full-time away from home, Cowen found himself 'alone in a strange town, in a strange house, in the depths of winter'. On top of that, an economic recession ripped the rug from under him; the job he had moved for disappeared, leading him to the alarming realisation that the economic, social and political circumstances on which we rely are changeable. His need to escape became urgent. 'I had to get out, away from the madness of a crumbling human world. So, one evening I shut the door and headed for the nearest open space'.

He made his way across a ring-road, through housing estates to an edge-land, an overgrown tangle of woodland, hedge, field, meadow and river. Crossing into this inglorious but 'weird and wonderful patch of ground' changed him. He had a profound sense of other-worldliness, of being away from it all. He found his senses being graced by the scream of a fox, the call of a tawny owl, the river's murmuring and the knocking together of tree branches, all marking the beginning of a process of reconnection. He visited this place of refuge again and again and, in doing so, found 'it was impossible to hold onto the concerns of town-life. Life became simpler and happier'.

Earlier in his life as a writer on nature, Cowen had sought wildness in the farthest reaches of the world. But his 'weird patch' led him to understand that nature isn't a distant and separate thing but is all around us, and that a wilder existence doesn't necessarily mean going off grid or living in a shack in the woods. It's more about just getting outside, slowing down and being attentive. In his words, it is:

> To be still and hear the unexpected, bright choruses of birdsong, swifts returning or butterflies drifting between wildflowers, to be delivered into the possibility of escape from the constrictions of modern living. Such moments of

'wildness' provide portals into the greater rhythms—the seasons, day and night, the slow spinning of stars—and other, vivid lives that exist in parallel to our own. And we need that as surely as we need anything.

So if you're feeling a little lost, depressed and untethered, try 'rewilding' yourself a little.

Cowen offers some simple ideas for getting started on your rewilding (or connecting with nature) journey. These are equally good ideas for making the most of your times of refuge in nature.

- Walk wild (attentively). Walk slowly with pauses to look around and listen. Linger in places that particularly catch your eye. If track conditions permit, try walking barefoot.
- Learn about nature. Notice what is around you, the obvious and not so obvious. Use field guides and similar resources to find out more about the things that catch your attention.
- Try foraging for forest foods (bush tucker in Australia), ensuring first that you can identify what is safe to eat and what is not; use indigenous food guides if these are available.
- Sleep under the stars. With modern equipment and aids to comfort (insulated sleeping mats, 4 season sleeping bags, double-skin tents, for example), camping can be an enjoyable as well as an immensely effective way of 'getting away from it all'. There is no better portal to the rhythms of nature than to be woken by the dawn chorus of bird calls and to wind up the day around a campfire.

Nurturing

In broad terms, nurturing is helping things to grow. So, any activity that aids the growth of a living thing is a nurturing activity. Green activities that involve looking after animals or plants are nurturing activities. These activities are good for the nurturer as well as the nurtured. This is so for several reasons, but the exchange of positive feelings is prominent among them. Even tiny babies take advantage of this mechanism, having a range of signals at their disposal to keep their nurturers happy and all too willing to carry on nurturing, a win-win situation.

But even in the absence of emotional signals like a baby's smile or a pet dog's affectionate lick, we humans seem to find nurturing other living things intrinsically appealing and rewarding. We are almost certainly hard-wired to be nurturers. Hobby gardeners, for example, are rewarded as much by the 'growing' of their gardens as by the flowers and vegetables produced. Apart from the testimony of gardeners themselves, there is scientific evidence that gardening can be therapeutic, reducing stress and improving mood[3]. In a notable Norwegian study, people who had been diagnosed with depression, persistent low mood, or bipolar 2 disorder spent six hours a week growing flowers and vegetables. After three months, half of the participants had experienced a measurable lessening of depression symptoms, with improvements in mood lasting for more than three months after the gardening program ended.

For Anne Halvorson, gardening helped her survive the ravages of grief [4]. When her common-law partner, Kevin, died, she was left feeling hopeless. At the time she was a military servicewoman and a mother of two young children. With her closest family halfway across the country (the USA), she felt very much alone in her grief and her anxiety about the future of her family. Her distress was compounded by having to fight legal battles arising from the common-law nature of her relationship with Kevin. On top of that, she was diagnosed with multiple sclerosis and advanced Lyme disease. In addition to depression triggered by her grief, she was also suffering panic attacks that caused her to isolate herself socially.

Formidable as her distress and problems were, Anne set her foot on the recovery road when she and a neighbour began harvesting maple sap to make maple syrup, not a universal green activity but a green activity none-the-less. After 10 days of collecting, potting and boiling (over an outside fire in the icy Pennsylvanian winter), two litres (half a gallon) of syrup were produced. 'I felt great for the first time since Kevin's death', Anne recalled. The sequence of syrup-making activities gave her something to look forward to each day. Even though the pain of grief and concern endured, she woke on each of the syrup-making days knowing that something had been accomplished and that there was something worthwhile still to do.

The memory of how she had been helped by the sap-harvesting and syrup-making prompted Anne to plant a small garden in the following spring. She describes three ways in which this venture into gardening helped her manage her grief.

- It helped her to value self-care. The daily nurturing of her garden made her aware of the plants' dependence on her. 'My kids needed me', she noted, 'but on a bad day, the plants didn't talk back or argue. It was my therapeutic me time'.
- It changed her attitude and perspective. Apart from the immense satisfaction that the harvest gave her, Anne found that 'the continuous flow of down days lessened'. 'Focusing on this garden gave me a more positive outlook on life'.
- It pushed her to move forward and create goals. The following garden season, Anne expanded her garden and attempted unsuccessfully to grow plants from seed. But instead of giving up, she planted out alternative crops. The end of the season brought with it the realization that her mindset had changed for the better, a change she summed up this way:

> This garden hadn't healed me of any of my physical conditions, but it had become a source of therapy and healing in my grief journey. I still had days when I wanted to be a hermit and left alone, but knowing I needed to tend the garden was enough to challenge me to get off the couch and face the day.

Shawna Coronado also testifies to the therapeutic power of gardening[5]. A major turning point in Shawna's life occurred when she had the 'genius idea' to build a garden around the mailbox at the front of her property. At the time, she was very unwell, stressed and had poor eating habits, all on top of being a single mother. She suffered from endometriosis, high blood pressure, asthma, migraines and back pain. She was also affected by allergies that constantly triggered bronchitis. At one point, she took over a dozen prescription medications a day. Weighing only 44 kg (96 lbs), she was skeletal in appearance. Her back trouble would flare up frequently, leaving her unable to walk for days at a time. She was only able to work from home, which she rarely left. Hers was a grim existence.

Her modest first venture into building and nurturing a garden marked the beginning of a remarkable journey of emotional and physical recovery. Within a few years, she had become a professional garden designer and writer. Many gardens later, she felt and looked better than she ever had. Her weight had increased by (a healthy) 14 kg (30 lbs) and she was down to three prescription medications daily. She attributes much of the marked improvement in her health to gardening and the green lifestyle that flowed from it. Both, she says, helped her to cope with stress and made her body more resilient to allergies and other conditions. Gardening also led her from social isolation to vibrant community life. She found that gardening was a natural step towards community. Gardening encourages sharing of plants, produce, compliments, ideas and assistance. Shawna Coronado places great value of the social aspects of gardening.

> While making the physical effort to get out into nature and build a garden is important, it is the act of following through with community which will truly make a difference for your emotional health.

Restoring her health through gardening was such an amazing experience for Shawna that in 2008 she published *Gardening*

Nude, a book about achieving mental and physical health through gardening and living green[6].

Green activities that engage us in nurturing are not confined to the care of plants, of course. Looking after an animal, especially a pet, can also provide the social and emotional benefits of nurturing. Kathryn Oda discovered this after an adolescence and young adulthood plagued by crippling anxiety and depression[7]. Both had been a constant presence in her life, like a chronic cough that seemed to be getting better only to recur worse than before. But unlike a cough, which is not usually debilitating, Kathryn's anxiety and depression would hit 'like a ton of bricks', making getting out of bed each day a progressively more difficult task. Her days were spent ruminating, regretfully about her past and anxiously about the future.

She sought relief from doctors, in books, through gym membership and by trying many 'cures' including anti-depressants, special teas, yoga and vitamins. She even tried to become her own therapist by studying mental health at university. Another of her futile strategies was to move to a different city in search of a new beginning. Her life during this time oscillated between lighter and darker periods, between hope and despair. She was contemplating a life with the dark cloud of depression always hanging over her.

But then she read an article that prompted her to buy a dog, a corgi she named Buddy. When Buddy first joined her, she did not anticipate how much he would change her life. The transformation did not happen overnight. The other dog, the 'black dog' of depression, continued to visit. There were still days when getting out of bed was difficult. On one such day, Buddy's excited jumps and licks in anticipation of a walk could not be ignored. Kathryn responded and during the walk that day she realised that her mood had lifted, and she had the realisation that something new had begun.

From then on Kathryn did not experience a day paralysed by fear and regret. She still had down days, but the companionship of Buddy helped her finally to manage feelings of sadness and anxiety. In Kathryn's view, he did this in three ways: by motivating her to exercise, by making her laugh and by being a loved and loving friend. From her mental health studies, she knew that the way her brain was responding to Buddy—releasing the feel-good chemical serotonin and the love hormone, oxytocin—was also an important factor. And Buddy was also doing well out of the relationship. He was receiving nurture as well as providing it.

Dwelling

Grieving the loss of a child surely ranks among the most difficult of difficult times. In 2006, Maureen Hunter, then a nurse working in a small country town in Western Australia, lost her 16-year-old son, Stuart, in a car accident[8]. Stuart's death was the third and cruellest tragedy Maureen had to endure. Her husband had also lost his life in an accident and both of her parents died from carbon monoxide poisoning. For a time, her grief was overwhelming, almost blotting out hope and the will to carry on. But a point was reached when she said to herself, 'No, I will not become a victim of my circumstance. I will not let pain be all that I know. I don't know how but I will…somehow get through this'. Get through she did, eventually realising that she could draw on her own experience of profound grief to help others find life after theirs.

One of the things that Maureen found particularly helpful, and encourages others to consider, is spending times of quietness and reflection out-of-doors:

> I went outside every day. I listened to birds, held out my hands to the fury of the wind and sat on the veranda and felt the rain come in. Nature connected me to life, to renewal and to simple pleasures again. I also looked for signs. I saw messages in clouds, picked up butterflies with a smile and rejoiced when I saw an eagle soaring, taking strength from something greater than myself.

Here is an example of the kind of green activity I refer to as 'dwelling'. Basically, dwelling is opening yourself to the sights, sounds and other sensory ingredients of the natural world—just letting yourself be present in nature. Simple as it is, dwelling can be amazingly enjoyable, calming and restorative. Often it takes only a few minutes of dwelling to settle distressed emotions or troubling thoughts. Dwelling in sensory gardens can reduce agitation and anxiety in people suffering some forms of dementia, for example. As one woman diagnosed with early onset dementia remarked, 'To smell, see, touch, taste, these are all really important things for dementia people as their senses break down. To go somewhere to experience it is a marvellous thing to do'.

Dwelling is an opportunity simply to savour the moment or take advantage of the 'me-time' by reflecting on the difficulties being faced. Not to be confused with rumination, which is unhelpfully stewing over things, reflection can set your thoughts on healing pathways. In Maureen's case, she seems to have used times of dwelling to seek meaning in her loss, to rage at the futility of it and to find comfort in her memories.

Extending

The film, *Wild*, is based on Cheryl Strayed's account of her hike along the Pacific Crest Trail, which runs from Mexico to Canada. As someone who has trained over 500 people for backpacking and camping activities, I cringed watching the scenes showing how unprepared Cheryl was for the venture and the initial difficulties she had as a result. I had to remind myself that her grieving and despairing state of mind left little room for thoughtful and thorough preparation and planning.

Cheryl embarked on the expedition as an escape but mainly as a way of doing something sufficiently 'heroic' to repair her crushed spirit and shattered self-image. She found herself on an archetypical hero's journey—a venture into a novel world, valiant struggles against adversity and a fulfilling reward at the end. As a hero's journey, her undertaking was among the more ambitious. It was nothing short of audacious, given how completely unprepared she was. She certainly chose a green activity (really a whole combination of such activities) that was extending physically, mentally and in other ways as well. She did not complete all the Pacific Crest Trail but psychologically she reached her destination.

In the film, the part of Cheryl Strayed is played by Reese Witherspoon. The film's director insisted that Reese came to the role as much a novice about extended wilderness hiking as was Strayed in the early days of the actual walk. This meant that Reese experienced some of the mental and physical hardships that Strayed endured.

It also meant that she had the opportunity to experience the special joy and satisfaction that comes from meeting challenges in the natural world. This is how she recalls one of these challenges, that of starting a fire without matches or a lighter:

> One day, when I set up camp off the trail, I rubbed sticks, made fire, and started screaming. (There is no scene of her doing this in the film.) I was in the middle of the woods screaming, 'Yes! Yes! Yes!' at the top of my lungs. I was jumping up and down for joy. If you saw me in that moment, you would have thought that I'd lost my mind.

Why did this sophisticated young woman find lighting a fire without modern aids so exhilarating? The exuberance of her reaction suggests her success meant more to her than simply getting a fire started. I know from first-hand experience that lighting a fire with sticks, even using the bow and drill method, can be a physical and technical challenge. As green activities go, it is one of the most 'primitive' in the sense that it is alien to civilised technology and practices. But it is one of humanity's basic survival skills and learning it provides a 'powerful and direct way of re-connecting with the earth'.

This was a discovery Australian journalist and environmental activist, Claire Dunn, made[9]. Burnt-out by the pressures of work and city life, Claire opted to spend a year alone in the bush with only the amenities she herself crafted from the wilderness. She found that learning the required survival skills made her feel 'truly alive' and was very satisfying. I believe that a large part of Reese Witherspoon's elation was an expression of just this kind of satisfaction. Making *Wild* gave Reese many other opportunities to undertake personally extending green activities, including wading streams, scrambling rocks, and plodding through knee-deep snow. Even some of the hiking she had to do on location would have involved some degree of primitiveness, especially as she was carrying a massive backpack, sometimes over steep and rough terrain. But I am not at all surprised that she found the challenges and hardships of acting in *Wild* transformative. It was so liberating, so freeing, she said, adding, 'Yes, I can survive this, so maybe I can survive anything'.

Challenging green activities were responsible for a similar but more dramatic transformation in the life of Michael, an Australian teenager, whose story features in an inspiring television documentary about a remarkable school[10]. By the middle years of his secondary schooling, Michael was facing alarming difficulties, personally, academically and socially. The documentary introduces us to Michael when he was a member of Darrabi, a class formed to cater for year 9 boys with serious behavioural and learning issues. Like most of his classmates, Michael joined Darrabi with negative attitudes about himself, learning and the school. Despite the best efforts of his class teacher he, along with most of his classmates, failed to respond to the Darrabi program, despite its laudable emphasis on one-on-one attention, respect, expectation raising and confidence building. Academic performance went backwards and a couple of serious behavioural meltdowns, one being a classroom break-in involving Michael, finally compelled the teacher and the school's assistant principal to devise a relatively radical remedial strategy.

Although few, if any, of the boys had done any bushwalking, the two staff members elected to take them on a four-day full-pack hike in a scenic coastal wilderness area. Michael was not at all excited by the prospect. 'At the time they told us, I said, 'No damn way', he later reported. I had never walked further than going to the shops or going to my mate's house. That's two kilometres', he recalled.

The 62.5 km walk challenged the boys mentally as well as physically. They had to dig deep at times, arriving at the campsite after dark on one occasion. There were blistered feet and fatigued muscles in abundance but also displays of endurance and co-operation. Around the campfire at the end of each day, the teachers were able genuinely to commend the boys for their efforts, resilience and support of one another.

The physical and mental challenges of the walk, the immersion in nature, the camaraderie that developed and the patient encouragement and counselling from the teachers had an astonishing impact on the boys. They finished the four days with a new and more positive image of themselves and their capabilities. This is what Michael had to say about the experience: 'Physically, it [the four-day walk] sucks, but I feel so proud of myself'. Very significantly, he also said: 'If you can get to do a 62.5 km hike without crying, you can do anything'.

These are the remarks of a boy who had grown in self-respect, confidence and resilience. Indeed, for Michael, the experience was life changing. He returned to the regular Darrabi program with a commitment that brought not only academic success but also made him a better person (his words). Such was his transformation that he wanted to share his story for the benefit of others. In a speech marking his graduation from the program, he said, 'I want to show other kids how Darrabi has helped me'.

But there is more to Michael's metamorphosis. The boy, who was once called a rank outsider, who once broke into a classroom, who once was a menace to himself and others, was selected for the prestigious leadership position of sub-school captain. It is hard to find the words to describe Michael's delight on learning of his election.

Michael and his classmates had received and benefited from wilderness adventure therapy, even though the teachers responsible may not have used that label for the experience. But the experience had all the hallmarks of an adventure for the boys—perceived by them as risky (even though the actual level of risk was low), physically and mentally challenging and an unfamiliar outdoor location. Accomplishing the walk, made the boys heroes to themselves.

All manner of nature activities can draw out the heroic in people. A day-walk along a wide bush track can be a hero's journey for one person as much as a full-pack trek in trackless terrain can be for another. What matters is not the activity as such but its meaning to the individual.

As the story of Michael and the other Darrabi boys illustrates, adventurous or extending green activities can have positive, powerful and enduring effects. Studies of formal and informal wilderness programs including Outward Bound have consistently found that wilderness activities, especially ones of longer duration (two to three weeks), produce noticeable improvements in independence, self-esteem, personal sense of control and other personal attributes that strengthen self-belief and confidence. Interestingly, there is evidence that such benefits are likely to be greater for adults than for young people[11].

Consider including a wilderness adventure or two in your nature connectedness journey. There are plenty of organisations that can help you do this. Outward Bound immediately comes to mind, but there are other options including joining a group or club that is engaged in outdoor activities such as bushwalking, canoeing and canyoning. If you are prepared to spend a little time getting yourself walking fit, why not think about a supported walking or trekking holiday in Nepal, India, New Zealand, Canada or Patagonia?

Creating

Erica Cirino describes herself as a 23-year-old full-time freelance writer who tells stories about the environment and its creatures, about 'what broken parts make up the whole of the Earth'[12]. Erica has had her own experience of brokenness. Five years earlier, when she was about to enter her senior high school year, she learned that her parents' frequent loud and angry clashes harboured the secret of her father's infidelity. Her once close relationship with her father was seriously damaged by this knowledge.

In addition to the family instability and her emotional distress, she was dealing with a mysterious illness. She was rapidly losing weight; her bones were weakening; bruise-like blotches were appearing on her shins; everything ached, and she was constantly tired, her doctors being unable to tell her why. 'I was hurting, psychologically and physically, she recalled. I felt trapped in a situation I didn't want to be in, trapped in a body that was failing me. It was a broken time'.

Her high school studies included a course in art for which she had to prepare a portfolio of 12 works that were related both in content and medium. She knew what the content would be about: wildlife rehabilitation. Time spent assisting in a local wildlife hospital helped her to forget what was going on in her life. It also encouraged her to contemplate the possibility that, like many of her 'patients', she would someday be made whole and freed once more to resume a normal life.

Erica's decision about the artistic medium to use was both fortunate and fortuitous. Her class schedule gave her time to walk in a nature reserve near her school. She took photos of the landscape and its plant and animal inhabitants as she went, often scribbling down her thoughts at the same time. On one of her hikes and after a particularly difficult time at home that prompted thoughts of leaving, she felt the need to lie down. She chose a spot among tall grasses and flowers that were overlooked by green and gold reedy plants.

As she gazed upwards, she noticed that the tall grasses divided the sky into narrow panels. The panels were occupied by the crawling clouds as well as the blue sky. She took many photos of the display. Looking at the photos that evening, she discovered that the black-and-white setting on her camera had been flicked on. Gone were the blue sky, golden haze and clouds that she had seen. Instead, she had pieces of black and white, held in place by various shades of grey. Her artist's eye immediately saw the 'epitome of a collage: a juxtaposition of shapes and shades, parts making up a whole'.

This was an epiphany for Erica. She saw the collage-like image of the sky as a mirror that was reflecting the brokenness of her life. At the same time, the mirror reassured her that wholeness can emerge from brokenness. She had found her artistic medium: collage.

The next day she began work on her portfolio. Using pieces torn from coloured magazines, she filled in a sketch of the face of a wild hawk, frozen in a fierce scream (the image can be seen by visiting her blog post). From this first collage image, eleven others were born. Together the twelve tell the story of a wild hawk's illness, rehabilitation, return to health and eventual release. For Erica, creating the nature-inspired portfolio was life-changing. 'I learned more about coping with what is broken while working on these twelve pieces in that one year of high school than I had in my previous 17 years of existence'.

Among the most important of all the lessons she learned is that she could still move forward picking up the pieces of her life and fitting them together in the best way possible. At the time of writing her blog post, Erica's family remained divided and there was still uncertainty about her health, although it had improved. But through nature-inspired creativity, she was finding the resolve and strength to cope.

Meditating

Saneum Healing Forest is near the South Korean capital, Seoul. South Korea is richly endowed with vast natural areas, forests of towering pine, oak and maple trees. Saneum is one of 37 state-run recreational forests scattered across the nation. The forests offer citizens easy and enjoyable access to the country's vast natural resources, with cheaper entrance fees than other private or government-owned recreational forests.

Saneum is also one of three similar forests where healing centres have been established. These centres offer programs based on the ancient Korean saying, *shin to bul ee* ('body and soil are one') as well as scientific evidence linking forest-based activities, especially walking, to a range of health benefits. In this respect, the programs are like ones provided in Japan under the umbrella of the *shinrin-yoku* (forest bathing) movement. In addition to walking, the healing programs include activities that are more often practised indoors rather than outdoors such as yoga, dancing, poetry reading, *GiCheon* exercising and meditation. Undertaking these activities in forest settings is believed to enhance their effectiveness.

Author and mental health advocate, Matthew Johnstone, probably shares this view, if his approach to meditation is anything to go by[13]. Having had a long struggle with depression, Matthew spent time as the creative director at The Black Dog Institute, an Australian organisation dedicated to understanding, preventing and treating mental illness. Matthew has been greatly helped by what he calls eyes-wide-open meditation (EWOM). This, he says, is a form of mindfulness meditation that is for people who are not drawn to conventional *vipassana*, mindfulness meditation (MM), or who find it difficult.

MM involves quietening the mind by channelling attention onto an object, such as a candle flame, a feeling, a word or mantra ('om' is a popular one) or one's own breathing, and then observing in a non-judgemental way the thoughts and feelings that pop into your head. According to Dr. Craig Hassed, founding president of Meditation Australia, the key ingredient of mindfulness is being conscious of what is going on, but not in a self-conscious way— paying attention rather than thinking about ourselves[14].

In contrast to inward-looking MM, EWOM turns our observing to the world beyond ourselves. It requires us to slow down, look around, and let our attention be attracted and held. It centres our awareness on the 'out there' and enables our senses to dwell on 'beautiful light, beautiful shapes [and] beautiful colours'. It locates us in the present and in the here and now and, in so doing, quietens the sometimes unpleasant and damaging busyness of our minds.

Matthew found that a camera can be a great aid to EWOM.

> A camera in your hands is the reminder to consciously slow everything down from your breath, to your walk, to your thoughts... To take photographs, we have to stop, look around, focus and capture. It brings our awareness to what's going on.

The camera does not have to be a fancy one. The cameras built into most mobile phones are quite adequate for the purpose. Indeed, a mobile phone camera is the perfect tool for EWOM, Matthew says, especially for people on-the-go. A great advantage of your phone camera is that you probably have it with you all or most of the time. It is also convenient to carry and easy to use.

Drawing on Matthew's writings, I have identified several key guidelines for using your camera phone as an EWOM tool:

- Switch the phone to aeroplane mode so that you're not distracted by texts, tweets and the like.
- Let the camera remind you to slow everything down, your breath, your walking, your thoughts, and to take time to look.
- Imagine the camera is asking you questions like, 'What can you see that no-one else can?' 'What grabs your heart?' 'What makes you smile?'

This last guideline underlines the importance of photographing only what resonates with *you*, what you are drawn to spontaneously. These will be subjects that you find intrinsically interesting and attractive; subjects that you attend to effortlessly and without direction from your conscious mind.

Matthew Johnstone practises EWOM in all kinds of settings. But I think that natural settings have more to offer than most as far as EWOM is concerned. In my view, there are no better places than natural ones for being in the present and the here-and-now. If the phone camera can help with EWOM, then there is a case for taking a mobile phone (switched to aeroplane mode) on a nature walk. I never thought I would think, much less say, such a thing, given that mobile phones have become technological tyrants in the lives of many people. Sure, they are a great communication tool, but they are an insistent source of distraction that can almost run our lives if we are not careful. I was once convinced that they have no place in nature-based activities undertaken to find stillness, inner calm and tranquillity, but Matthew's story has changed my mind. Used in the way he suggests, mobile phones can serve a useful function on a nature walk.

6. CARING FOR NATURE

After several chapters talking about green activities we do for *ourselves*, our family and our friends, the focus shifts in this chapter to green activities we can do for *nature*. Many green activities are good for nature as well as ourselves. Beautifying the world with gardens is an obvious example. It is equally true that anything we do to safeguard nature's well-being we are also doing for ourselves. Science tells us that all living things are biologically enmeshed in an unbelievably complex web of life. Eco-psychologists go further by proposing that we are also deeply bound up with nature psychologically. So deep is this bond, they say, that we cannot separate our own well-being from that of nature. Whatever benefits or damages nature, also benefits or damages us. In a similar vein, Stephen Kellert wrote:

> In society estranged from the natural world, our sanity becomes imperilled, no matter the material comforts and conveniences we enjoy. By contrast, a life of affirmative relation to nature carries the potential to be rich and rewarding[1].

Clearly, connecting with nature must include activities that nurture nature as well as ourselves.

I am writing this chapter against a background of growing alarm about climate change and global environmental degradation. In 2015, Pope Francis released an encyclical in which he called for action to heal the environment and combat climate change. Responding to the encyclical, Nobel Laureate, Professor Brian Schmidt wrote an article with the arresting title, 'I fear for my grandkids and humanity if we don't tackle this'[2]. The 'this' referred to is climate change and other threats to the integrity of the natural environment.

The encyclical attributes the environmental crisis to the rampant consumerism and greed of rich nations and the associated struggle in poorer nations to secure the basics of existence, adequate food, safe water, shelter and security. But the encyclical takes the analysis of the problem a step further—into our mental emotional and moral relationship with the natural world. First, it challenges the ancient Biblical notion of human dominion over other creatures. Second, it points to humanity's increasing disconnect from nature because of increased urbanisation.

I believe that this second point is the sleeper in the whole conversation about combatting climate change and restoring planetary health. We are hearing more and more about decarbonising the atmosphere largely by transitioning from fossil fuels to renewable energy sources. That is great and not to be contested, as decarbonising addresses a major source of accelerating global warming and climate change. But it only partially addresses a wider problem, that of the massive ecological damage being wrought by human attitudes and activities.

At the core of ecological health and productivity is biodiversity, the variety of all living things—the different plants, animals and micro-organisms, the genetic information they contain and the ecosystems they form. Human life is totally dependent on nature's biodiversity for food, dietary health, the sustainability of livelihoods and quality of life. It enables nature to provide us with our oxygen, regulate our weather systems, pollinate our crops, produce our food, feed and fibre and furnish us with pharmaceuticals. At least 40 percent of the world's economy and 80 percent of the needs of the poor are derived from biological resources. That is just one of many reasons why declining biodiversity has become a major concern and correcting it, equally with arresting climate change, a foremost goal of the 21st century.

As we are all part of the problem, we must be part of the solution. The encyclical identifies the root cause of the problem as the growing disconnect between humanity and nature. Reversing this disconnect is a vital step in building a practical, wholehearted and enduring commitment to planetary well-being. The green activities described in this section foster such a commitment. They do this by enabling us to discover that caring for nature is enjoyable and rewarding. They also do it by cultivating our empathy for, and understanding of, the natural environment.

Three kinds of caring green activities are described. My labels for the three are: 'wooing', 'greening' and 'activism'. The wooing and greening activities engage with the natural environment directly. Most of the activities in the activism category are different. They are not necessarily activities we do with and in nature, but for or on behalf of it. For this reason, some might say that they are not actually green activities. But they are activities that connect us with nature, nevertheless by heightening our environmental awareness, sensitising us to the needs of nature and furnishing us with insights that help us to relate to nature empathetically.

The wooing, greening and activism categories do not cover all the environment-friendly actions that are available to us. They do not include, for example, the familiar 'reduce-reuse-recycle' lifestyle practices such as:

- using energy-efficient household appliances and devices
- avoiding products that have been produced in environmentally unsustainable ways
- purchasing products in reusable containers
- making full use of opportunities to recycle products
- purchasing products made from recycled materials.

It is quite possible that such practices raise environmental awareness and may even foster nature connectedness. At the very least, they complement the caring for nature actions described in the following sections.

Wooing the Earth

On the shores of the magnificent Sydney Harbour, there is a much visited and much appreciated garden. The garden is the creation of Wendy Whiteley, who lives on the ridge above the garden in a house she once shared with her ex-husband, the internationally famed artist, Brett Whiteley, and their actress daughter, Arkie. The house backs onto state government land where there is a disused railway line. Two decades ago, the piece of this land immediately behind the house was a weed-infested and overgrown dumping ground.

Soon after Brett's death in 1992, Wendy set about building a garden on this very unpromising patch. She had no authority to do this and risked seeing her efforts swept away, as the government had refused to commit to keeping the land as a reserve or park. But caught up in the creative nature of the project, she pressed on, spending a great deal of time and money and eventually employing the services of two gardeners. The result is a beautiful place, Wendy's 'secret garden'. Wendy thinks that Brett and Arkie, who died nine years after Brett, would both approve of the garden. The ashes of both are buried there. Happily, the future of the garden has been assured by a government decision to lease the land to the local council on a 30-year renewable basis.

More than a beautiful place and the realisation of a dream, the garden is an example of what the Indian poet, Rabindranath Tagore, described as 'the wooing of the earth'. Like the wooing of one person by another, the wooing of the earth is the forming of a bond of love and respect that is achieved through reciprocity and mutuality. Wooing is being moulded as well as moulding. For Tagore, the wooing of the earth is the 'perfect union' between humanity and nature. He arrived at this idea when marvelling at the beauty of the English landscape and realising that it was the product of centuries of collaboration between people and the elements and processes of nature.

The eminent microbiologist and pioneer in the development of antibiotics, the late René Dubos, made wooing nature the centrepiece of his environmental thinking. In his book, *Wooing the Earth: New Perspectives on Man's Use of Nature*, he points out that many of the landscapes which we admire and seek because of their naturalness are the result of successions of adaptations of people to nature and nature to people[3]. This process, which has been going on for tens of thousands of years, rests on the belief that we can manage the Earth in ways that make nature more appealing and helpful. In her secret garden, Wendy not only restored nature but enhanced it. This is the essence of wooing the earth, working with rather than exploiting nature to achieve a result that benefits Earth as well as ourselves. Wooing is more than nurturing simply to help something to grow. It is nurturing that affects nature more broadly. Wendy helped things to grow, but she also transformed a place in nature from disorder to order, from dullness to colour and from ugliness to beauty.

Dubos described himself as a 'despairing optimist' as far as the future of Earth is concerned. He was as alarmed as anyone about the environmental crises that we have brought upon ourselves. But he drew optimism from his conviction that by working lovingly, respectfully and insightfully with nature, we can satisfy our needs while taking care of nature at the same time.

Any green activity undertaken with the mind-set Dubos describes is likely to be a wooing activity. Both home and community gardening are rich in opportunities to woo the earth. So too are voluntary, hands-on nature conservation projects that can be joined through agencies such as Landcare Australia, The Conservation Volunteers (in the United Kingdom and Australia) and the American Conservation Experience, USA. There are also relatively simple ways of wooing nature around the home and in the neighbourhood, such as:

- maintaining or planting bird-attracting trees and hedges
- planting herbs and shrubs that attract birds, butterflies, ladybugs, and bees and other pollinators

- installing a bird bath and bird feeder in your garden
- using compost to maintain the structure and fertility of garden soil
- building a garden pond with sheltering places for frogs and fish
- attracting lizards to your garden by providing lots of dry, dark hiding places, large flat rocks (for sunning) and nooks and crannies
- educating yourself about noxious and invasive plants and keeping them out of your garden
- keeping your garden weed-free, lawns mown and plants contained and pruned (one untidy garden can really detract from an otherwise attractive streetscape)
- collaborating with neighbours and local council to establish ornamental or vegetable gardens on street verges or any vacant public land that may be nearby
- collaborating with neighbours and the local council to have trees maintained or planted.
- watering your street trees in summer and keeping them mulched to maintain soil moisture and to keep weeds at bay.

Greening

In several Western countries, enlightened town planners, educators, and others, including politicians, are promoting the greening or 'naturalising' of urban environments. The goal of this movement is to maximise the greenery in cities and towns. Creating 'urban forests' is one way this is being done. This involves preserving or increasing the number of trees along streets, around dwellings and in public spaces. In some cities, urban forests have been joined up, not only to provide green environments for footpaths or cycleways but also to establish wildlife corridors. The increasing presence of vertical and roof-top gardens in commercial and public buildings is another sign of the greening movement. Particularly important targets of the movement are playgrounds and schools, and for good reason. Children are happier and play and learn better in green surroundings.

In some urban locations, schools are the greenest places in the district. Patrician Brothers College in the Sydney suburb of Blacktown is an example. Blacktown is not the greenest suburb in Sydney but the boys at the college have planted more than 11,000 native trees. Apart from enhancing the attractiveness of the campus, the greening has brought other benefits. 'Having trees around makes everyone so much happier', one year 10 student said, adding:

> Because we live in a very urbanised area, when we come to school it's nice to see so much green. It creates such a nice atmosphere, and it makes it much easier to concentrate because it is so peaceful[4].

These are perceptive and inspiring words.

It is easy to follow the lead of these young people and become part of the greening movement. A place to start could be your own home patch. Perhaps there is room in your garden for large shrubs or a tree or two (go for native species that suit the intended site, I suggest). There may also be scope for some co-operative neighbourhood greening projects, establishing verge gardens along your street, for example. If there is a patch of neglected public land nearby, it may be possible for this to become a community garden of some kind. I have seen the surrounds of a suburban stormwater drain transformed into an amazing wetland by some enterprising locals.

Apart from hands-on greening activities, there may be opportunities for you to support community organisations and government agencies that are sponsoring, promoting or undertaking urban greening initiatives. You may find that your local school or service clubs, such as Rotary and Lions, are moving on this front.

Activism

Late in the afternoon of Christmas Eve 1910, the 19-year-old Myles Dunphy was at a lookout at Katoomba in the Blue

Mountains of south-eastern Australia. The view of vast, blue-green valleys and towering sandstone cliffs glowing orange in the afternoon light filled him with such awe that later he wrote, I had never seen such a scene before. 'It is hard to grasp the stupendous immensity connected with all things relating to the scenic part of the Mountains'[5]. Myles' experience that day fired a passion and sparked a mission. The passion was for bushwalking and the mission was the preservation of bushland for the pleasure and well-being of everyone. By the end of his life, Myles had become a legend among bushwalkers and a towering figure in the Australian conservation movement.

Myles Dunphy's love of the bush was boundless. When his first son, Milo, was still a babe in arms, Myles modified a pram, nicknamed the *Kanangra Express,* so that Milo could accompany him and wife, Margaret, on bushwalks (the pram is now kept at the National Museum of Australia in Canberra). Myles and Margaret were obviously very keen to have their son experience nature from an early age. The impact this must have had on Milo is a story itself because he became, like his father, a legendary bushwalker and one of Australia's foremost conservation advocates. Among his successes was the creation of the Greater Blue Mountains National Park and its listing as an area of World Heritage value.

The Dunphys, father and son, appreciated that an authentic friendship with nature is reciprocal. Their relationship with the natural world was one of giving as well as receiving. They gave an enormous amount of time and energy to the preservation of the natural areas that had given so much to them. They understood that natural environments are essential for our well-being. They also accepted that we all have a moral obligation to preserve such environments. Both Myles and Milo played leading roles in promoting the expansion of Australia's system of national parks.

Most of us are living in countries where there are international environmental and conservation organisations, such as World Wildlife Fund, My Green World (appropriate for children as well as adults) and Greenpeace. Many countries have their home-grown organisations as well. In Australia, for example, we have the Australian Conservation Foundation, Australian Wildlife Conversancy and the Australian Marine Conservation Society, as well as chapters in each state of the National Parks Association[1]. Joining or otherwise supporting such organisations is an important way of following the Dunphys' lead.

If you want to be actively involved in environmental and conservation projects, you will find volunteer recruitment organisations helpful. Such organisations are likely to be found in most developed countries. In Australia, for example, there are: Conservation Volunteers Australia, Eco-shout and Go Volunteer. Be on the lookout as well for opportunities to help with government or community sponsored nature surveys. This might involve you in counting birds, animals or insects at a particular time and in a particular place, for example, or reporting sightings of wildlife.

How's this for a great idea?

Since 2013, the people of Finland have celebrated their connection with nature with the Finnish Nature Day holiday. This celebration is held at the height of summer on the last Saturday in August. On Nature Day, the Finnish flag is flown in honour of the country's natural environment, making Finland the first country in the world to acknowledge its natural scenic and recreational resources in this way.

One aim of the Nature Day campaign is to have the Finnish flag in as many places as possible, including on nature trails and as decorations for hiking food packaging. Many activities are conducted in natural settings, including choral concerts in national parks and 'dinners under the sky'. People are encouraged to organise independent events such as having family and friends together for a campfire meal, taking an elderly person on a parkland walk or arranging family reunions in natural settings. Apart from fostering national pride and nature awareness, the

Nature Day campaign also aims to promote conservation and to encourage nature play in children.

Deservedly, Nature Day has attracted international interest. Finland is greatly favoured by an abundance of beautiful landscapes and by the drama of radically changing seasons, but it is not unique as far as having natural assets is concerned. Even the most densely populated countries on the planet have their wild and urban green spaces.

I believe that the concept of Nature Day could be made to work in other countries, my own included. What is required is enthusiastic leadership and the active support of community organisations, the media and government agencies. Note what has happened to the Clean-up Australia Day movement. From small-scale regional beginnings, it has grown to become a model for similar campaigns in other countries. A local council, service group such as Rotary or Lions Club, church or school could get the ball rolling. This could be even better perhaps than having the lead come from the state or national government.

But you don't need a national Nature Day, to be wholeheartedly connected with nature. Every day can be a nature day for you because connecting with nature is easy. There are green activities you can enjoy right now and many others you can move onto when you are ready. Remind yourself that connecting with nature is a 'blue-chip investment' in well-being. Nature knows nothing of market volatility, fiscal crises, recessions and scams but is, as John Burroughs observed, 'constant and always at hand'[7]. When embraced humbly, openly and as a friend, nature changes who we are and how we function. It enriches our mental, emotional and spiritual capabilities in ways that are unique. It makes us more the person we are capable of being.

PART 2

THE GOOD THINGS TO EXPECT WHEN YOU DO

7. AESTHETIC PLEASURE, AWE AND WONDER

As I indicated in Chapter 1, learning about the benefits of nature connectedness *after* I had experienced them gave me a new and deeper appreciation of what had happened to me. It prompted me to re-live my nature experiences and to enjoy them in a new way. If you are well into your nature connectedness journey, I hope that reading the second part of this book will do the same for you—that it will validate your experiences of nature and help you to see them through eyes that are fully opened to their value and significance.

Even if you have still to begin your journey or have not progressed far, Part 2 can still be of interest and help. You may be aware that nature is good for you, but still be wondering, how good is 'good' and feeling the need to know more about the goodness that nature connectedness can deliver. 'What's in nature connectedness for me?' is a reasonable question for you to ask, especially if you are asking it with a concern for nature as well as for yourself.

Part 2 of this book answers that question by describing the good things to be expected from a nature connectedness journey. The good things take a variety of forms. Some are emotions that expand our mental and emotional boundaries, making us smarter, kinder and more spiritual (this chapter). Others help us to de-stress, regain vitality and deal with life's rough patches (Chapter 8). Still others are enduring building blocks of well-being such as self-understanding, self-esteem, emotional resilience, camaraderie and a sense of oneness with the natural world (Chapter 9). The good things also include sunlight, fresh air and other health-giving physical and biological elements of nature (Chapter 10). For children, the good things include experiences that are essential for their optimal physical, mental, emotional and social development (Chapter 11). The last chapter in Part 2 (Chapter 12) is about a good thing that is especially important to the present and future well-being of the natural world. The chapters in Part 2 can be read separately, but the chapter on health (Chapter 10) draws a little on content from earlier chapters. Hopefully, reading Part 2 will leave you feeling: 'I really would like some of that'.

Aesthetic pleasure or the beauty buzz

Enjoying natural beauty is one of our commonest pleasures, and is easily taken for granted for that reason. Beauty can be found in almost all forms of nature, including presentations of it in pictures and photographs. But there is a great deal that is extraordinary about this ordinary experience. There is much more to natural beauty than meets the eye.

The enjoyment of natural beauty is called aesthetic pleasure or less formally by me, the 'beauty buzz'[1]. Aesthetic pleasure is a feel-good and rewarding emotion that ranges from gentle pleasure ('Isn't that pretty?') to heady euphoria ('Isn't that stunning?'). It is also a 'get-up-and-go' or arousing emotion that stirs our minds by heightening awareness, sparking curiosity, stimulating inquiry and inspiring creativity. For many people, beauty is also strongly linked with spirituality. The Christian theologian Keith Ward, for example, says that one of the divine purposes of human existence is the creation and contemplation of beauty[2].

While aesthetic pleasure is itself a pleasant and rewarding experience, it evolved as an essential means to an important end. Without it, says evolutionary psychologist Gordon Orians, humanity would not have survived[3]. It helped our ancient forebears identify what was good for them in the natural world and what could cause them harm. Their brains had evolved to associate beauty with beneficial and hospitable aspects of the natural environment, such as water and woodlands. On the flip side, their brains told them to regard unattractive features and objects like dense vegetation and putrefying carcasses, as things to be avoided. Like us, our earliest ancestors found panoramic views especially engaging. For them, panoramas combined beauty with opportunities to gather important survival information about safe routes to follow, the presence of danger and the availability of food, water and shelter[4].

Our forebears have passed their ability to experience aesthetic pleasure on to us. The ability is strikingly displayed in the ease with which natural beauty is perceived. For people everywhere, nature, beauty and pleasure go together and the capacity of nature to delight and enthral us appears to be limitless. For the Lobar people from the Upper Mustang region of Nepal, the word for beauty and happiness is the same. We find beauty in the minutiae of the natural world, in a butterfly or an autumn leaf, for example, just as we do in the vastness of a sunset or the night sky. We readily recall encounters with natural beauty, and we enthusiastically keep a record of them with cameras and otherwise. Our genes ensure that aesthetic pleasure is something we are all destined to experience.

The beauty of nature has a special value for the Australian journalist, Jeff McMullen. As a foreign correspondent for many years, he covered several horrifically violent events, including the civil war in Rwanda. Asked in a TV interview how he coped with the horrors he had witnessed, he replied:

> You've got to go looking for the wonder and the beauty. If you see a lot of horror, and you want to stay balanced, you've really got to seek out the beauty. So I went to great extremes to find the naturalness in the Galapagos Islands, or in particular for me, Antarctica. And I came out of that unearthly kind of beauty thinking, 'God, it's good to be alive,' and in love with every minute, every day. That's what extremes do to you, they make you relish the now. The everyday, the opportunity of, 'Don't waste it,' you know, 'Use every breath.' That's what the beauty does to you as well'[5].

Jeff McMullen's testimony to the balancing and healing power of natural beauty echoes a common theme in writings about nature.

John Muir, the 19th century pioneer conservationist, naturalist and writer, insisted that 'everybody needs beauty'[6]. Renowned biologist, Rachel Carson, made much the same point: 'Those who contemplate the beauty of the Earth find reserves of strength that will endure as long as life lasts'[7]. This is so, she said, because the 'affinity of the human spirit for the earth and its beauties is deeply rooted'[8]. It is an affinity that unites all of us with the rest of nature. This affinity is forged by biophilia (Chapter 11), the trait in all of us that makes other creatures our kin and the environments they inhabit places to which we are drawn.

Beauty and the beholder

Natural beauty (or beauty of any kind) is not something we encounter or discover. Beauty is not *in* nature waiting to be observed. Rather, beauty is a quality that our brain 'gives' to things; it is behind our eyes in our brain. The beauty of a flower, a sunset, a mountain panorama or anything else exists totally in the activity of brain cells. Beauty is not a thing we *find,* but a response we *make*. And the fact that there is such a response and that we can appreciate beauty at all is one of the most intriguing aspects of the human brain.

Our brains can experience beauty because they can detect the forms, patterns and relationships that make an otherwise incomprehensible universe meaningful. They are sensitive to the symmetry, balance, proportion and ratios (especially the Golden Ratio) that are displayed in nature's more orderly structures such as crystals, water droplets, snowflakes, flowers, seed heads, shells, spiral galaxies, faces, beehives and lava columns[9]. They are also attuned to the underlying regularity (the fractal geometry) within the seemingly chaotic complexity of trees, forests, mountain ranges, clouds and coastlines[10]. We humans can find meaning in what would otherwise be nature's mind-blowing complexity.

There is some truth in the saying that 'beauty is in the eye of the beholder', but it is not the whole truth. The uniqueness of our personalities, life experiences and backgrounds ensures that no two of us will experience beauty in the same way. But this does not mean that everything about beauty and the pleasure it gives is unique to the individual. Our tastes in beauty may differ, but a great deal of what is experienced as beauty in the world is shared. Much of what is beautiful for you and me will be beautiful for others as well.

This is particularly so where natural beauty is concerned. A landscape seen as beautiful by an Australian will likely be regarded in the same way by someone from the United States of America, Indonesia or Scandinavia, for example[11]. Natural landscapes are almost always preferred to urban scenes and the features that people find attractive are strikingly similar. Everywhere it seems beauty is associated with streams, lakes, ponds, waterfalls, cascades, areas of grasslands and trees, vistas that recede into the distance and paths that invite exploration. All these are features that are linked with securing the essentials of human well-being such as food, water, shelter, safe routes and security.

Over the last 60 years, studies of landscape quality and scenic attractiveness have generated close to 1500 research articles and reports. The foundations of a science of scenery are certainly in place[12]. Two general features that are known to strongly influence people's perception of nature's beauty are 'naturalness'—having the appearance of unspoiled nature—and diversity. A mixed species forest of moderate density with spacious clearings clothed in groundcover, for example, is much more likely to be admired than one where there are signs of human management such as cutting and clearing. As for the trees themselves, the picture is much the same; those that are preferred are likely to have low branches (and thus easy to climb) and to be tall, thick, healthy, aged and without signs of having been cropped or pruned.

The buzz of aesthetic pleasure

Many experiences of aesthetic pleasure in nature give us an unforgettable emotional buzz. This buzz is a mix of delight and arousal[13]. The feelings of delight are a reward for being somewhere that is potentially beneficial. The feelings of arousal encourage us to take advantage of the situation, especially by getting to know more about it. The buzz is triggered by our brain's own chemicals. Endorphins produce the feel-good glow and dopamine is mainly responsible for the get-up-and-go effect. Dopamine also makes us more alert and improves our memory of the circumstances in which we experience aesthetic pleasure. Little wonder, then, that encounters with nature's beauty can have a deep and lasting impact, sometimes healing and sustaining us when life is humdrum, bland and even grim (as Jeff McMullen's testimony illustrates).

As we experience the buzz of aesthetic pleasure, our attention is captured by whatever it is that has attracted us. For a time, we are 'lost' in the experience. There is a suspension of self-awareness. We can give it our full attention without trying, which is to say that we are fascinated by it[14]. Eventually, our conscious mind kicks in and we become aware that we are experiencing beauty and feeling an urge to enhance the experience by devoting more time and attention to it. We smell the flower, for example, we stop to listen to the bird call, or we interrupt our walk to watch the waterfall.

More than a buzz

As a salesman might say, 'But there's more!'. Aesthetic pleasure can be much more than an emotional buzz. Part of the wonder of aesthetic pleasure are its major psychological offshoots: happiness, inspiration and kindness.

Aesthetic pleasure and happiness.

Aesthetic pleasure makes us happier in two ways. First, it adds to the credit or positive side of our emotional balance sheet. When we are harbouring more positive than negative emotions, we experience happiness in the 'feeling good' or hedonic sense. Second, aesthetic pleasure can evoke the kind of happiness that comes with the sense that life is going well. I recall, for example, the reaction of a walking companion when she had her first view of the widest canyon in the world (the Capertee Valley in Australia's Wollemi National Park): 'It makes you glad to be alive!' she exclaimed. We both stood for minutes utterly lost in the scene. We were caught up in what Mihaly Csikszentmihalyi (pronounced cheek-sent-me-hi) calls a state of flow. To be in this state, he says, is to experience a deep form of happiness. All our senses can tap into the beauty of nature but Csikszentmihalyi singles out 'seeing' in particular. A wonderful view can provide an experience of 'extreme joy, a moment of ecstasy', he says[15].

Aesthetic pleasure and inspiration.

At the same time as it brings joy, aesthetic pleasure gives us a message to 'do' in order that we might enter the experience more fully. The message may be simply to pause and gaze, but it can also launch us on one or more of the following journeys of mental and spiritual growth and enrichment:

- *Recreation and restoration.* Aesthetic pleasure prompts many of us to journey, quite literally, into natural environments in search of recreation. When people are asked why they visit natural places, the beauty of scenery may not always top the list, but it is usually close.
- *Discovery.* The allure of natural beauty is a call to seek and to search. When a beautiful flower or bird catches our eye, for example, what do we often find ourselves doing? We examine it closely to discover more about it. Even brief encounters can provide the spark that ignites deep and abiding interests.
- *Creativity.* Aesthetic pleasure can also inspire people to take a creative journey. From the early days of humanity, people have been moved to make representations of nature, sometimes for religious and social purposes but also as a way of expressing aesthetic pleasure. We see something of this in the enduring popularity of landscape

paintings and nature photographs, in their contemplation as well as their creation.

- *Spirituality.* An encounter with natural beauty, especially an intense one, can be a transcendent experience that forges a sense of union with the universe, with a higher entity or both[16].
- *Nature conservation.* The power of aesthetic pleasure to inspire the protection and preservation of nature was strikingly demonstrated in the campaign to save Tasmania's Franklin River. This wild river runs through a region that very few Australians ever visit. Nevertheless, when a project was launched to dam and drown the river, the outcry of protest was nationwide. A powerful underlying sentiment was that a natural feature of such beauty should never be destroyed. This same sentiment has driven other conservation efforts in Australia and elsewhere. The work of John Muir and Galen Clark on behalf of the Yosemite Valley in California is a famous example. The valuing of natural beauty for its own sake is a major driver of the conservation movement. Conservationists need to be passionate and aesthetic pleasure can fire that passion.

Aesthetic pleasure and kindness

Don't be surprised if a dose of natural beauty makes you feel kinder towards others. Encounters with beauty activate brain pathways and chemicals, mainly oxytocin, that are associated with empathy, openness and co-operative behaviour. An experimental study of the link between natural beauty and kindness found that the greater the beauty, the kinder was the behaviour[17]. The same study also found that the effect was stronger in people who were more open to natural beauty (just as are nature-connected people). The conclusion drawn from this study is worth sharing: 'Human civilization has had a profound and ancient relationship with the natural world. In this research, we asked the question, does nature help promote the greater good? Our studies reveal that it does'.

A pleasure to be savoured

To be opened fully to the benefits of aesthetic pleasure, we need to savour natural beauty. Savouring is the process of being deliberately mindful of pleasure and attentive to its source[18]. There are three techniques of savouring that are particularly relevant to aesthetic pleasure.

> *Absorption.* Go with the flow. Stay with your feelings and try not to think about what is happening and why. Dwell in the moment and be aware of your oneness with the object of your contemplation. Ignore the presence of others and shut out distracting thoughts. Don't rush for the camera. Give priority to making a 'heart and mind' record rather than a photographic or electronic one.

> *Sharpen perceptions.* Accept aesthetic pleasure's implicit invitation to discover more. Let your attention take you deeper into the experience. Observe mindfully; listen, taste, feel, smell as well as look. Follow Rachel Carson's suggestion to focus as if this is the last time you will have the experience.

> *Build memories.* After allowing time for absorption, take a photo, make a sketch or write a diary or journal entry. Reminisce about your experience with a friend. If appropriate (and legal) keep a physical souvenir (a rock, feather or leaf, for example).

Wonderful awe and awesome wonder

Even though they are commonly spoken of together, awe and wonder are different. But they can be discussed together because they are similar in several important respects. Both are highly beneficial, feel-good emotions, and both are triggered by something that is unexpected, astonishing and amazing[19]. Amazement, accompanied by incredulity, marvelling and admiration, is the emotional hallmark of both awe and wonder. It is triggered when expectations or predictions based on our knowledge of the world are violated. Successful magicians, for example, are experts at amazing audiences by violating expectations. They are usually highly skilled at appearing to make possible what we know is impossible.

Everyone's behaviour is guided by expectations. If this were not the case, we would be in a hopeless state of bewilderment because everything would be novel, and nothing would be familiar and predictable. We depend confidently on our expectations because they are based on our knowledge of how things are and how the world works. So, a violation of our expectations is a challenge to some of our trusted knowledge. This may not trouble us if the violation is of no consequence or is easily explained or rationalised away, because it is a magic trick, for example. But if the violation unveils a perplexing gap in our worldly knowledge, we can be left feeling puzzled, incredulous, mystified and even close to fear, close enough to make us uneasy, vigilant and wary. Usually, though, having our mental comfort disturbed in a challenging but not a menacing way leads to positive feelings, such as joy, excitement, admiration, respect and reverence.

Amazement works in both awe and wonder to arouse our interest, curiosity and desire to explain the unexpected, and to update our knowledge if necessary. The energy for this work comes from the powerful drive in all of us to resolve uncertainty. While a little uncertainty can be stimulating, exciting and even thrilling, a lot of it can be stressful. That is why our brains are programmed to seek the comfort of certainty. Awe and wonder serve this purpose by stirring us to 'fix' our knowledge so that the unexpected is explained and certainty is restored. Along with love, the need to resolve uncertainty makes the world go round.

In serving our brains in this way, awe and wonder have the power to make us smarter, kinder and more spiritually aware. Both emotions have long been recognised as the foundations of inquiry, understanding and wisdom. It has been suggested, in fact, that 'awe-inducing events may be one of the fastest and most powerful methods of personal change and growth'[20]. As well as being uplifting emotions, awe and wonder are broadening and building ones. Our ability to experience them is truly a gift, one to be cherished and nurtured.

The wonder of awe

I still vividly recall an episode of awe I experienced over 40 years ago. It happened at the end of a long day of uphill trekking in central Nepal. I was walking a little apart from my companions, weary and looking forward to reaching the campsite. I arrived at a small saddle, the final hurdle of the day, and there in front of me was the immense eastern face of Mt Dhaulagiri rising the best part of 6000 metres from the valley of the Kali Gandaki River. I was overwhelmed and I remember exclaiming, 'It can't be true!'. Time stopped for me as I was totally caught up in the scene. I have no idea how long I remained there, utterly transfixed (I can still get goosebumps recalling it). When I finally made my way to the camp, I had completely forgotten my fatigue and my mood had lifted. Somehow the world seemed a better place.

I call this experience a 'high moment', a term I borrowed from Mark Gibbard, who believed such experiences have a spiritual dimension[21]. My high moment was certainly a transcendent experience that gave me a sense of oneness with the universe, the 'cosmic sense' as Pierre Teilhard de Chardin called it[22]. While I sat gazing at Mt. Dhaulagiri, I felt drawn out of myself and into the grandness before me. This was a powerfully charged experience that went beyond aesthetic enjoyment. The panorama was beautiful, most certainly, but it was also challenging and exciting, I sensed immensity beyond the scene itself, something to which I was connected in the core of my being and something that I had to acknowledge in my understanding of the cosmos. I felt humbled and deeply conscious of my 'smallness' and relative insignificance.

Awe, vastness and accommodation[23]

Awe is a 'goose-bumpy' feeling we get when we perceive that we are in the presence of *vastness*—in the presence of something that is both beyond our current understandings and imaginings and dwarfs us physically or psychologically[24]. The actual or measured scale of the vastness is not what matters; it is how it seems to us that is important. If vastness is perceived, then vast it is, regardless of whether the vastness relates to physical size or another dimension such as force, power, achievement, leadership, altruism, heroism and, of course, beauty. Vastness, like beauty, is in the eye (or, more accurately, the brain) of the beholder. If you perceive vastness, then the vastness is real for you. I was not aware that any of my trekking companions were awed by the vastness of Dhaulagiri in the same way that I was. That did not make my perception of vastness and my experience of awe any less valid or real.

Confronted with the towering face of Dhaulagiri, I was moved to say, 'It can't be true!', because my mind struggled initially to accept the reality of the scene before me. My 'mental model' of the characteristics of mountains was challenged; it had to be changed if I were to accept or *accommodate* the new reality before me.

My high moment, my experience of awe, also changed me as a person. I came away from the experience with a new belief about myself and my place in the cosmos. This was not a fleeting change but an enduring one that has influenced my approach to other people, nature and life in general. Without the change, it is highly unlikely that this book would have been conceived, much less written.

Awe is different from other positive emotions such as joy, gratitude, serenity and amusement. The difference can be observed. The genuine (Duchenne) smile that is a feature of other positive emotions is not a characteristic of awe. The typical outward signs of awe are raised inner eyebrows, a bright-eyed stare, an open mouth, a slight forward jutting of the head and an inhalation of breath[25]. These signs all indicate heightened attention, alertness and mental arousal, just what a larger-than-life encounter would be expected to evoke.

The distinctiveness of awe has also been detected in the workings of the brain and nervous system[26]. When awe is being experienced there is diminished activity in brain regions associated with self-awareness and self-preoccupation but heightened activity in the parts of the nervous system controlling attention, alertness and concentration. This is an unusual combination of neurological responses, but it matches the sense of uplift, mental absorption and loss of self-awareness typically mentioned in reports of the awe experience.

The awesomeness of wonder

While awe is a relatively rare experience, wonder is experienced far more commonly and often in ordinary situations. When Natalie Maras, a distinguished Australian polymer clay artist, was explaining to me where she found inspiration for her work, she produced an object I had never seen before or knew existed. The object was the external skeleton of the glass sponge commonly known as Venus' Flower Basket (*Euplectella aspergillum*). The glass sponge is so named because its vase-shaped skeleton is made of pure glass produced by the sponge itself from silica it extracts from the surrounding seawater. My interest in the delicate but incredibly strong structure turned to wonder when Natalie told me how the sponge anchors itself to the ocean floor. It uses hair-like fibres that can carry light far more efficiently than any human-engineered optic cable. The sponge makes these fibres at extremely low temperatures using natural materials, something scientists are still unable to do but hope someday to mimic. When Natalie had finished, I showered her with questions, my curiosity in overdrive. Following the visit, I read all I could find about *E. aspergillum,* discovering other examples of nature's brilliant engineering along the way. I felt compelled to share some of what I had learnt in a blog post I entitled, not surprisingly, 'The genius of nature'.

My response to the glass sponge and Natalie's explanation displays all the mental and emotional elements of wonder: amazement, interest, curiosity, marvelling and a desire to know more. It also points to the connection between wonder and what we know (or think we know). Prior to being told about the sponge, I did not believe (or 'know') that primitive creatures were capable of such incredible feats of engineering. But because *E. aspergillum* amazed me and then ignited wonder, my store of biological knowledge has been updated. Along with specific information about the creature, I have added items of more general knowledge, that nature has already solved many of humanity's technical and scientific problems, for example. With Natalie's help, *E. aspergillum* made me a little bit smarter.

Like awe, wonder is a response to a mismatch between beliefs and expectations, between reality and our mind's version of reality. That is why wonder is often accompanied by utterances like 'I don't believe it!' or 'That's incredible!'. I once heard a friend say after a bushwalk, 'I just didn't believe wildflowers grew like that'. Her amazement and wonder were justified because the display of wildflowers she saw was as unusual as it was spectacular. The flowers were massed in a way far more typical of lush grasslands than the dry and infertile sandstone plateaus of eastern Australia. All of us on the walk were affected in the same way. The delight of the experience spilled over into an afterglow of joy, satisfaction and bonhomie (the 'bushwalker's glow').

Despite being similar in some important respects, wonder and awe are different, a distinction that is not always made. Some dictionaries, for example, include 'wonder' in their definition of 'awe' and vice versa, and sometimes wonder appears to be regarded merely as a less intense form of awe. But the perception of vastness and the feeling of reverence that are present in awe are absent from wonder. Nor does wonder challenge us to 'change our minds' in the way awe does. Both prompt us to fill gaps in our knowledge and to *refine and extend* our mental models but awe alone induces us to *transform* old models into something different. Awe leads us to new mental and emotional territory in ways that wonder does not.

Awe also induces feelings of humility that arise from a sense of smallness relative to something vast or great[27]. Not to be confused with humiliation, humility is a feeling that helps us to see ourselves more objectively and realistically[28]. It is an emotion that counters self-centredness and heightens our awareness and appreciation of others, of their circumstances, feelings, needs and rights. Humility is an emotional link between awe and caring and altruistic behaviour[29].

The humility that accompanies wonder is different. It is not a response to vastness but to a reminder of how little we know and how ignorant we are. We feel wonder when our knowledge and expectations are challenged—when something we expected to happen, didn't or something we didn't expect to happen, did. Either way, we are confronted with a reminder of the limits of our knowledge and understanding.

Being different from awe does not make wonder the poor relation. Wonder may not have awe's 'Wow!' factor, but it stands alongside awe as an important agency in human mental development. 'Wonder is the beginning of wisdom', Socrates taught[30]. For children, wonder is especially important. They are born to wonder just as they are born to experience awe. 'There are not seven wonders of the world in the eyes of a child', says Walt Streightiff. 'There are seven million'[31]. Among the most important things we can do for our children, Rachel Carson advised, is to nurture their innate capacity for wonder[32].

What awe and wonder do for us

Awe and wonder are themselves wonders. They add so much to life that it is hard to imagine existing without them. In fact, without them, we might not exist at all, at least not nearly as successfully as we do. They became part of our human make-up back in the distant evolutionary past of our species. This happened, scientists believe, because they are emotions that helped our species survive in two ways:

- by both emotions sharpening our ability and motivation to seek knowledge and understanding (and so reduce the discomfort of uncertainty)
- by awe inclining us to be empathetic, generous and co-operative and better equipped to foster cohesive communal life.

It is highly likely, as well, that awe can awaken and deepen religious and spiritual feelings. And let's not forget that joy is a powerful ingredient of both emotions. Clearly, awe and wonder are highly beneficial, either one or both helping us to be happier, smarter, kinder and more spiritual.

Awe and wonder make us happier.

Awe and wonder are called positive emotions for good reason. The strong feelings of pleasure that accompany them arise from activity in the brain's reward or dopamine pathway. Even a brief experience of awe or wonder is noticeably mood-lifting and likely to leave a positive after-glow that makes the world seem, for a short time at least, more interesting and attractive. The world is imbued with an 'alluring quality', says Robert Fuller[33].

Awe and wonder make us smarter.

To experience awe and wonder is to learn something, and to do so very effectively. We all learn best when our attention is focussed on the content to be learned, when we understand the content, and when we take the content on board in a memorable way. All three of these boxes are ticked when awe or wonder is driving learning. When I was introduced to the glass sponge, for example, my attention was grabbed immediately by the object itself, mainly by its 'unexpectedness', its strange shape, lattice-like structure and 'glassiness' (the first box ticked). As I found more to wonder at in Natalie's account of the sponge's engineering capabilities, my curiosity was aroused and 'how' and 'why' questions sprang to mind (the second box ticked). Finally, the novelty of the situation and the interest it aroused in me left a lasting memory (third box ticked). By strengthening learning in this way and by arousing our curiosity, interest and urge to overcome ignorance, awe and wonder make us smarter.

Awe makes us kinder.

Awe leaves a surprising emotional legacy. I came away from my high moment in Nepal with what I can only describe as an afterglow of goodwill. 'The world seemed a better place', as I recalled. For a short time at least, I was a nicer person, more amiable and gracious.

There is nothing mystical and mysterious about the link between awe and kindness. It has been demonstrated experimentally[34]. The link has at least three strands. First, the emotional lift from awe makes us feel better about ourselves. You have probably noticed yourself that when you are in a good mood, you are more content and friendlier and more open and accepting of others. Second, awe has the effect of absorbing us into the present moment and diminishing our awareness of the passing of time. As a result, we perceive that we have more time available for others as well as ourselves. This lifting of time pressure enables us to be more generous in providing for the rights, needs and concerns of others. Third, by shrinking us down to size, awe enables us to see ourselves more objectively and realistically in relation to others. This, in turn, helps us to identify with other people, to see the world more from their point of view, and to empathise with them.

Awe makes us more spiritual.

You do not have to be religious or 'spiritual' in any conventional sense to experience the transcendence of awe. For everyone, awe is a response that lifts consciousness from the familiar and ordinary to the exceptional and extraordinary. It is a response that calls on us to consider the possibility of 'something more' beyond the reality we know. But awe does have an association with religious spirituality as well. It is a desired and valued element in many religious traditions, rituals and texts. Awe has also inspired the designers and builders of cathedrals, mosques and temples through the ages. The first thing that strikes you when you walk into Westminster Abbey, for example, is the sense of vastness created by the towering columns and arches, the vaulted roof and the huge stained-glass windows.

Finding awe and wonder in nature

There is no shortage of things to amaze us and to be marvelled at, especially in nature. We can be amazed by the tiny and the massive, the animate and the inanimate, the created and the natural, by abstract ideas as well as physical events. We can be amazed by things as diverse as the crystalline beauty of a snowflake, a vast mountain panorama, a sporting victory, and even a fact about nature. A fact I find amazing, for example, is that our bodies are made from chemicals manufactured in dying stars billions of years ago.

There is nothing surprising, then, in the fact that nature is our richest source of awe and wonder experiences. This is especially so for children, which is why scientists and educators advocate nature-based play throughout childhood and the incorporation of nature into school environments and curricula. The physical, academic, mental health and social benefits of 'naturalising' childhood in this way are beyond dispute. And what is good for children is good for us adults as well. Nature is a source of awe and wonder for us as it is for them. For children, it is potentially a richer source, but for everyone, regardless of age, nature is where the triggers for wonder and awe are most abundant. To seek awe and wonder is to put yourself in the way of new information that surprises, amazes and challenges. There is no better place to do this than in nature.

So, in seeking to enrich your life with wonder and awe, the first and strongest piece of advice you can follow is to connect with nature wherever it is to be found, and it can be found almost everywhere. A second important piece of advice is to approach nature with an open and receptive mind. Consider adopting an approach that is shaped by the anticipation of pleasure (you are more likely to enjoy yourself if you expect to) and a readiness to:

- use all your senses and to stay focussed on the present
- look deeply as well as widely; zoom in as well as zoom out
- be absorbed by experiences and savour them.

8. RELAXATION, RESTORATION AND TRANQUILLITY

One of the main reasons people say they spend time in nature is to find peace and quiet. According to several United Kingdom surveys, people place a high value on natural places that are remote from cities, towns and human activity[1]. In such places, people feel they can relax, recover from mental fatigue and enjoy the deep comfort of tranquillity. 'Few elixirs have the power and punch to heal, restore, and rejuvenate in the way that nature can', says Professor Timothy Beatley, an expert on the greening of cities[2].

The relaxation response and destressing

Relaxing is generally associated with taking it easy in some way, having a lie-down, for example, watching TV, reading a magazine or novel, strolling through a park or lounging on a beach. We expect that passive activities like these will rid our minds and bodies of tension and leave us feeling calm and content, and so they can. But the same effects can accompany much less passive, even vigorous, activities. Within seconds of setting out on a walk in the bush, I start to sing or hum a snippet from my favourite opera. It is as if a switch is turned on in my head. What is happening, I am sure, is that I begin to unwind emotionally and the music, which I associate with pleasure and relaxation, springs into my mind. It is intriguing how quickly and reliably this happens. The response usually persists throughout the walk and its calming or de-stressing effect may persist for hours or even days afterwards.

I am not alone in experiencing nature as a 'stress-buster'. The experience is common and very well documented. Many studies of the impact of recreational activities in wilderness and urban nature show that reduced stress is one of the most important benefits. For over 30 years, for example, Japanese scientists have been studying the effects of forest bathing or *shinrin-yoku*, the simple practice of spending time mindfully taking in all the sights, sounds and odours of forests[3]. The findings have been so consistent and compelling that health practitioners in Japan are advocating *shinrin-yoku* as a main-stream therapy to combat stress and its symptoms.

Why stress is distressing

Reducing stress in our lives is essential for physical and mental well-being. It is not that all stress is bad. Stress—or more accurately the stress reaction—does a necessary job for us. Often called the 'fight-or-flight' reaction, it equips our bodies and minds for urgent action in the face of danger. Without this instinctive reaction, our species would not have survived. Confronted by a large and hungry predator or a club-wielding stranger, for example, our early ancestors faced a stark choice: stay and fight or leave in a hurry. Both options require a very rapid mustering of physical and mental resources. Whether it is for fleeing or fighting, you want to have all your wits about you and your body poised to work fast and hard. This is what the stress reaction achieves.

Herbert Benson, an expert on stress and relaxation, likens the stress reaction to a fire station responding to a call[4]. Immediately the call is received, a set of co-ordinated actions begins. When our brain detects or believes that we are facing a 'stressor' (a threat of some kind), it goes into emergency mode. It becomes more alert and vigilant. It sends high-speed nerve and hormonal messages throughout our body telling our heart and lungs to work harder and faster. It shunts blood away from our gut, hands and feet to the big muscles that will be most engaged in the fighting or the fleeing. It stirs the body's energy factory, the liver, into increased production to ensure that our muscles will have the fuel they need for a big effort. In anticipation of injury, it increases the supply of endorphins, the body's natural pain killers.

Few of the stressors we face in modern life warrant such a full-on, all-stops-out response. Yet, because the stress reaction is programmed into us, there is little we can do about it. If operating as originally intended, the reaction is over and done with quickly and the excess energy that is generated is burned up in physical exertion. As a result, there is no long-term harm to health and well-being. That is how it was for our nature-dwelling ancestors.

For us, however, things are different. The stressors in modern life tend to be sustained rather than brief. Short bursts of aggression or running away cannot dispose of the threats and challenges that typically stress us. We may occasionally face physical dangers but the stressors most familiar to us relate to work, relationships, financial security, study and the like. These stressors of modern life are often unavoidable and persistent. The threat of redundancy, for example, has become an enduring fact of many people's working lives, often accompanied by the challenge of servicing a mortgage and staying on top of parenting and other family demands. And then there are the hassles that are also part-and-parcel of our time-driven and complicated existence. These are irritating and frustrating small-scale stressors such as spilling coffee over yourself or misplacing your mobile phone. In themselves, hassles aren't potent threats to well-being, but their cumulative effect can be.

Persistent stress exacts a toll. The strain it imposes increases the risk of heart disease and stroke. It also interferes with the immune system, making our bodies more vulnerable to infectious diseases, kidney damage and possibly some forms of cancer. Stress has been found to play a role in literally dozens of diseases. In some, stress is totally or partly the cause; in others, it slows recovery or aggravates symptoms. Apart from the damage it can do to physical health, chronic stress accelerates the aging process. Chronic stress is also detrimental to psychological health, often leading to disabling levels of anxiety, depression and anger. During stress, our minds remain in a state of vigilance and urgent activity, so we have trouble thinking clearly or solving problems. To make matters worse, stress tends to be self-perpetuating. A chronically stressed mind keeps the body tensed for action; the tensed body keeps the mind on alert and so the cycle goes on.

As well as undermining individual well-being, unrelieved stress is damaging socially and economically. Stress-related illnesses cost Western economies billions of dollars each year. Not surprisingly, the provision of services and the production of books, programs and medicines to prevent, manage and relieve stress have become big business. But there is a way of managing stress that requires no special knowledge or training, no courses of instruction or gurus, no life counsellors or psychologists. It simply involves engaging with nature. Nature has a remarkable power to counter stress by eliciting the *relaxation response*. How good it is, then, that something as simple and cheap as looking at a nature poster, spending time in a garden or going for a walk in a park bush can combat stress by helping us to relax?

The 'natural' way of relaxing and de-stressing

The relaxation or 'rest-and-digest' response is nature's way of unwinding the fight-or-flight reaction and allaying its potentially damaging effects. The stress reaction and the relaxation response cannot occur together because they are in opposition to each other. Whereas the stress reaction involves increases in blood pressure and heart, breathing and metabolic rates, for example, in the relaxation response, these are lowered. The stress reaction diminishes the resources of our minds and bodies while the relaxation response restores them.

This natural way to relaxation has been known for a long time. The ancient Greeks applied this knowledge in their temples of healing. But it was largely ignored by modern medicine until the late 20th century. That situation has changed because many studies have confirmed that exposure to nature triggers the relaxation response. In one of the first studies to demonstrate the connection, stress was induced in young adults by showing them a gory film about workplace accidents[5]. After viewing the film, the stressed young people watched a 10-minute movie of an everyday outdoor scene. Some of them then watched films of natural scenes (open forest with birds and no people, for example) and others viewed urban scenes, such as a commercial street with traffic. Measures of stress were made before and after the screening of the film and then after the recovery videotape had been viewed. The results were impressively consistent. Recovery from stress, assessed using measures of muscle tension, stress hormone levels and brainwave activity, was faster and more complete in the subjects who saw the videos of natural settings rather than urban ones.

This study, like most others of its kind, demonstrates the effect of visual nature on stress. But the story does not end there. Natural sounds such as birdsong, running water, soft wind and the roar of surf also reduces stress levels. They spur the brain's anti-stress and 'rest-and-digest' networks into action. They also activate the network in the brain associated with healthy mind-wandering and reflective thinking (the default mode network)[6].

Japan is no longer the only country where doctors are prescribing 'doses' of nature to treat stress and related disorders. More broadly, scientific confirmation of the calming effect of nature is reflected in the increasing presence of gardens and other forms of natural greenery in hospitals and other health care facilities. It is also prompting the greater use of plants, nature photographs and the colours green and blue in places where nervous people are likely to congregate, such as dentists' waiting rooms. Even exam jitters, a familiar form of high-level stress, can be calmed by viewing pictures of nature[7]. Virtual nature may also reduce the perception and stress of pain[8].

Workplaces are often stressful environments so it is encouraging to know that even in many of these, a little touch of nature can make a difference. In one study, staff who had Dracaena plants placed in their offices showed reductions in stress levels, negative feelings and fatigue in the order of 30 to 60 percent. In stark contrast, those staff with no plants to look at recorded increases in stress and negativity of 20 to 40 percent over the three-month test period[9]. The presence of just one plant made a difference. This is not a one-off result. There are numerous studies reporting higher productivity and increased job satisfaction in workplaces with views of greenery or displays of indoor plants or nature images[10].

It is also easy to experience the calming effects of nature images and sound without setting foot outdoors. An Internet search using terms such as, 'YouTube relaxing nature sounds' will locate videos, some lasting hours, that combine delightful scenic imagery and the sounds of running water and birds[11]. When you are free of distractions, spend a few minutes with one of these videos. Sit comfortably just focussing on the scene and the sounds. According to some evidence it may take 10–20 minutes for you to feel the effect.

Restoration from mental fatigue

Fatigue is another of the great bugbears of our fast-paced way of life, not the usual sleepiness or tiredness we feel at the end of an ordinary day, but unhealthy fatigue. This is the fatigue that tells us something in our body or brain is not working properly or is being overburdened. There are many causes of unhealthy fatigue including disease, mental disorders, stress, poor diet, too little exercise and demanding work conditions. But there is one cause that we all need to contend with because it is an inescapable and common part of modern urban life.

I am reminded of this cause every time I see road-safety signs with these messages: 'Fatigue kills', 'Stop, revive, survive' or 'Take a break every two hours'. The fatigue these signs warn us about can simply be from lack of sleep. But it is frequently caused more insidiously by the physical and psychological load that driving imposes on our senses and nervous system. Even a drive along a familiar road is a major exercise in receiving, screening and processing information. As we drive, our eyes are constantly having to focus and re-focus, gathering the information that the brain needs to control our actions. Because the scene through the windscreen is continually changing, we must deal with an endless and potentially overwhelming stream of information.

Directed attention fatigue (DAF)

We are usually relieved from information overload because we can pay attention selectively. But doing this when there is a lot of information to deal with or for long periods of time can be very draining. Sooner or later, we struggle to concentrate, our eyes feel heavy and perhaps sore, and we may become impatient and irritable. These are the symptoms of what is called directed attention fatigue (DAF).

I am confident that DAF will be familiar to you. In addition to driving a car, you may associate it with the close reading of documents for work purposes rather than for pleasure, or with staring at a computer screen for hours. You may know it from being in a job where your attention is constantly demanded by others. Even negotiating busy footpaths and shopping malls requires directed attention. All such situations set us up for DAF because they require us to maintain attention in the face of many potential distractions. Carefully focussing on information from one source while we try to block out the information from others involves mental effort.

This effort uses resources that must be restored if DAF is not to become a chronic condition, possibly leading to mental and physical 'burn-out'. If we don't restock depleted mental resources, we are less able to function effectively. Our mental productivity can be reduced, and we can become more prone to errors and accidents. We can become less emotionally resilient and this, in turn, can make us irritable and impatient. Attention fatigue has been linked to several forms of dysfunctional behaviour including aggression, crime and incivility among residents of high-density public housing estates[12]. It is also likely that DAF worsens the symptoms of Attention-Deficit Disorder (ADD)[13]. And I suspect that hours spent on electronic game consoles are placing many children and teenagers at risk of DAF.

Because DAF is impossible to avoid in our 21st century world, we must deal with it to safeguard our well-being. The obvious thing to do is to take a break from tasks that require directed attention. This gives the parts of our brain that control concentration the chance to recover. But there is another option that does more than provide recovery time; it makes it more likely and rapidly to happen. All this alternative strategy requires us to do is to look (quite literally) to nature.

Fascination and restoration (A sight for sore eyes)

When we find ourselves mentally and emotionally fatigued, one of the best things we can do is to spend time in nature. Going for a walk in a quiet park where there are plenty of shrubs and trees would be ideal but just sitting in an out-of-the-way spot in a garden could do just as well. Time spent this way will be more helpful than resting indoors or doing similar activities surrounded by bricks and mortar, concrete and bitumen[14].

The special value of nature for combating DAF was first recognised by Rachel and Stephen Kaplan[15]. They believe that nature restores tired minds by enabling the brain to switch off directed (voluntary) attention and to switch on a form of attention that rebuilds rather than uses up mental resources. This second form of attention operates involuntarily. Imagine you are concentrating on preparing a meal (using voluntary attention) when you hear an unusual bird call through the kitchen window. Without any conscious effort on your part, your head would turn, and your eyes would be directed at the window and beyond. You would not be able to resist the attraction of the sound. You would be under its spell, so to speak. The attention that is captured irresistibly and involuntarily is referred to as fascination (from the Latin word for 'spell', *fascinum*). Fascination promotes recovery from DAF because it rests our brains from the task of resisting distractions. That is why it restores what directed attention depletes.

Interest is the major driver of attention. We are most likely to pay attention to what interests us (Remember your school days). High interest induces us to attend involuntarily and closely. Low interest, on the other hand, gives the brain the option of paying attention or not doing so. What happens will be largely a matter of choice. Because it is associated with high-level interest, fascination is sometimes spoken of as attention. Directed attention, on the other hand, is described as choice-driven.

In the workings of our minds, nature and fascination go together. Just as directed attention is an inescapable part of life in modern environments, fascination is the spontaneous and usual form of attention in natural places. Natural environments are rich in features that are spontaneously interesting to us. These are features that are aesthetically pleasing and gentle on our senses and emotions, such as flowers, lakes, grassy woodlands and birdsong. The fascination that such features evoke is called soft fascination to distinguish it from a second and less restorative kind of fascination. This is hard fascination, so called because it is 'hard' on our senses, minds and emotions. Hard fascination is stimulated by natural objects and circumstances that arouse fear, anxiety, apprehension and other mind-focussing emotions. Examples include snakes, spiders, aggressive animals, the edges of cliffs and violent surf. Outdoor activities like rock climbing, abseiling and trackless walking can also evoke hard fascination.

Soft fascination is more restorative than hard fascination because it does not take over our minds. During soft fascination, there is much less emotional energy driving attention. In addition, soft fascination enables the mind to spend time with itself engaging in reverie, reflection and introspection. Time spent this way sometimes spawns creative ideas and new and helpful ways of seeing problems and issues, or it simply may give a troubled mind a chance to recuperate.

Restorative environments

When it comes to having our mental energy restored, natural environments are the places to be. It is easy to recognise restorative settings because our brains are programmed to detect them. We just have to look out for them. What we are looking for could be as close as a window with a green outlook or a display of indoor plants[16]. But the more obvious places to seek restorative settings are outdoors in gardens, parks and other places with a mix of vegetation, and if water is present in the scene, all the better[17]. Playing fields consisting of grass without trees and shrubs may not work as well. It is also important to keep in mind that physical size is not critical. Not a lot of greenery is needed to provide our minds with a restorative sense of being in the presence of nature. Nor is restoration tied to particular activities. Any activity that allows nature to capture our attention will do, whether it is just sitting and contemplating or undertaking something more vigorous like cycling, hiking, or backpacking. And in the case of children, there is no better activity than free play. For children with Attention-Deficit/Hyperactivity Disorder (ADHD), for example, play in natural settings has been found to improve concentration, social behaviour and sleep patterns[18]. Children, in general, are likely to benefit in the same way and to perform better academically as a result.

While your preference should be for seeking restoration in real nature, 'virtual' nature in photos and videos can work for you as well[19]. They may not be as effective as real nature, but they can be a good alternative[20].

Tranquillity and solitude

I spend some of my leisure time rowing on a winding river estuary. The more sheltered stretches of the estuary can be mirror-like, still as a millpond, the water disturbed only occasionally by a leaping mullet or a passing boat. The serene stillness of the estuary reminds me of that pleasantly quiet state of mind called tranquillity. To experience tranquillity is to feel calm and at peace, and to be free of disagreeable sensations and thoughts. A tranquil mind is neither consciously busy nor idle, neither preoccupied nor inattentive. It is a mind that is present in the moment but free to wander into its own inner world of thoughts, memories and feelings.

Contemplating this inner world is known as reflective thinking or reflection. Reflective thinking can be completely freewheeling, as in daydreaming or reverie, or channelled in directions of our choosing. We can be reflective about ourselves—about our past, present and future, our actions, attitudes, values and feelings, our work and play, our bodies and our relationships. Whether unrestrained or channelled, reflective thinking can be both productive and therapeutic, sometimes leading us to new and helpful perspectives on problems, issues and possibilities in our lives. Reflective thinking, along with an awareness of beauty and feelings of serenity, makes tranquillity the distinctive and important experience that it is. Tranquillity belongs with aesthetic pleasure, awe and wonder as one of nature's most appealing and sought-after experiences.

By facilitating mind-wandering and reflection, tranquillity sets in train important processes of self-discovery. It does this by activating connections in our brain that neuroscientists call the default mode network (DMN)[21]. This network links parts of our brain that provide us with a sense of who we are based on our memories, our social awareness and our ability to imagine and contemplate the future. The DMN is where we generate our own story, our own autobiography.

When switched on, the DMN is active (even though our conscious mind is working relatively quietly). Until recently, it was assumed that our brain is busiest when we are engaged with the external world, addressing tasks and solving problems, for example. But studies have revealed that the DMN is possibly where most of our brain work is done[22]. Our brains, it seems, are built for 'day-dreaming' as much as for learning, planning and problem-solving.

This tells us that reverie and free-roaming reflection are important for our mental and emotional well-being. A switched-on DMN not only rests and restores our brains but it also unlocks them for creative and imaginative thinking[23]. On the negative side, faulty or inadequate DMN activity has been linked to attention deficit disorder, schizophrenia and depression. Perhaps inducing tranquillity is one of nature's ways of keeping the DMN in good working order.

There are situations, of course, where day-dreaming is inappropriate, harmful and dangerous, when we are meant to be paying attention to someone, operating machinery or driving a car, for example. But times spent in the tranquil contemplation of nature are not among them.

As well as feeling good, tranquillity is obviously good *for* us—by helping us to recover from mental fatigue and the effects of stress and, very importantly, by creating the physical and psychological space that supports reflective thinking. As the famous Roman statesman, Marcus Cicero, declared: 'A happy life consists in tranquillity of mind'[24]. Cicero would have known that expecting a lifetime of unbroken tranquillity and happiness is unrealistic. Nevertheless, seeking regular 'doses' of tranquillity to fortify ourselves for the hurly-burly of modern life is a wise thing to do. Fortunately, the question of where to look is an easy one to answer.

The tranquillity of place

The word 'tranquillity' has come to mean different things to different people. It is often used in the relatively narrow sense of being relaxed or not stressed. Taking it easy by a swimming pool or on a beach, for example, would be many Australians' idea of tranquillity. It is also commonly given the same meaning as 'peaceful' or 'quiet'. A parent of young children, for instance, might describe a childfree period as tranquil. People who meditate sometimes use the term to describe the special feeling of mental stillness that is achieved when their mind is finally centred. Practitioners of *Tai Chi* do much the same, although in their case the stillness is experienced in the pause between stylised and symbolic actions. Theirs is a tranquillity of movement.

Then there is the tranquillity of place, possibly the most common interpretation of all. People, in general, tend to describe tranquillity by referring to a specific location or type of place. 'Tranquillity is a place where you feel at peace', they might say, or 'Tranquillity is found in areas you can visit to leave all your troubles behind and escape life's hustle and bustle'[25]. In linking tranquillity and place, people are recognising that what goes on in their minds is influenced by their surroundings. The sights, sounds and activity of a typical city or town, for example, can bombard our minds with information and put stress and strain on our emotions. In contrast, there are places that have the opposite effect, gently stimulating rather than overloading our mind and soothing rather than taxing us emotionally. Settings of the second kind enable our minds to switch from being effortful to being (almost) effortless. Not surprisingly, these are the kinds of environments most people associate with tranquillity.

These tranquil places can sometimes be in unlikely settings. They can be in the heart of urban busyness, for example. City churches, mosques, temples, art galleries and other buildings that give people an attractive space for quiet contemplation can all be tranquil places. So can urban gardens and parks. The Japanese have made an art form of creating gardens that promote tranquillity. Sima Eliovson tells us that the intention of a Japanese garden is 'to provide tranquillity so that the people of the house can obtain peace of mind and escape from the strains of living in the contemplation of nature'[26]. The Japanese are not alone in their urge to 'domesticate' nature to enjoy its beauty, tranquillity and other non-material benefits. The same urge is expressed in ornamental gardens and parks the world over and has been for centuries.

What makes a natural place tranquil?

What is it, then, that makes a garden, urban park, stretch of rural countryside or a pristine mountain lake a place of tranquillity? Happily, we have an authoritative and helpful answer to this question from landmark work being done in the United Kingdom. This work is proceeding along two distinct but merging paths: one is the production of tranquillity maps of the British countryside; the other is the development of the Tranquillity Rating Prediction Tool (TRAPT) for predicting the 'perceived tranquillity of urban open spaces'[27].

The starting point for both paths is evidence that people want and need access to places where they can experience peace and tranquillity. Such places have two defining properties. First, they are completely natural in the sense of being as nature intends them to be. Second, they are free of the presence and signs of people and, for this reason, are experienced as remote, even if, in terms of distance or geography, they may not be.

Naturalness.

We are experiencing naturalness when we are aware only of the sights and sounds of nature. This can happen in genuinely wild places or in green oases within built-up areas. Naturalness is a property that nature alone can create. This is true even in the case of a fully landscaped garden. The architecture of the garden, its location, form, size and style, along with the provision of essential resources such as water and fertilisers may be the work of humans, but whether the garden feels authentically natural depends ultimately on nature's contribution to the enterprise.

Naturalness cannot be divorced from beauty. This may suggest that beauty is the key to the strong association between naturalness and tranquillity. While beauty is part of the story, the overlap between beautiful and tranquil places is not complete. People do not always describe beautiful places as tranquil[28]. A scene with a dominating feature such as a thundering waterfall is more likely to be described as beautiful rather than tranquil. People find tranquillity in natural places that are attractive but are also relatively gentle in their demands on the senses. Tranquillity is not usually experienced in settings that are strikingly awesome or interesting, even if they are beautiful. We are more likely to find tranquillity in places where aesthetic pleasure can be experienced in combination with soft fascination[29]. This combination lures us into tranquil places and holds our attention once we are there.

Remoteness.

Remoteness is often taken to mean being a long way from anything or in the middle of nowhere. Remoteness as it relates to tranquillity, however, is a matter of psychological rather than geographical location, of perception as well as reality. It refers to having a sense of 'being away from it all' regardless of where we happen to be.

Remoteness is a critical attribute of tranquil places. The tranquillity that people seek and expect in nature requires a place where there are few people and virtually no signs of human activity—a place that feels remote from 'civilisation' in other words. It only takes one or two signs of people to prevent, weaken or destroy that feeling of remoteness.

Solitude

Remoteness or time away from other people enables the mental quietness and emotional calm of tranquillity to expand into a sense of being contentedly with oneself. Although we are social animals, we all need time by ourselves and for ourselves. We value the oases of private space in our daily lives and often actively seek such spaces. Many people say that seeking solitude is a major reason why they visit wilderness areas and other natural environments[30].

Unlike loneliness or involuntary aloneness, which is usually thought of as undesirable, solitude is typically a positive experience. In solitude, there is little or no sense of deprivation or of missing out. Quite the contrary, solitude is a satisfying journey into the world of our own thoughts and feelings. Such a journey of self-reflection is possible only when we are free from the claims of others. This does not mean that we must be completely alone. We can be in the physical presence of others but mentally in our own space. Solitude is not measured by the distance from other people but by the place they occupy in our attention and thoughts. Many bushwalkers I know often walk 'alone' but very rarely by themselves. They walk in companionable silence. A bushwalking friend, Susan, is typical. A busy professional person, she values her bushwalking for rest and recovery as well as recreation. 'I love walking with my own thoughts', she told me, 'but I need to have the security of a safe group to do so'. Providing the number of other people in our space is small and providing that they do not linger in our company or demand our attention, we can keep them on the margin of consciousness and still enjoy the sanctuary of solitude [31].

We are not alike in our enthusiasm for solitude or in our ability to take advantage of it. For people who live alone, for example, solitude may not be an attractive prospect. Others may feel that solitude is a luxury they cannot afford because they lead busy lives. And there are those who believe that they cannot live without the company of others. But being contentedly alone has benefits for all of us. To enjoy those benefits we first must take ourselves to one of nature's tranquil places. Once there, all that is left to do is to welcome the solitude. The consequences can be surprising as well as valuable, as one 47-year-old woman discovered on her first trip into a remote wilderness area:

> The water and trees became more beautiful when I was able to go off by myself and just sit, perched on a rock away from the rest of the group. Not that I didn't like the other women and all, it's just that being alone is when I found my centre. Times when I did that was like returning to a place deep inside me and visiting an older and wiser me even though I felt young and vitally alive too[32].

Others in her group found that, after periods of solitude, they felt rejuvenated and had a renewed sense of hope about the challenges waiting for them back home.

These are not one-off or exceptional experiences. Solitude in natural settings offers potential benefits for everyone.

- We can learn more about ourselves, about our values and goals, beliefs and prejudices, strengths and weaknesses, hopes and ambitions.
- We can discover new and creative ways of seeing situations, relationships and problems as our mind shifts from purpose-driven thinking to the spontaneity and unpredictability of musing and meditation.
- We can have a sense of being part of a greater whole, which may be interpreted by some as being closer to God.
- We can feel closer to, and more appreciative of, others, especially those we care very deeply about.
- We can discover what the acclaimed Australian novelist, Tim Winton, describes as the great power of 'being happily alone harbouring secrets in special places'[33].

Perhaps the most important benefit of nature's solitude is simply the peace and quiet it brings. Life in cities and towns imposes an unnatural and sometimes heavy burden on our brain and nervous system. Tranquillity is an escape from the clamouring sights and sounds of urban life and having time with and for yourself, as much as it is aesthetic pleasure, fascination or anything else. In a tranquil place, we are gently drawn from one world into another. The 'whole new world' we enter is the world of lakes, streams, woodlands, grasslands, birdsong, wildlife and all the other things that express naturalness. The world we leave behind is the so-called modern world. This journey of the mind—from a world that requires our attention to one that facilitates reflection—is a worthwhile journey for everyone. It is a necessary journey because there is always part of the human psyche that yearns for the primal world of our forebears. Only in places where remoteness and naturalness occur in combination can this yearning be genuinely satisfied. Perhaps the gift of tranquillity is nature's way of encouraging us to visit such places and to be nourished by them.

9. CONNECTIONS

Some years ago, five women went on a professionally guided seven-day canoe trip in the Boundary Waters Wilderness Area in northern Minnesota, USA. All the women were in their forties, but this was the first time they had made such a journey. Two environmental scientists, Laura Fredrickson and Dorothy Anderson, made the women's experiences the subject of a research project and asked the women to keep personal journals during the trip[1]. Journal entries were then discussed in follow-up interviews. Several clear themes emerged from the information the women provided. One of these themes had to do with 'connections', that is, with the sense of being in close touch with someone or something else.

For example, one woman said:

> …[A]t the end of the day, when we were left on our own to go and explore, that was when I felt like I was in-touch. Those certain areas where the moss was real thick and you just felt your foot squishing around—it all felt so natural and real. That kind of stuff, the feeling of being in natural surroundings and getting back in-touch with all the really important stuff of life[2].

She obviously experienced a deep sense of connection with her surroundings, an 'earthing' that provided a new lens through which to view her life.

One of her companions also spoke appreciatively of times spent alone, but for her, these were times of connection with herself and with others.

> It was marvellous and wonderful those times when I could go off on my own, you know, after we got into camp and

all at day's end, or early in the morning before everyone else was awake. I noticed more, I felt more connected to myself and even to the other people on the trip after I took these momentary periods of solitude[3].

We are not told exactly what being more self-connected meant to this woman. But from my own experience, I imagine she was talking about getting in touch with her thoughts and feelings and with the things that really mattered to her. She might also have found that thinking about the day's events and accomplishments made her feel good about herself. The fact that her times alone also strengthened her bond with the other women in the party is not surprising. Solitude does strengthen feelings of attachment to loved ones and friends[4]. Perhaps being alone makes us more conscious of others and appreciative of what they bring to our life.

For a third woman, the social connection she experienced was a highlight of the trip.

> The strongest part, the thing that I remember the most is just the interaction with all the other women which to me was equally important as being in this beautiful setting. You know, the natural setting was a wonderful place, but it was the interaction with all of these women that was truly inspirational to me. I have just never encountered that kind of cooperation in such a gentle manner. Maybe, it was the place, the setting itself washed away all the other stuff, all the artificial barriers that get in the way of first just being comfortable with yourself and then being with a group of people you haven't met before[5].

It is sad that this woman had to wait until her forties before discovering just how unstinting and unconditional kindness can be. But it is good that she did not miss out altogether, thanks to her companions and the power of shared wilderness experiences to foster empathy and caring behaviour. We can also relate to her pleasure in having been part of a supportive group. The women accepted one another as equals. Differences in their educational, social and economic backgrounds, 'the artificial barriers', that might have separated them in their ordinary lives were set aside as irrelevant or were 'washed away' as the woman expressed it. The experience of being accepted unreservedly would have boosted her self-confidence and sense of worth.

The canoe trip was in a beautiful and rugged wilderness area. The women usually paddled their canoes for several hours at a time, from one campsite to the next. The only stops were at places where the canoes had to be unloaded and carried around rapids and waterfalls, sometimes on rocky, uneven and muddy tracks. The trip certainly required the women to accept nature's terms and conditions and to do much more than observe and admire the beautiful environment. For these novices, the trip had all the elements of the archetypal hero's journey that is re-told in countless legends—a venture into a novel world, valiant struggles against mental and physical challenges and a fulfilling reward at the end[6].

The connections described by the women happened because the canoe trip possessed these elements [7]. Imagine their feelings of uncertainty and apprehension at the beginning of the trip and the gutsy resolve they needed to cope with fatigue and other discomforts. Imagine the teamwork that was demanded and the socialising around the campfire at the end of each tiring but rewarding day. Also imagine the joy they shared at journey's end in the knowledge that they had 'done it'.

Other wilderness activities such as backpacking, ski touring and trekking can work in the same way—not because they are adventurous or risky but because they take place in a wilderness setting and are seen as challenging as well as appealing by those taking part. A day-walk along a wide bush track can be a hero's journey for one person as much as a full-pack trek in trackless terrain can be for another. It is not the activity as such that matters, but its meaning to the individual. If it draws out the hero in us in some way, then it can help us become more connected with ourselves, with others and with the cosmos.

Connection with your inner self

The late Irene Gleeson, an Officer of the Order of Australia (the country's second highest honour), was an extraordinary humanitarian. I met Irene when she enrolled as a mature-age teacher education student at the college where I lectured. I recall her telling me that she felt weighed down by many years of being a carer, first as the surrogate mother of several younger siblings and then as the mother of five children. She lamented that, years of being at the beck-and-call of others had not allowed her to be her own person. Beginning tertiary studies in mid-life was an attempt to restore some autonomy to her life and to combat self-doubt and feelings of inadequacy.

At the end of her studies, she joined me and four others on a trek in the Himalaya of Nepal. She saw the trek as an opportunity to take time-out doing something of her choosing away from the demands and constraints of suburban family life. A delightful companion, she coped well with the physical demands of the trek and the four weeks of tent life involved. In a reflective moment near the end of the trek, she said to me, 'I came on the trek to draw and write, but I keep thinking about God'. It was to be many years before I realised the full significance of that remark.

Apart from one brief encounter, I lost touch with Irene but I sometimes wondered whether she had found the liberation and fulfilment she was seeking. My answer came decades later in a newspaper report of her death. The report spoke of her humanitarian work in establishing schools for thousands of Ugandan children. The flood of tributes that followed her passing spoke of a person of great selflessness, faith, courage and resourcefulness. Her achievements were clearly those of a woman who had found both herself and the freedom to be the person she had discovered. A reference in Irene's obituary to her Himalayan trek suggests that the experience was a landmark on her journey to self-realisation and self-fulfilment. I feel greatly privileged to have known Irene and to have had a small part to play in her remarkable story.

Based on my own experience and that of many others, I suspect that the trek helped Irene to forge a deeper connection with her inner self. This enabled her to discover more about herself, to become more internally self-aware. As we grow in self-awareness, we understand better why we do what we do. This gives us the opportunity and freedom to become more like the person we want to be, living the life we want to live. Being clear about who we are and what we desire (and why we desire it) empowers us to take more control of our lives. We are much less likely to be controlled by unrecognised and unexamined beliefs, attitudes, values, expectations and prejudices. How can we make wise decisions and choices if we don't understand what we want and why? And how can we begin to understand others if we are a mystery to ourselves?

Internal self-awareness is an important goal to pursue because it is good for our mental and social well-being. But the busyness and distractions of everyday life can make this difficult. Seeking self-awareness requires time alone and the mental space for reflective thinking. A solution is to take time out from our ordinary lives and go somewhere and do something that supports and encourages self-reflection. As the women on the canoe trip discovered, wilderness activities are ideal for this purpose. Wilderness activities take us to places where solitude is easy to find. These are almost always beautiful places, and the mix of solitude and beauty sets the scene perfectly for contemplation, reverie and reflection. Nature writer Quentin Chester believes that the combination of beauty and solitude encourages us to 'take a peek at the big picture'[8]. He means by this that we are more inclined to think about the deeper issues of life, such as relationships, emotional well-being, job satisfaction and spiritual needs. Even while physically engaged in a wilderness activity, some inner journeying may be possible.

When full concentration is not needed, walking rhythmically along a wide, well-graded bush track, for example, the mind can easily slide into a freewheeling and reflective mode.

As well as providing opportunities for self-reflection, wilderness activities can expand self-awareness by teaching us about ourselves. In natural environments, we are not in charge; nature calls the shots. We are often required to cope with novel, unpredictable and challenging situations and to stay concentrated on what we are doing. The women on the canoe trip would have been doing this constantly as they managed changing river conditions, carried their canoes and gear around obstructions and adapted to the business of camping, all with little or no previous experience. They would have learned a great deal about themselves as they responded to these demands. They are likely to have become more aware and appreciative of their physical capabilities, mental resilience and ability to adapt. As canoeing novices, they had plenty of room for personal growth and self-discovery. But everyone, inexperienced or otherwise, can learn something of value from wilderness activities.

David Cumes, the founder of Inward Bound, a wilderness healing and self-discovery program, shares this view. He also believes that some wilderness activities help us to connect with what he calls 'our higher self'[9]. This is a state of 'inner peace, calm, harmony and oneness' that is reached when we have set aside concerns about self-worth, acceptance, prestige and power[10]. To manage this, we need to escape the clamour of our ego—the streetwise part of our psyche that values power, possessions, popularity and other sources of recognition and status.

This is not easy, but Cumes believes that 'if we spend extended periods of time in nature with the right intention, it is easy to let go of ego and let the higher self emerge'[11]. We can do this, he says, by participating in wilderness activities such as backpacking, canoe touring or trekking for a period that is long enough for the activity to become familiar and routine. This may require weeks rather than days. The activity itself must not be driven by ego-serving objectives and aspirations to do with learning or achieving. The focus of the activity should be on *being* rather than doing and it needs to be modest in its call on equipment and provisions. We should aim at 'keeping as little between us and the wilderness as possible'[12]. This does not mean foregoing all creature comforts, just confining ourselves to the basics. It is surprising how little is needed to stay dry, warm, well-fed and secure in the wilderness.

A wilderness experience that affects us very deeply may be difficult to leave behind. The return to ordinary life can be a massive letdown. It can trigger a reaction described by Cumes and others as re-entry depression. This can range in intensity from feelings of regret to a sense of having left part of oneself behind[13]. But a temporary sense of loss and sadness is a small price to pay for the mental and spiritual capital that is built up during extended wilderness activities. This is evident from the way such experiences are often recalled by people as life-changing, and sometimes as the best thing they had done in their lives.

Connection with others

The highlight of the canoe trip for one of the women was the connection she forged with the other women. She mentioned particularly the acceptance, kindness and empathy she had received. She had experienced the kind of trusting and supportive companionship that is forged among people who share positive but challenging nature activities. I am very familiar with this kind of companionship, having mentored many people undertaking backpacking and other demanding wilderness activities. It is a wonderfully egalitarian relationship, one in which social, educational and cultural differences play little part. The canoe trip was a shared challenge and the 'gentle' co-operation and the 'washed-away artificial barriers' of which the woman speaks are references to the empathic support and friendly acceptance that wilderness companionship typically provides.

Companionship is an example of a primary relationship[14]. More than other kinds of social connections, a primary relationship provides warmth, familiarity and closeness. Primary relationships are often established in wilderness activities because it is usual in these activities for a small number of people to be pooling their efforts and working very closely together. Both the location and challenge of a wilderness activity virtually ensure that people come to accept one another, warts and all. As Quentin Chester learned from his extensive bushwalking and camping experience: 'There's nothing quite like being in the middle of nowhere for putting a different spin on how people interact. Thankfully, many of the social niceties simply don't amount to much in the wild'[15].

As primary relationships are formed, bonds within the group become stronger and the members more willing to share and to be open with one another[16]. People are helped to feel that they are valued and supported, fulfilling a need that is not always met in people's daily lives[17]. Relationships within the group can become family-like and the 'washing away' of social barriers can prompt individuals to question their own preconceptions, attitudes and values (especially as these relate to other people)[18].

Wilderness activities also help people connect with one another because they are a form of play. I have come to realise that my adult bushwalking is no different fundamentally from my adolescent wanderings in the bushland near my home. I went off to play in the bush as a boy and I am doing the same as an adult. I just call it bushwalking. I delight in exploring, just as I did when much younger. I still scramble up rocks simply because they are there. I remain just as interested in overhangs, caves and vantage points. And playing with the campfire (on the pretext of looking after it) is as much fun now as it was in my youth. The more I see others engaging in these and similar wilderness activities, the more convinced I am that these activities draw people together because they are a form of play, the kind that Fred Donaldson calls original play[19].

Unlike competitive 'them and us' play, original play involves just 'us'—us together, not competing but co-operating, us sharing equally in the rewards of an experience and us accepting one another unconditionally and not for what we can contribute to winning. This is the essence of wilderness activities. The philosopher, Johan Huizinga, says that play is 'inspired by the feeling of being apart together in an exceptional situation, of sharing something important, of mutually withdrawing from the rest of the world and rejecting the usual norms'[20]. This could just as easily be a description of wilderness activities. People say that bushwalking and other wilderness activities are great levellers. This is true but more than that, they are great unifiers because they encourage us to engage in original play. It doesn't much matter how wealthy you are, how important your day job is or how many university degrees you have when you are collecting firewood with your mates or looking for an easy route through a cliff line or cooling your feet in a creek. The people with you are simply companions in an enterprise that requires nothing more than a desire and an ability to join in, for the sake of the activity itself.

Connection with the cosmos

There is an important sense in which we are already connected to the cosmos, to everything that exists. Every single atom in our bodies and every molecule that sustains our lives are from the universe, the origin of all that was, is and will be. We are made, quite literally, from the dust of stars that disintegrated billions of years ago.

But there is another kind of cosmic connection that we must establish for ourselves. This is the connection that is forged from a sense of oneness with the cosmos. Talking about this oneness or acknowledging it in our heads is not enough. We need to experience it emotionally as wonder and awe, and intuitively as a sense of being part of something vastly bigger than ourselves. For many, the experience also has a spiritual dimension, serving as a window on the sacred and divine. Bede Griffiths, writer and Benedictine monk, recalls how this window opened for him:

> Now I was suddenly made aware of another world of beauty and mystery such as I never imagined to exist, except in poetry. I experienced an overwhelming emotion in the presence of nature, especially at evening. It began to wear a kind of sacramental character for me. I approached it with a sense of almost religious awe, and in the hush that comes before sunset; I felt again the presence of an unfathomable mystery. The song of the birds, the shape of the trees, the colours of the sunset, were so many signs of this presence, which seemed to be drawing me to itself[21].

Connecting with the cosmos begins with our senses. No one appreciated this more than the late Dot Butler, a legendary figure in Australia's bushwalking and climbing communities. She was renowned for spending much of her time barefoot, even when bushwalking, rock climbing or engaging in other wilderness activities. Her career as the 'barefoot bushwalker' began when she was quite young. In her autobiography, she writes, 'I found in bushwalking the adventure I had known as a child, trailing barefoot through the bush with my brothers, feeling, smelling and dancing my way into the blood and bone of Australia'[22].

The young Dot, 'feeling, smelling and dancing' her way through the bush is a delightful image of what it can mean to connect with the natural environment and the wider cosmos via the senses. We do not have to be bushwalking (barefoot or otherwise) or enjoying any other wilderness activity to connect with the cosmos at this level; the simplest encounter with a work of nature can do it for us. Wilderness activities, however, enlarge the scale and richness of the encounter. By requiring us to engage intensely with nature, these activities provide a degree of sensory intimacy that is hard to experience otherwise. We are much more likely to feel the texture of dry vegetation when preparing a campfire, for example, or to enjoy the refreshing coolness of a mountain stream if we need to take our boots off to cross it. And it is only in a forest that we will hear the full splendour of the chorusing of birds at dawn.

Yet there are situations and activities away from wild nature where we can feel intimately connected with the cosmos. Sometimes working hard in the garden can do it, as Michael McCoy, a landscape designer and writer, discovered while making a garden for his own home. This is part of his account:

> There came a point when my body was in autopilot, and my mind just sufficiently occupied to retain a single focus. It was at these times, and when I least expected it, that I stepped into some new relationship with my surrounds. I was suddenly a part of them, no more foreign for my consciousness than a weed seed blowing in; an inhabitant as the old trees around me and the microbes under my feet…[23]

Beyond the sensory contact with the cosmos there is a deeper level of connection. We experience this as an awareness of being part of all that is. This awareness may deliver the realisation that the cosmos is indivisible, that it is one seamless, dynamic whole. Our minds may be accustomed to seeing and relating to things as separate but in the cosmos, everything is connected to every other thing.

It is both a rich and an enriching experience to have a sense of oneness with the cosmos. With it comes:

- a consciousness of being in the presence of some greater power or entity
- strong positive emotions such as joy and excitement
- absorption in the moment
- feelings of lightness and freedom and of transcending the limits of everyday life
- a sense of timelessness.

Connecting with the cosmos at this higher level is a form of transcendence; our consciousness shifts from the here-and-now to a place beyond the limits of our senses. Wilderness activities help us to connect with the cosmos because they access natural places and situations that promote transcendence.

Nature provides two kinds of transcendent experiences, but only one is associated with feelings of belonging and oneness [24]. This is the form of transcendence that occurs in natural environments that are beautiful and gentle on the senses. They are also environments that are novel in some respects but familiar in others. Seascapes and forests often fall into this category. Both bring together familiar elements, the sea, sky, trees and grass, for example, but always in distinctive and unique ways.

In the second form of transcendence, there is not the same sense of familiarity and belonging. Feelings of insignificance and humility are prominent, sometimes in the company of apprehension or even fear. Transcendent experiences of the second kind occur in environments that are strikingly novel, complex and hard to understand. These are often environments in which there are imposing or dramatic features such as tall trees, thundering waterfalls and immense cliffs. I recall, for example, being transfixed by the South Annapurna Glacier in Nepal but feeling uneasy at the same time. The rumbling and creaking of the glacier evoked a sense of menace that I could not ignore even though I was in one of the grandest mountain settings on the planet.

For most of us, transcendental experiences are short-lived, but their positive impact can survive in our memories for a lifetime. Their effects can also be carried forward in our lives in other significant ways. They can inspire changes in our attitudes towards nature, for example. Participants in wilderness activities often develop a greater respect for, appreciation of, and affinity with the natural world. This leads to a stronger commitment to conservation and care of the environment. But we need to nurture our sense of connection with the cosmos to make sure that this strengthened commitment leads to action[25].

Connecting with the cosmos gives us a sense of the unity of all things, so what is spoken of in this chapter as three separate connections—with self, others and the cosmos—are not different connections at all. They are aspects of the same all-embracing oneness. As the stories from the canoe expedition reveal, the same wilderness activity can promote all three connections singly and in combination. Such is the power of nature to speak to our minds and souls.

10. A HEALTHIER YOU

Being healthy is more than not being sick. The World Health Organisation defines health as 'complete physical, mental and social well-being and not just the absence of disease and infirmity'[1]. Health in this sense is certainly about illness and injury but it is equally about such things as happiness, stress, burnout, self-esteem, social relationships and satisfaction with life. It is about the oneness of body and mind and the seamless effect each has on the other. It is about the whole person in other words. To be 'really well' is to be living fully while having an illness-free mind and body. It is to feel that we are realising our potential, coping with the normal stresses of life, working productively and contributing to our communities. Being illness-free is an important part of health, but only part. A complete sense of well-being is essential to make the picture complete.

The previous three chapters have shown that connecting with the natural world increases happiness, empathy and kindliness; stimulates awe, wonder, curiosity, interest and learning; reduces stress, restores mental energy and induces us to engage in healthy reverie and self-reflection. It encourages activities that increase self-understanding, self-reliance and self-esteem; and activities that bring us closer to others, the natural environment and the cosmos. But does having a connection with nature lead to better health? Does it strengthen well-being beyond the short-term? Does it significantly reduce the risk of physical diseases as well as mental illness? Will becoming more nature-connected result in a healthier you?

The likely answer to these questions is, yes. There is abundant evidence that contact with nature is *associated* with higher levels of well-being, fewer illnesses and a reduced risk of developing and dying from a range of physical diseases and mental disorders[2]. Some of this evidence comes from population studies involving a million or more people[3]. But strong evidence of a link does not necessarily mean that nature exposure 'causes' us to be healthier. There may be other reasons for the link. It is possible, for example, that the association arises because healthier people choose to live in leafier towns and suburbs and visit nature more frequently. The kind of research needed to resolve this issue (experiments, clinical trials and long-term studies) is still a work in progress. Nevertheless, many health practitioners, planners and policy-makers are moving forward assured that exposure to nature is a cause of better health. I am happy to do the same, the more so because science has identified pathways by which nature connectedness could, and very probably does, influence well-being and health.

Knowing about these pathways and how they work has practical value for us. Awareness of the pathways helps us to take full advantage of them. This is important if we are to maximise the well-being and health benefits of our nature connectedness.

Nature connectedness and well-being

Well-being is one of those rubbery terms that can mean different things to different people. This hasn't stopped the United Kingdom Office of National Statistics from conducting regular national surveys of well-being[4]. The survey asks people these four questions:

> Overall, how satisfied are you with your life nowadays?
> Overall, how happy did you feel yesterday?
> Overall, how anxious did you feel yesterday?
> Overall, to what extent do you feel the things you do in your life are worthwhile?

People are asked to answer these questions using a scale of 1–10, with 1 representing 'not at all' and 10 'completely'. A person enjoying an optimal level of well-being, for example, would select numbers close to 10 for all the questions apart from the third one. They would respond to that question with 1 or a number close to it. In an ideal world, people's 'scores' on the survey would be nearer 31 than 13, the highest and lowest possible, respectively.

The questions provide a good idea of what psychologists and health practitioners have in mind when they talk about psychological well-being. The Oxford English Dictionary defines well-being as 'the state of being comfortable, healthy, or happy'. What this state actually 'feels' like varies from one person to another, as we all have different personalities, backgrounds, ambitions and life circumstances. It is also important to bear in mind that there are different forms of well-being, physical, mental, social and economic, for example, all contributing to overall or general well-being. Nature connectedness makes its greatest impact on mental well-being, although other forms of well-being, especially social and physical, benefit from it as well.

Mental or psychological well-being is widely thought to comprise five interwoven strands[5].

- *Happiness*: experiencing fun and pleasure more often than sadness, fear and other negative feelings ('feeling good' or hedonic happiness); and experiencing life as satisfying, purposeful and meaningful ('functioning well' or eudiamonic happiness)
- *Low mental distress*: being free of chronic stress, unhealthy mental fatigue and feelings of loneliness, alienation, and low self-esteem
- *Resilience*: having a sense of competence, autonomy and self-reliance accompanied by a commitment to a higher cause
- *Social connections*: having close social relationships
- *Self-realisation*: being the person we feel we can be, accomplishing what we feel we can accomplish

Gains affecting any of these strands strengthens psychological well-being. This is what nature connectedness does for us. It enhances our psychological well-being by promoting happiness, reducing stress and mental fatigue, strengthening resilience, building togetherness (social relationships) and fostering self-realisation.

Promoting happiness

Many studies from Canada, USA, Europe and several other countries show that nature-connected people are more likely to be happier in both the feeling good (hedonic) and functioning well (eudiamonic) sense of the word[6]. A happy person in the first sense feels good more than they feel bad and are generally satisfied with how their life is going. Such a person is usually cheerful and content. A happy person in the second sense finds life meaningful, purposeful, fulfilling and shaped by their deepest values. They are also comfortable with themselves and others and can handle the complexities of modern life with energy and vitality. If you think that being happy in both senses adds up to a state of high-level well-being, you are right. It is quite acceptable to think of happiness as well-being, especially in the case of eudiamonic happiness.

The measured effect of nature connectedness on both forms of happiness is small but is comparable with that of wealth, size of income, education level, religious faith and other accepted 'causes' of happiness and well-being. The finding of a small effect is not surprising. Happiness is determined by many factors, all competing with nature connectedness to exert their influence. But we can be confident that the effect of nature connectedness on happiness (or well-being) is real because there are at least two pathways by which the effect is known, or is likely, to be delivered. One involves a process called *broadening and building*. The second facilitates *maintaining a positive emotional balance.*

Broadening and building

As recently as 30 years ago, the prevailing view in psychology was that positive emotions served no purpose. If they were good for anything, it was merely to 'undo' the impact and consequences of negative emotions, such as fear, anger, sadness and disgust. These negative emotions were known to be important because they had obvious survival value. Fear, for example, helps us to avoid threats to life and limb.

But positive emotions are no longer regarded as useless psychological 'accessories'. This is largely due to the insights and persistence of Barbara Fredrickson, the Kenan Distinguished Professor of Psychology at the University of North Carolina. As a young researcher in the early 1990s, she could not accept that positive emotions served no purpose. She reasoned that, as they had evolved along with the negative emotions, they must also be relevant to human survival and well-being. Her initial attempts to make the case for positive emotions were ignored or rejected. Determined to hold her ground, she developed the broaden and build theory to explain how positive emotions strengthen our ability to survive and thrive[7]. She has spent the past 30 years testing the theory and successfully demonstrating its validity. Her accomplishments make her a leader in the study of positive emotions.

She found that the most frequently experienced positive emotions are joy (or pleasure), gratitude, serenity (or tranquillity), interest and hope. Less often experienced are inspiration, amusement, awe, love (or affection) and pride (not the 'sinful' kind but the kind that arises from a worthy accomplishment or act). Nature-connected people experience all these emotions, not all at once of course, but over the many and varied activities that form their nature connectedness journey. Some, notably pleasure, awe, interest and tranquillity (chapters 7 and 8), are regularly reported. But the other positive emotions are also part of the mix. Sharing nature activities with others, for example, often fosters close and enduring bonds of affection (Chapter 9). I continue to enjoy (and cherish) many of the friendships I formed during my own nature-connectedness journey.

According to Barbara Fredrickson, positive emotions are broadening because they make us more responsive to experiences.

They increase awareness, awaken interest, excite curiosity, encourage learning, stimulate thinking and promote creativity. They also incline us to be more socially sensitive, generous and caring. As they broaden us, positive emotions prompt us to interact with the world in ways that extend or build our knowledge and abilities. We become more capable of leading happier lives and taking care of ourselves. In the broaden and build process we have an account of how positive emotions 'cause' happiness and well-being.

The previous chapters in Part 2 provide numerous examples of the broaden and build process at work. Indeed, most of the 'good things' arising from nature connectedness deliver their goodness by this process. Awe (Chapter 7), for example, broadens by focussing attention, arousing curiosity, supporting learning, fostering humility and stimulating empathy. The building that follows encompasses a range of capabilities including knowledge and understanding, learning and thinking skills, interests, openness to experience, social sensitivity and tolerance. Each of the positive emotions has its own way of broadening and building but the general outcome is the same. Both happiness and well-being are enhanced.

As I look back on my own journey to nature connectedness (Chapter 1), I see a vast array of experiences that exposed me to the full range of positive emotions, especially joy, awe, serenity, gratitude, interest, inspiration and fulfilment. I am gratefully aware of how these experiences have enlarged me as a person, expanding my mental, emotional, social and spiritual horizons in ways I never expected. What began as an avenue of family recreation became a rich pathway of personal growth.

Maintaining a positive emotional balance

One idea of happiness is having more good feelings than bad ones meaning that, on balance, positive emotions such as joy outweigh negative ones like sadness. According to this (the hedonic) view of happiness, the road to well-being lies in maximising happy times and minimising unhappy ones. This is often easier said than done, as many life events and their emotional consequences are beyond our control. Nevertheless, doing all we can to have positive rather than negative experiences is a guideline worth following.

Nature is an abundant source of positive emotional experiences. Nature-connected people tap into this source regularly. Every time they do, they add to the credit or positive side of their emotional balance sheet. When this happens, their sense of well-being or wellness gets a boost. They are more likely to appreciate this effect when they are feeling down, when they are sad, lonely, anxious or angry, for example. It is hard to feel completely well when life is being coloured by negative emotions, but if a dose of happiness brings relief, even if it is short-lived, we usually feel better for it.

On its own, a one-off positive emotional experience in nature will usually have only a small and passing impact on well-being, but the effects of such experiences can be cumulative. In Chapter 2, I introduced you to the ideas of neuropsychologist, Rick Hanson, who insists that we must make 'taking in goodness' (or experiencing positive emotions) a constant ingredient of life[8]. This, he says, will counter the tendency of our brains to remember bad memories and forget good ones. Remaining aware of the bad or damaging things that could happen to us may be good for survival but there is a cost. It can incline us to expect bad or negative things from life rather than good or positive ones. This can make us wary and unduly vigilant, anxious, suspicious and inward-looking.

To avoid this, Hanson advises, we must make the most of positive emotional experiences by engaging in them mindfully. By this he means extending them, savouring them and unpacking them to find all the goodness they have to offer. In relation to nature's good things, the SPE strategy described in Chapter 2 is a good way of doing this.

Whether or not taking in goodness rewires the brain, as Hanson suggests, has still to be determined. But there is no question that positive emotional experiences in nature increase happiness and reduce stress, sadness, anxiety and depression[9]. In a world where there is so much to feel bad about, getting the most from the good things that happen to us in nature and elsewhere makes a lot of sense.

Reducing stress and mental fatigue

Nature offers direct relief from both stress and mental fatigue. By doing this, it enhances well-being in the short-term and probably helps to prevent long-term health problems. The calming and restorative power of nature has been observed in many studies[10]. Just a few minutes of exposure to greenery are calming and restorative. Longer periods spent in settings that are perceived as tranquil and remote (even if physically they are not) produce even stronger effects.

It is not difficult to discover for ourselves how best to use nature as a counter to stress and fatigue. As explained in Chapter 3, there are many different and convenient ways to choose from, ranging from contemplating photos of landscapes through to climbing mountains. If you are not already a nature-connected person, begin with simple home- or neighbourhood-based activities and consider moving into wild nature later. Aim to connect with real nature as regularly as possible. A few minutes spent in a garden or park each day would be a good start.

Strengthening resilience (or hardiness)

People who keep their heads (stay calm) in the face of threats or challenges tend to be healthier[11]. A major reason, it seems, is that they are hardy or resilient, a quality that enables them to take upsets and difficulties in their stride and not be excessively stressed by them. Consequently, their bodies are less likely to suffer the wear-and-tear that increases the risk of disease. And there may be more to the story. Resilience has been linked to better immune functioning and higher levels of HDL, the good or protective cholesterol[12].

There are two main aspects to resilience: first, a 'can-do' attitude or sense of competence and second, a sense that life has purpose and meaning[13]. A sense of competence enables people to view change and problems as challenges rather than threats and to retain a sense of humour in the face of difficulties. People with a sense that life has meaning and purpose have an incentive for managing the problems and difficulties that come their way. They have something that justifies getting on with life. That 'something' usually ranges beyond self-interest. It might be the welfare of family, for example, an artistic endeavour, a religious or spiritual commitment or a humanitarian cause. The combination of a sense of competence and a sense of purpose is an effective weapon against stress. And nature contributes to the development of both.

Nature activities like backpacking, camping and canoeing are particularly good ways of building a sense of competence. They provide opportunities for us to be 'heroes' to ourselves by venturing into unfamiliar territory, confronting challenges and achieving goals[14]. This is powerfully illustrated in the stories of the women canoeists in Chapter 8 and Michael in Chapter 5. In the process of extending ourselves in nature, we are likely to gain new skills and discover attributes we didn't know we had. Wilderness activities, especially ones of longer duration (two to three weeks), produce noticeable improvements in independence, self-esteem, personal sense of control and other personal attributes that strengthen self-belief and confidence[15]. These improvements are displayed by adolescents as well as adults and are maintained and may even grow over time. Quite apart from boosting competence and resilience, all these gains are valuable contributors to well-being in themselves.

Nature provides us with a sense of purpose primarily by inspiring the journeys of the mind and heart of the kind described in chapters 7 and 8—journeys of intellectual discovery, creativity, spiritual exploration and the conservation of nature, for example. All such journeys are inherently purposeful and guided by values and ideals that emerge on the way. Recall the story about Miles Dunphy I recounted in Chapter 6. He was so moved by the beauty of the Blue Mountains of New South Wales that he made exploring, mapping and preserving the region his life's work. There are many similar stories of people finding in nature the inspiration and purpose that guided and energised their lives. Celebrated figures like John Muir, David Thoreau, David Suzuki, Dian Fossey and David Attenborough readily come to mind. The list could be extended to embrace countless others representing many fields of human endeavour including literature, painting, photography, science, conservation and even politics.

Building togetherness (social relationships)

People often say that the relationships with others are the most important things in life. There is no question that close and supportive relationships are essential to well-being. Family and friendship ties are usually a potent source of love, pleasure, interest, stimulation and fulfilment, and people can cope with most life crises if they have social support to call upon. It is not surprising, then, that loneliness or a lack of social intimacy is damaging to health, rivalling the effects of well-established health risk factors such as cigarette smoking, blood pressure, blood lipids, obesity and inadequate physical activity[16]. People who have rich social contacts feel healthier, have a lower risk of developing cardiovascular disease and live longer [17]. Elderly people with adequate social contacts are less likely to experience depression and mental impairment[18]. Social contact not only prevents loneliness, but it also results in more social support and practical assistance in difficult situations.

There are two ways nature builds personal relationships. The first is providing settings where people are likely to meet and interact. The second is drawing people into activities that break down social barriers and promote friendship. The two processes often work together. People are likely to meet in gardens, parks and other natural settings because these are attractive places to gather. Whether friendships grow from such meetings obviously depends on other things apart from the setting. But studies by Frances Kuo on the impact of living in a public housing estate confirm that green spaces do have the potential to bring people together and to promote a sense of community[19]. Organisers of community garden projects would agree. Many community gardens have become valued and informal community meeting places[20]. Some, like the ones in the bushfire-devastated Australian town of Toolangi, are helping people to cope with the trauma of the disaster and other forms of mental distress.

The second way that nature promotes social well-being involves a special kind of interpersonal chemistry. When people are together in nature, what they have in common matters far more than what makes them different. Differences in socio-economic status, cultural background, education, age and temperament, which are bases of division in the wider society, are irrelevant. This is because nature is impartial. Nature is the great leveller, the great disregarder of social status and pretensions. In natural settings people are freer to be themselves, more able to be accepting of others and more disposed to relate empathically and generously.

In the previous chapter, we saw how this special chemistry worked for a woman on a challenging canoe trip, providing her with an experience of co-operation and empathy she had not encountered previously. This same sharing-and-caring togetherness is fostered in any joint activity that is centred in nature including community gardening and land-care and bushland rehabilitation projects.

Fostering self-realisation

Capertee Valley, in the northern Blue Mountains of eastern Australia, is the widest canyon in the world, not nearly as deep as Arizona's Grand Canyon but much wider. Its vastness is breathtaking. One approach route to the cliffs rimming the valley provides no hint of the panorama until you are suddenly upon it. I remember vividly the reaction of a bushwalking companion when she arrived at the spot for the first time. 'It makes you glad to be alive!' she exclaimed, and then gazed silently at the scene for several minutes.

I am confident that she had a moment of self-realisation. Seeing the panorama had made full use of her capabilities to perceive beauty and grandness and to feel pleasure and joy. She almost certainly had what Abraham Maslow called a 'peak experience', a meaningful and transforming moment of intense joy[21]. I can't be certain, of course, but I suspect that as she stood there silently looking, she was lost to herself and feeling a deep sense of fulfilment.

Peak experiences are encounters with excellence or greatness in some form. It can be the greatness of a work of art, for example, a building, a musical performance, a physical achievement, an altruistic action, or an instance of inspiring leadership. Such encounters make us feel more complete, self-realised or self-actualised because they connect us with greatness[22]. While everyone can have peak experiences, personal, social, educational and cultural factors make a difference. Peak experiences are more common in people who are open to experience, less anxious and freer of tension, for example. Nature is the source of the most common and universal triggers of peak experiences. These can be encounters with wildlife as well as with beautiful and awe-inspiring features and events. As exposure to nature increases, so too does the likelihood of having peak experiences.

But peak experiences are only part of the link that connects nature with well-being. A second pathway exists because nature provides distinctive and unique opportunities to challenge and extend our mental, physical, mental and creative capabilities. As the account of the canoeing expedition provided in the last chapter illustrates, these opportunities take the form of activities that require us to move beyond the familiar and comfortable. These can be adventurous activities such as wild-water canoeing, trekking, backpacking and scuba diving but there are other nature activities that serve the purpose. Some forms of gardening, for example, can be mentally, physically and creatively challenging. For a dedicated and highly motivated gardener, establishing and maintaining a beautiful garden could be as fulfilling and self-actualising as an epic trek could be for an ardent bushwalker. By looking to nature for ways 'to push the envelope', we give ourselves scope to do what we are capable of doing and to be what we are capable of being.

Nature connectedness and the prevention of illness

Doctors in several countries, including the USA, Finland, Japan and the UK, are now prescribing 'doses' of nature. Health authorities in Scotland's Shetland Islands, for example, have launched the Nature Prescription Project to help with a range of afflictions, including high blood pressure, anxiety and depression. Doctor's surgeries on the islands have leaflets listing nature walks and activities. The leaflets have been produced to make it easier for doctors to prescribe nature activities. While new to modern medicine, using nature as a remedy for illness is a centuries old practice. Physicians in ancient Greece, for example, used the beauty and wonder of gardens, along with that of art and music, to bring peace and joy to the minds of their patients. Nearer our own time, the 19th century author and naturalist, Henry David Thoreau, described nature's impact on our well-being as the 'tonic of wildness', a tribute to the way time spent in natural places can clear the head, stir the spirit and refresh the body[23].

Even Thoreau could not have anticipated how busy health scientists have been over the past 20 years exploring the association between exposure to nature and physical and mental health. Many studies have been undertaken, most comparing the health of people living close (within 300 metres to one kilometre) to some form of wild or everyday nature with that of people living farther away[24]. Some studies have made the comparisons across entire national populations, those of Denmark, the Netherlands and the United Kingdom, for example.

All these studies tell a similar story. People living closer to natural or urban greenspace are more likely to report that they are in good health and to be at reduced risk of:

- dying prematurely from any cause
- dying from cardiovascular disease
- developing type 2 diabetes
- suffering from anxiety, depression, stress disorders and schizophrenia.

They are more likely, as well, to enjoy better sleep and to score well on important health markers, such as cortisol (a stress hormone) level, heart rate, HDL ('good') cholesterol level and blood pressure. For expectant mothers who are exposed to nature, there is additional good news. Their babies are at less risk of being born pre-term or underweight. And this is probably a conservative picture of the benefits associated with the nature-health connection. Mounting immunological and other evidence raises the real possibility that nature plays a beneficial role in relation to other threats to health, including some forms of cancer.

Some of the associations between green space and health have been found in children as well as adults and many have been observed across different cultures, ethnic backgrounds, socioeconomic circumstances and levels of education. Interestingly, there is some evidence that the less advantaged economically and educationally stand to benefit most from contact with nature.

Some scientists are so impressed by the evidence of a link between exposure to nature and a reduced risk of illness that they speak of 'vitamin N' (for nature) if they are from the USA or 'vitamin G' (for green space) if they are European. There is certainly abundant evidence of an association. It is also becoming clearer how the health benefits of nature are delivered. Three likely pathways have been identified: the mind-body pathway, the biological or physiological pathway and the physical activity pathway.

The mind – body pathway

Your mind can make you sick and shorten your life. Before the 1990s, such a statement would have been medical heresy. Well into the 20th century, most medicine was practised in the belief that what happened in our minds had little or nothing to do with the state of our bodies. Physical diseases and bodily malfunctions were thought to be totally biological and had to be treated accordingly. By 2000, that belief had been overturned. The evidence left no doubt that a distressed mind can disrupt and impair every system in the body, including the immune and healing systems. Correspondingly, a happy and untroubled mind helps to invigorate, heal and protect the body from harmful agents, including viruses and bacteria. Best practice health care now requires approaches that involve our minds and everything influencing our mental well-being.

Connecting with nature is one approach that must be included. As explained in the previous section, when we connect with nature we are dosing ourselves with happiness, deepening our satisfaction with life, mitigating the damaging effects of stress and mental fatigue, strengthening resilience, broadening our social relationships and meeting our need for self-realisation. In all these ways we will be resourcing our minds to promote and protect our physical and mental health.

The biological pathway

The biological pathway linking nature and health exists because the natural world contains many agents that interact directly with our respiratory, cardiovascular and immune systems. Some of these natural agents of health are easily recognized: clean air, sunshine and natural sights and sounds. Others are invisible or minuscule in size: negative oxygen ions, phytoncides and micro-organisms in the soil.

Clean air

The air we breathe in green spaces is usually less polluted than the air in built-up areas, making it less likely to introduce toxins, irritants and carcinogens into our respiratory and cardiovascular systems and our brains[25]. Even merely the presence of vegetation near sources of toxic gases and dangerous particulates, such as freeways and factories, can improve air quality. As well as pulling carbon dioxide out of the atmosphere and replacing it with oxygen, vegetation can screen out dangerous chemicals and other airborne muck.

Negative oxygen ions

You may have noticed that being near surf, waterfalls and other forms of moving water is invigorating. There is something in the air it seems. That 'something' has to do with the property of the air around moving water. When water is moving vigorously, electron from some of the oxygen atoms in the water are stripped away and freed to join oxygen atoms in the surrounding air. This creates electrically charged particles called ions. Losing an electron turns oxygen atoms in the water into positive ions. But those in the air gain an electron and become negative ions.

The energising and refreshing lift we can experience while sitting by a waterfall or strolling near the surf is partly caused by the abundance of negative oxygen ions we are breathing in. An overload of positive ions, however, produces a contrasting effect. Dry and windy days can make us feel out-of-sorts. Normal fresh air has about 2000 – 3000 negative ions per cubic centimetre (the size of a sugar cube) but around a waterfall, by the ocean and in heavily vegetated areas the count can be in the tens of thousands!

Why air loaded with negative ions lifts our sense of well-being is still being investigated. It may be because negative ions increase the levels of the feel-good chemical, serotonin, in our brains[26]. It may also be because they improve cardiovascular, respiratory and immune function by activating protective cilia in our airways, dilating blood vessels and increasing the alkalinity of our blood.

But when it comes to helping to clean the air we breathe, the contribution of negative ions is clear[27]. They improve air quality by removing mould spores, dust and other particle pollutants from the atmosphere. They manage this by attaching themselves to the positively charged polluting particles making them too heavy to stay airborne. Removed from the air, the particles are no longer dangerous to our airways and lungs.

Phytoncides

Phytoncides are airborne chemicals manufactured by many plants as a defence against insects, bacteria and fungi ('phytoncide' means exterminated by the plant). Pines, oaks, eucalypts (gum trees), melaleucas, along with many other plants, are known to emit these chemicals. The exact nature of the chemicals varies from one plant species to another. As you would expect, phytoncides are abundant in forests but scarce in urban environments. Taking in the atmosphere of these forests is one reason for the popularity in Japan of *shinrin-yoku* or 'forest bathing'. Researchers led by Professor Qing Li have shown that phytoncides found in Japanese forests increased the activity of human natural killer (NK) cells. NK cells are front-line warriors in our immune defences against cancers and viruses. In one study they found that breathing in phytoncides during a three-day forest walk increased NK cell activity in both men and women, an effect that lasted for as long as 30 days[28].

Micro-organisms

The natural environment abounds in micro-organisms that play an important role in building our resistance to disease and reducing inflammation caused by allergens and free radicals. Children exposed to bacteria and allergens during early infancy, for example, are less likely to suffer from allergic reactions and asthma later in life[29].

Graham Rook, a microbiologist at University College London, refers to these helpful organisms as 'old friends'. Some of these old friends (which include parasites as well as microbes) are almost totally absent from urban environments because of excessively zealous hygiene practices, dietary changes and the over-use of antibiotics. Consequently, the incidence of illnesses associated with faulty immune and inflammatory regulation is rising in urbanised countries, especially the high-income ones. This increases the dependence of many of us on old friends derived from our mothers, other people, animals and the natural environment. In Rook's view, improving immune and inflammation regulation could be one of the main ways by which nature contributes to health. It is certainly a powerful reason for protecting biodiversity[30]. The part played by micro-organisms may prove to be the most important aspect of the biological pathway between nature and health[31].

Sunlight

Dusk is my favourite time of day, especially when I am outdoors. I love the mellow light and the red, pink and mauve hues of the sky. Add the dancing orange and yellow flames of a campfire and all is right with the world as far as I am concerned. I enjoy the bright yellow and blue light of early morning but dusk delights me more. It is important for our health to be aware of the different light and colours of sunrise and sunset. As well as cells that enable us to see the world and in 3D and colour, our eyes have a second set of cells. The cells in this set register the brightness, yellowness and blueness of sunlight. Information from these cells is sent directly to the organ in our brains responsible for regulating the circadian and other rhythms of our bodies. Relatively intense blue and yellow light signals daytime and prompts wakefulness while its absence triggers the production of the sleep hormone melatonin. The circadian rhythm is called the 'master' rhythm because it regulates sleep and orchestrates other bodily rhythms including those affecting immune function, appetite and hunger regulation, temperature, blood pressure and mental efficiency. Adequate sleep is crucial for good health. Apart from restoring energy, it facilitates the repair and healing of body and mind. Sleep deprivation, on the other hand, has been linked to several very unwelcome health outcomes including obesity, cardiovascular disease and cognitive disorders, among them dementia[32].

Access to green space encourages spending time outdoors, which helps to keep the circadian rhythm in sync with the natural patterns of daylight. An Australian study found that people living in greener neighbourhoods had a lower risk of insufficient (fewer than six hours) sleep [33]. A comparable study in the United States reported a similar outcome; access to natural environments lowered the prevalence of sleep deprivation among adults, especially men[34].

The modern way of life often disrupts the match between natural light conditions and our circadian rhythm. Many of us work all day in artificial light. Almost all of us experience light well beyond sunset. Using iPads, tablets and other appliances with back-lit screens at night is especially disruptive as these mainly deliver blue rather than red spectrum light. One major effect of artificial lighting is to create a lag between the natural light-dark cycle and our circadian rhythm.

There are simple ways to avoid this and claim the sleep and other health benefits of exposure to natural light. These include:

- replacing indoor recreational activities with outdoor ones such as cycling and gardening
- taking a short walk in the early morning sunlight
- using sunglasses sparingly in the morning
- softening domestic lighting and avoiding using back-lit appliances in the hour before bedtime
- having a sunshine break during the day (particularly important if you spend the day in artificial lighting).

Having a sunshine break is also important because it exposes us to the ultraviolet (UV) radiation that our bodies need to produce vitamin D. With too little vitamin D, children fail to develop bone strength and adults risk developing the bone-weakening condition, osteoporosis. But UV radiation has a sting in its tail (almost literally). As people living in sun-drenched countries like Australia know only too well, excessive UV radiation can be seriously damaging to the skin causing several forms of cancer including life-threatening melanoma. However, UV radiation's effect on the skin may not be all bad. Recent research suggests that it induces the release of nitric oxide from the skin, which may have health benefits, including lowering the risk of high blood pressure and cardiovascular disease[35].

The physical activity pathway

Physical exercise is essential for health. Regular exercise helps prevent obesity, cardiovascular disease and several other disorders. Among older people, it helps maintain independence and prevents injury from falls. Active people are sharper mentally, have a lower risk of dementia, have more energy, enjoy higher self-esteem and are less prone to anxiety and depression. Unfortunately, however, most of us are not getting enough exercise. Only about one-third of adults in most First World countries have the amount of regular activity required to safeguard their health.

Natural settings are often excellent places for active pastimes. Many people spend time in nature for that reason. But it does not follow that spending time in nature necessarily makes people more physically active. This is true for nature-connected people as much as for anyone else. Nature connectedness may induce you to spend more of your leisure time in green spaces that are suitable for walking, cycling and other healthy activities. But it does not follow that you will undertake active pastimes when they are there. To be surrounded by nature is one thing but to use it as a setting for health-promoting physical activity is quite another.

But if you are nature-connected, you are more likely to find yourself in places and situations that encourage and require you to exert yourself. You may discover that natural settings add to the appeal of fitness activities such as walking, jogging and cycling. Perhaps there are local urban green spaces that could work for you in this way. Ideally these spaces should have the following features:

- a convenient distance from home or work, walking distance preferably
- has the facilities required for physical activity, appropriately surfaced walking or cycling tracks, for example
- aesthetically pleasing gardens, lawns and trees, with little or no visual pollution
- well maintained
- safe
- no traffic hazards
- favoured by local people for meeting socially and for exercising together[36].

The last criterion in the list is a particularly important one, as it highlights the value of having the company of family and or friends when using green spaces for exercise. Many of us find exercising with others safer, more pleasurable and sustainable than plugging along alone. Whether you do it alone or with others, however, you are likely to find that green exercise is more enjoyable and beneficial than exercising in gyms or other indoor settings[37].

Nature connectedness can also help you become a regular exerciser by giving you a compelling reason for doing so. Given a choice, we opt for those things we want or desire to do. The desire to be physically active largely depends on the pay-off the person gets from activity[38]. If it is worth it, we will make the effort. In my own case, for example, I enthusiastically built physical activity into my lifestyle once I discovered the joys of bushwalking and trekking. I was happy to swim laps or jog around the neighbourhood knowing that the time and effort involved meant that I obtained even greater enjoyment from my active leisure activities. I saw much the same thing happen with my daughters, neither of whom was very 'sporty'. But a passion for bushwalking prompted them to become joggers to develop the fitness required, and after 40 years they are both still exercising regularly and loving it.

Similarly, gardeners have little difficulty finding the motivation to be active. They know that their digging, raking, planting and other horticultural activities will have a rewarding pay-off. Many people get direct enjoyment from gardening activities; being busy in the garden is fun for them. For people with the opportunity and incentive to garden each day, there is little difficulty getting the amount of exercise required for health.

oOo

Connecting with nature should be as much part of a healthy lifestyle as eating sensibly, getting enough exercise, reducing stress, having close personal relationships and avoiding environmental hazards. Edward O. Wilson is so convinced of this that he says we require daily contact with nature if we are to be healthy and productive individuals[39]. According to Jules Pretty and his associates at the University of Exeter, our lives are shaped by the choices we make in relation to two 'life pathways', a healthy and an unhealthy one. People taking the healthy pathway usually live longer and enjoy a better quality of life. They are healthy eaters, physically active and connected to people and society. And unlike those who choose the unhealthy path, they are engaged with nature[40].

11. A PRECIOUS LEGACY
(To share with the children in your life)

One of my favourite wild places is a confined and almost hidden valley where days can be spent exploring canyons, caves and chasms. On one of my visits there, a family comprising mum, dad and two young boys, set up their camp near mine. Having similar plans, we decided to join forces and share activities. I learned that, although the family was from the city, nature outings were a regular and high-priority feature of their lives. I now realise that both parents, Jim and Judy, were deeply nature-connected individuals. They told me that they were long-time enthusiasts for outdoor activities, and they were hoping to pass their enthusiasm onto the boys.

It seemed to me that they were succeeding. Their boys, Chris and Michael, were off exploring by themselves almost from the moment they arrived. I wasn't surprised when the older boy, Chris, told me that he enjoyed outdoor activities more than sport and indoor games. Outdoors 'you can have adventures', he explained. Both Jim and Judy worked in demanding professions. They had limited leisure time, which had to be budgeted carefully to accommodate the boys' sporting and social commitments. But I was struck by their determination to ensure that time spent in nature brought balance to the boys' lives. They had consciously and deliberately chosen to pursue that path and had adjusted their priorities accordingly.

Biophilia: The precious legacy

Jim and Judy were helping their boys claim a precious legacy. Like the rest of us, Chris and Michael were born with a predisposition to be attracted to nature. Labelled 'biophilia' ('bio', life; 'philia', friendship) by Edward O. Wilson, this disposition lies at the core of our 'humanness'[1]. It is also the foundation of nature connectedness. To be connected to nature is to be nature's friend, to relate to it affectionately, respectfully, empathically, ethically and caringly. It is to have made nature part of yourself, to have identified with it and to value it unconditionally just as you do a friend. Such a relationship is impossible without the motivation and abilities that stem from biophilia.

Biophilia is in our genes. It inclines us to think, feel and act in ways that connect us with nature. It gives us a nature bias, you might say. The story of our biophilia is as least as old as our species. Our human ancestors emerged in savannah woodland and possibly other natural environments 300,000 years ago. Biophilia enabled them to survive and thrive in nature. It gave them an affinity or a 'oneness' with nature on which they built their success as hunters, gatherers, naturalists, nomads, and explorers. This affinity ensured that they would learn about the natural world and how to make it their home. Biophilia also enabled them to draw from nature the stimulation and inspiration for much of their art, dance, music and spiritual beliefs and practices. Living illustrations of this can still be seen in long-surviving indigenous cultures like those of Australia's First Nations peoples. Without biophilia, our human ancestors would have found surviving in the wild extremely difficult and developing rich and diverse cultures even more so.

Biophilia endures in us even though most of us live in cities and towns. Our change of address has been too recent for our genes to adapt. As far as they are concerned, we are still creatures of nature.

We should be extremely grateful for this. Biophilia holds the key to all the 'good things' discussed in previous chapters. Without it, nature's beauty, awe, wonder, serenity and sacredness would elude us as would its power to calm, restore and heal. Far from being a genetic relic, biophilia is a priceless legacy. I was reminded of this by a fascinating character called Kenny Salwey, who is featured in a BBC documentary, *Mississippi: Tales of the Last River Rat*. Kenny lived on the shores of the Mississippi

River, subsisting mainly by fishing and hunting. He understood the instinctive connection we have with nature. At the end of the documentary, he remarks: 'Even though we live in an artificial world, we belong to the natural world. That is our true calling. We are fellow travellers with all things in that great circle of life. That is our legacy and it is a precious one'[2]. Kenny may not have heard of biophilia, but that is what he was talking about. And how right he was in calling it a *precious* legacy!

Biophilia is a legacy that must be claimed by being used. When claimed, it becomes a life-force; ignored and neglected, its influence wanes. We claim the legacy by becoming nature connected. When we do, we benefit from the 'good things' described elsewhere in Part 2. Having nature in our lives decreases the risk of a range of physical and mental illnesses, including, cardiovascular disease, diabetes type 2, depression and anxiety. It also opens the door to one of the most potent sources of mental, emotional and spiritual nourishment available to us. To experience pleasure, joy, awe, wonder and tranquillity—connect with nature. To reduce stress, recover from mental fatigue and restore vitality—connect with nature. To know yourself better, to forge enduring friendships and to experience a sense of unity with the cosmos—connect with nature.

For children, the positive effects of a nature connection are even more important and pervasive. Nature has the power to nurture all aspects of their development. Children, who can play in and with nature, enjoy an advantaged childhood. This is what Judy and Jim are giving their boys by helping and encouraging them to connect with nature.

An advantaged childhood

Compared with others, children who have regular, rich and varied contacts with the natural world, especially through nature play, stand to enjoy many advantages[3].

Physical

They are more likely to
- have superior aerobic and musculo-skeletal fitness
- display better developed fundamental motor skills that form the basis of an active lifestyle and sporting competence
- have a reduced risk of obesity.

Biological

They are more likely to
- have a lower risk of myopia or short-sightedness (because natural light stimulates healthy eyeball maturation)
- have healthy patterns of sleep and hormonal rhythms (because of exposure to natural variations in daylight)
- receive the sensory stimulation needed for the development of full visual powers
- encounter immunity-developing soil and airborne micro-organisms.

Emotional

They are more likely to
- experience lower levels of stress and anxiety
- have higher self-esteem, self-confidence, sense of autonomy, levels of independence and resilience
- display greater emotional control and self-discipline
- be free of unwarranted fears and negative attitudes about nature
- exhibit greater resilience.

Cognitive (Learning, thinking, problem solving, imagining, creating)

They are more likely to
- have better powers of concentration and attention
- receive the kind of brain stimulation that activates curiosity, a sense of wonder and efficient learning
- participate in creative and imaginative play

- be cultivating observation and reasoning skills
- perform better academically (because of reduced mental fatigue, better concentration, less stress, stronger self-discipline and greater engagement with learning tasks)
- display fewer symptoms of attention deficit hyperactivity disorder
- be laying the foundation of life-long interests and a commitment to the welfare of the natural environment.
- be gathering first-hand knowledge about the natural world and learning how to be part of that world.

Social

They are more likely to
- develop stronger feelings of empathy (through interactions with native animals and plants as well as pets)
- develop important social skills such as sharing, taking turns, and negotiating (especially through free play)
- exhibit leadership skills
- display better communication skills
- have more opportunities for private time away from adult supervision.

The more children are nature-connected, the more likely it is that they will experience all these benefits. But at least some of the benefits are available to every child who plays regularly in a variety of natural settings under appropriate adult care and guidance. The kinds of natural settings that most benefit children are described in Chapter 4 along with an explanation of what 'appropriate adult care and guidance' means.

If you can share your nature-connectedness journey with children, don't hesitate. You will be doing them a great service. Children who are deprived of nature contacts risk missing experiences that are essential for healthy growth and development. Sadly, this risk appears to be increasing because of changes that have occurred in the world of childhood in the past 40 or so years.

The changed world of childhood

Those of us who are grandparents or great grandparents can recall times when children made plenty of nature contacts independently. These were times when most houses had a backyard, usually with a garden of some kind; when nearby green spaces in the form of vacant lots or patches of remnant bushland were common; and when parental supervision of children's free time was much more relaxed. These were times when children's play was mostly out-of-doors; when they had fewer organised sporting or cultural activities, and when they were free to venture widely in the neighbourhood and beyond. These were times when parents could say something like, 'Go outside and play, but be back by teatime', with assurance and confidence. They were times when children encountered soil, plants, trees, water, frogs, birds, insects, spiders and other creatures as a matter of course.

With the world of childhood now shaped much more by technology, urbanisation, safety concerns and parental control, children have far less scope and freedom to encounter nature. As a result, they do not 'know' the natural world in the way earlier generations did. An 'extinction of experience' is taking place. Compared with their parents and grandparents, children today:

- spend much more of their time (from two to eight hours daily) in front of screens
- have less free and independent play
- are much more likely to engage in parent-organised sporting and cultural activities
- have a much more confined 'home' territory
- are much less likely to travel independently even within their own neighbourhoods
- have far fewer opportunities to play with nature.

This extinction of experience is placing many of today's children at risk of what Richard Louv calls nature-deficit disorder[4]. This is not a medical condition but the detrimental consequences of being disconnected from nature. Few areas of children's development and well-being are unaffected by these consequences and most have implications for adolescence and adulthood. The decline in children's physical fitness, for example, is heightening their risk of cardiovascular and metabolic diseases in later life. Their performance on tests of strength, agility, balance, co-ordination and the other fundamental motor skills is also deteriorating. This often translates in adolescence to diminished sporting competence and an aversion to physical activity. Less contact with nature also means that children's awareness and understanding of the natural world will be stunted, possibly leading to an alienation from nature and even contempt for whatever is not 'man-made, managed or air-conditioned'. The common association between unfamiliarity and fear applies to nature as much as to anything else. There is anecdotal evidence, for example, that children and adolescents are coming to outdoor education programs such as Outward Bound fearful of natural settings and reluctant to engage in wilderness activities.

Contact with nature is undoubtedly a major casualty of the changing culture of childhood. When after-school hours are dominated by indoor pastimes and organised activities, there is little time left for free-play in natural settings including the household garden. It remains to be seen what effect this will have on children's later development, but one thing we can be certain about is that a childhood without nature is a diminished childhood.

But all is not gloom and doom. Children have not lost their capacity and disposition to enjoy the natural world. With help from parents and other carers, they can forge a happy and healthy relationship with nature. Other good news is that helping children enjoy and benefit from a nature connection can be done in ways that do not add to the burden of parenting and caregiving. Many green activities can be shared because they are suitable for both adults and young people. This saves time as well as being a fun thing to do. Sharing green activities can also add to the quality of family life, often in ways that are as remarkable as they are unexpected. This was certainly my family's experience as I report in Chapter 1.

Nature is for children

An advantaged childhood requires both the companionship of nature and the companionship of other people. As a species, we evolved for a life to be shared with others and a life to be spent entirely in natural environments. As the young of that species, our children enter this world with brains that are primed both to establish social connections and to find the natural world a source of wonder, interest and pleasure. Virtually from birth, babies prefer to look at the human face and they are attracted to living creatures in general[5]. That is why representations of animals are among the favourite toys of infancy and early childhood.

Natural environments serve many of the basic needs of childhood. They prompt the kinds of physical activities—running, jumping, swimming, climbing, balancing, throwing and catching—that prevent obesity and related diseases and build fitness, physical skills and motor co-ordination. The richness, complexity and variability of natural scenery and phenomena are ideal for minds that thrive on sensory stimulation, wonder and satisfying curiosity. Children are highly receptive to the impact of nature on their senses, especially during the pre-school years. For them, nature experiences can be very intense, very involving and very memorable. Israeli researcher Rachel Sebba found that 97 per cent of the adults she surveyed recalled that their most memorable place was an outdoor location from their childhood[6]. What made the place memorable was not so much their scenic features as the activities that had been enjoyed there. Sebba puts this down to the intensity with which the natural environment is experienced in childhood. Children themselves have indicated that they are attracted to natural environments because these are both complex and manipulable. Elements such as trees, bushland and water can be particularly significant in children's play. Children also value the opportunities nature gives to claim territories through the building of cubbies and dens[7].

When children are building and playing in cubbies, they are learning how to work together, to share, to negotiate, to resolve conflicts and to advocate for themselves. They are creating a setting where roles they will need in later life can be practised comfortably and safely. Cubbies are also one of the settings in nature that encourages pretend play, which in turn promotes language development, creative thinking and imaginative reasoning.

Children can also use nature to have time-out from adults. Children require privacy and space to relate freely with their peers and to learn the give-and-take of social interaction. Reflecting on his own need as a child to have time alone, prize-winning novelist, Tim Winton, writes:

> Somehow, I needed the open-endedness of natural forms in order to cultivate privacy. Part of this, of course, was the simple ability to get away from people, to get peace and quiet, to escape other people's requirements and demands and rules. Some of it was about inhabiting somewhere without reservation, a place you could experience with only internal rules of your own devising. And part of this open-endedness came from the simple low-tech behaviour of contemplation aided by the exquisite rhythms of the natural world—the fugue-like chants you fall into as a child walking in the cool sand, the patterns of wind across water or the swaying crowns of trees, the sounds of cicadas or bees in the long grass, the slow stroke of your own freestyle, the hiss of the stick you trail in the dirt all afternoon. Do we ever see more clearly than during these aimless days without agenda, mission or purpose?[8]

The abundance of forms, materials and colours in nature also stimulates children's imagination. A bush cubby, secluded clearing or cave can be a marvellous theatre for make-believe. A sandstone overhang I often visited in my boyhood was variously the former hideout of bushrangers, a mysterious gravesite (there is a Latin cross etched in the wall) and my gang's secret headquarters. Writers of children's literature have been exploiting the fertile link between nature and imagination for generations. Most children's stories and books draw on nature in some way, often by featuring animals as characters. Young children have no difficulty admitting animals into their world of imagination. For them, animals and even plants can have feelings, motives and thoughts very much like their own.

Activities in nature can also accommodate children's enthusiasm for play that is exciting or adventurous. What makes an activity risky or adventurous for them is uncertainty about its outcome. Climbing a tree, for example, could be risky for children if they are not certain that they will be able to get back down. Faced with this uncertainty, children need to weigh up the benefits of attempting the climb, the likely thrill, the sense of achievement, the regard of their mates, for example, against possible undesirable consequence including injury and failure. But children can also turn benign activities adventures. I was reminded of this when watching an adolescent boy and his 10-year old sister having one such adventure. They were walking down a steep mountain track that recent rains had made into a watercourse. Their adventure was a game of 'avoiding the water'. They were having fun jumping puddles and keeping their feet out of the many rivulets that occupied much of the track. The wider or deeper the water, the better was the game. It was better because it heightened the challenge, allowing them to test their skill, agility and daring. No risk to life or limb was involved, no gung-ho heroics, just a pushing outward of personal boundaries. Children love to test themselves and to extend the range of their capabilities. Nature provides ideal settings and opportunities for this purpose.

One of the best things we can do for our children is to equip them to manage uncertainty—to handle situations outside their psychological (and possibly physical) comfort zone. Cocooning them is not the way to do this. Children can discover their capacity to deal with situations that they find unfamiliar, threatening and stressful only if they experience such situations with appropriate supervision and support, of course. Many activities in nature, climbing a tree, rolling down a grassy slope, stepping across rocks and investigating mysterious holes, for example, are right for this purpose. That is why they are a big part of Scouting, Outward Bound, Girl Guides, the Duke of Edinburgh Award scheme and most outdoor educational, rehabilitation and therapy programs for young people with social and psychological problems[9].

No one wants to see a child injured, of course, but quarantining them in totally risk-free environments denies them opportunities to learn how to assess risks appropriately and to avoid the hazards of foolhardiness. Enabling children to face the things that make them uncomfortable offers them a cluster of psychological benefits that family therapist, Michael Ungar, calls the risk-taker's advantage[10]. These benefits include resilience, confidence, happiness and a willingness to be engaged with life. Children who are confident about taking risks are ready to try new activities, explore new places and rebound well when things don't work out at first. They are more likely to keep trying until they master a situation that challenges them or judiciously step away from, if that seems best. 'To grow, we need to experience challenges', Ungar says, 'whether we're 4, 14, or 40'.

The importance of free play in nature

Free, unstructured play is the primary way by which children are meant to engage with their world[11]. For children, play is free when they are in charge. Adults can be on hand, even taking part, but only as followers, not initiators and leaders. Free play meets an astonishing range of developmental needs. The seemingly simple game of chasings, for example, is quite complex and wide-ranging in its contribution to healthy development. Think about the skills involved. There are motor skills such as running, turning, ducking under and climbing over obstacles and the social skills needed to organise the game in the first place and to keep it going safely, fairly and harmoniously.

Apart from motor or rough-and-tumble games, there are many other forms of free play including object play. This can be as diverse as making mud pies, floating sticks down a stream, fishing with a rod and flying a kite. As well as being essential for their physical, emotional and social well-being, free play is indispensable for children's cognitive and academic development. Despite this, pre-school educators in some countries, including my own, are being pressured to replace free play with teaching of the three R's. This pressure is coming from parents who mistakenly believe that play has no educational value. This belief ignores the fact that free play, especially free play in natural settings and with natural objects and living things, can stimulate the interest, wonder and curiosity on which optimal development of mental abilities depends. It also fails to acknowledge that some of the most successful educational systems in the world, in Finland, for example, conventional school instruction is delayed until children are seven years of age. Prior to then, play is the centrepiece of the curriculum. In fact, there is a strong movement in Finland and elsewhere in Scandinavia to provide education in 'forest schools'. As the label suggests, these are schools in natural locations, where classes can be conducted outdoors and abundant opportunities provided for nature play.

Writing in the *American Journal of Play*, Peter Gray attributes the rising incidence of young people's mental health problems to the sharp decline over the past half-century in children's free play[12]. Stuart Brown, a psychiatrist and leading investigator of play says something similar. He has observed links between deficient free play in childhood and lack of empathy, mental rigidity, diminished curiosity, workaholism, addictions, joylessness, anxiety and 'smouldering' depression in adulthood[13].

Without play, childhood goes wrong as surely as when there is a lack of love. 'The natural warm exuberance of the child begs not only for all-accepting love, but also for the deliciousness of all the senses, to reach out and grab from a safe and supportive place what the world has to offer'[14]. And in this world of ours, there is nothing richer on offer than the contents and opportunities of nature.

12. AN ENVIRONMENTAL CONSCIENCE

We have come to the last, but by no means the least, of the 'good things' we can expect from being nature-connected. This good thing is arguably the most important of all, because it is key to humanity's attempts to avoid global environmental catastrophe. I call it an environmental conscience because it is about doing the 'right thing' by nature morally and ethically. An environmental conscience guides us to value nature for itself, to see beyond what nature can do for us to what we can (and should) do for it. It obliges us to accept that all life forms have a right to exist and to flourish. It reinforces the disposition to love, appreciate and be inspired by nature rather than the inclination to exploit, dominate and even shun it. An environmental conscience makes protecting the planet a deeply personal matter, something we expect of ourselves.

When you become nature-connected, nature is woven into your sense of who you are. Nature becomes part of you, and you become part of it. There is a blending of nature and your 'self' that is expressed in such sentiments as, 'I think of the natural world as a community to which I belong', and 'I often feel a kinship with animals and plants'[1]. Your sense of affinity with the natural world will also make you sensitive to nature's rights, needs, vulnerabilities and hurts. You will readily agree with views of this kind: 'Plants and animals have as much right as humans to exist'; 'The balance of nature is very delicate and easily upset'[2].

For many people, feeling part of the natural world and valuing nature for itself are unfamiliar, even alien, sentiments. This is especially so in societies (such as my own) with a history of raping and pillaging the natural environment. But this is not the picture in many indigenous societies. New Zealand's Maori people, for example, have traditionally seen themselves as part of the natural environment and guardians of it, a world view captured in one of their proverbs: 'When the land, river and sea creatures are in distress then I have nothing to be proud of". In Australia, indigenous culture is founded on the belief that people and nature are created as one. Indigenous Australians feel a profound connection with nature or 'country'. This kinship is fundamental to their identity and entire way of life. They have a holistic engagement with a physical place that is both real and symbolic. For them, all living things are interdependent so that there can be no separation of person and country, no separation of culture and nature. Variations of the same Earth-centred wisdom are taught and practised in many other indigenous cultures. Nature connectedness serves as a pathway to this same wisdom, fostering the development of an environmental conscience along the way.

Environmental conscience = empathy + nature values

Environmental consciences hold the key to repairing the damage that humanity has done and continues to do to the Earth's biosphere, that thin layer of land, oceans and atmosphere on which we and all other life forms are totally dependent. An environmental conscience is our moral 'muscle' as far as nature is concerned. It lies at the heart of a considerate, compassionate and caring relationship with the natural world. It works this way because it is stirred by empathy and guided by nature-centred values.

Environmental empathy

Empathy is understanding and sharing another person's point of view and feelings. As a response to nature, it is being aware of the needs and 'feelings', especially the distress, of other living things. Empathy with nature is expressed in such sentiments as: 'I am aware of the nutritional and other needs of the animals and plants in my care'; 'I have tender, concerned feelings for the suffering animals and plants'[3]. Empathy can be triggered by thinking that plants and animals are like us, literally or metaphorically. Someone might say, for example: I imagine how I would feel if I were the suffering animals and plants; 'I visualize in my mind clearly and vividly how the suffering animals and plants feel in their situation'. Young children readily attach human thoughts and feelings to other living things in this way. This is a normal and should be encouraged because it is the forerunner of more mature expressions of empathy later in life.

The trick evolution used to make us empathetic creatures was to introduce the 'love' and bonding hormone, oxytocin, into our brains. Oxytocin was originally a body hormone with a range of functions relating mainly to reproduction. But in the brain, it triggers the discharge of neurocannabinoids, cannabis-like molecules that make us feel good. This chemistry works in the brain to foster attachment and empathy, the basis of a concern for others and of nurturing, comforting and supportive social behaviour. When someone dear to us is distressed, for example, oxytocin triggers a matching stress response in us, prompting us to come to their aid. It induces us to protect who and what we love.

Nature-connected people empathise with nature very easily. It is something they are disposed to do; it is part of their personalities, part of what their nature connectedness has made them[4]. 'Dispositional' empathy of this kind varies from one person to another, even among nature-connected people. In general, it is stronger in females than males, possibly because females more than males are socialised to be nurturers and carers or there may be some hormonal or other physiological factor involved as well.

Many things in nature trigger the oxytocin response in humans. Animals, especially small and cute ones, are good at doing it. Our brains usually respond to animals by reducing stress and increasing the output of oxytocin. This makes us more affectionate, open and caring. Experiencing beauty and awe in nature triggers the same reaction[5].

Empathy for other living things is often induced by horrifying instances of animal cruelty, exploitation and destruction. This is true for people who are not nature-connected as well as for those who are. The massive bushfires that destroyed vast swathes of south-eastern Australia in the summer of 2019–20 destroyed an estimated one billion native animals. Images of burnt, dehydrated and starving koalas, one of Australia's most loved, iconic and endangered animals, stirred outpourings of sympathy, sadness and assistance across the nation.

It is a short step from empathy to altruism. Altruistic actions are taken solely for the benefit of someone or something else; no *quid pro quo* expectation or any form of self-interest plays a part. An environmental conscience readily extends to environmental altruism—taking care of nature for nature's sake alone. Just as we are prepared to make sacrifices for the people we love, we behave altruistically towards the natural world if we regard it as 'kin', as something that is loved and valued.

Nature-centred values

We value what is important to us. We are especially important to ourselves, so we have many self-centred or egoistic values relating to our happiness, health, jobs, reputation and security, for example. Values are among the primary drivers of how we think, feel and act. They are among the strongest motivators of protective behaviour.

A powerful illustration of this is an event that saved one of Australia's iconic forests about 90 years ago. The Blue Gum Forest is a feature of the World Heritage listed Greater Blue Mountains National Park in south-eastern Australia. A mecca for bushwalkers, the forest consists mainly of towering mountain blue gums (*Eucalyptus deanii*). Standing among these giants is a truly awesome experience. Now accessible only by walking tracks, the forest was once reached by bridle trails suitable for horses. In Easter 1931, bushwalkers were camped in the forest when they met a farmer who told them that he had a lease on the forest and was intending to log it and plant walnut trees. Horrified at the prospect, the bushwalkers prevailed on the farmer to give them the opportunity to buy the leasehold from him. The bushwalkers managed to raise the £130 ($A260) the farmer was asking, a considerable amount, given that it was three years into The Great Depression. The bushwalkers' intervention saved the forest not only from logging but also damage from mining activities. It also launched Australia's conservation movement largely under the leadership of one of the bushwalkers, Myles Dunphy (whom I mentioned in Chapter 6). From the Blue Gum Forest project, Myles Dunphy went on to spearhead many other conservation projects including the World Heritage listing of the Greater Blue Mountains National Park. As a direct or indirect result of his work, tens of thousands of hectares of Australian wilderness are now protected for posterity.

No doubt, Myles and his bushwalking companions wanted to preserve the forest because they loved it as an area for bushwalking and camping. But almost certainly there was more to it than that. It is a safe guess that they were also motivated by both people-centred (anthropocentric) and nature-centred (biocentric) values. Anthropocentric values would have motivated them to preserve the forest for the well-being of current and future generations and the biocentric ones to safeguard the forest for itself as part of the living fabric of nature.

Both kinds of values lead to environment-friendly attitudes and actions, but biocentric values are more reliably and robustly related to environmentalism. Anthropocentrism promotes the preservation of the environment as a means rather than an end. Biocentrism on the other hand promotes environmentalism as a moral imperative, something you do as a matter of conscience.

Nature connectedness fosters both kinds of values. A review of 26 studies covering over 13,000 participants from several countries found consistent evidence of an association between nature-connectedness and pro-environmental values and actions[6]. The review also found that the relationship was little affected by age, gender and country of residence. The more nature-connected a person is the more likely they are to harbour biocentric values and engage in pro-environment activities[7]. They recycle items wherever possible, for example. They buy environment-friendly products; purchase energy from renewable sources; are members of an environmental or conservation organisation; and encourage others to protect the environment. But nature-connected people are not alone in their desire to conserve and safeguard the environment. Most people aspire to do the same. Many have good intentions as far as the environment is concerned but far from everybody manages to convert intentions into actions. Nature-connected people are among those that do, not just occasionally, but habitually and consistently. They have a stable commitment to 'green' values and actions that is woven into their sense identity. They are what Irish researcher, Mary Jo Lavelle, and her colleagues classify as 'ever-greens'[8].

Even if they are ever-greens, nature-connected people are not environmental 'saints', motivated entirely by nature-centred values. Like everyone else, they have values that are self-serving or self-centred. Such values are not necessarily unworthy. If we did not value personal happiness, well-being and sound health, for example, we would lack motivation to take care of ourselves. We are, in fact, hardwired to do just that—to look after ourselves—and to draw on the natural environment and the processes of nature for that purpose.

But nature-connected people are more likely to interact with the natural world in nature-loving, nature-valuing and nature-respecting ways. According to Stephen Kellert, who partnered with Edward O Wilson in developing the concept of biophilia (Chapter 11), humans relate to nature in eight ways:

- *affection*: loving nature and seeking its 'companionship'
- *attraction*: appreciating the beauty, awe and wonder of nature
- *knowing*: observing, understanding and thinking about the natural world

- *aversion*: feeling antipathy towards, and on occasions fearing, nature
- *exploitation*: utilising the resources of the natural world
- *domination*: mastering and controlling the natural environment
- *spirituality*: finding meaning and purpose in transcendental experiences
- *symbolism*: representing nature in art, language and music[9]

Take a moment before reading on to think about your own relationship with nature with these different ways of responding in mind: the form and depth of your love of nature, the strength of your attraction to natural beauty, the mental stimulation you get from nature and so on. These various ways of responding represent values as much as they do actions. Affection for nature goes with recreational, aesthetic and conservation values, for example, just as exploitation of the natural world is tied to economic, commercial and materialistic values.

Do not be surprised if you used all the eight ways to describe your relationship with nature. Even if you are the most ardent nature lover and admirer of natural beauty, you will also be involved in exploiting and dominating nature in some way, indirectly if not directly. Nature-connected people are no different to everyone else in depending on nature and being party to exploiting and mastering it. Similarly, if you love being in natural environments, there still may be aspects of nature that you seek to avoid. Likewise, people who feel disconnected from nature are unlikely to be completely indifferent to its attractions and benefits.

Kellert's eight ways describe how we all value and relate to nature. But what sets nature-connected people apart is how much more they value nature in terms of 'affection', 'attraction', 'knowing', 'symbolism' and 'spirituality' relative to 'aversion', 'exploitation' and 'domination'. Connecting with nature changes the balance of a person's environmental values, tilting the scales heavily toward affection and the other four pro-nature values. When these pro-nature values are partnered with environmental empathy, the result is a strong environmental conscience, one that is well-informed by empathy and well-formed by values.

An environmental conscience is not a hard task master. Far from it; following its guidance is rewarding. We get an emotional lift from doing what we believe is right and receiving affirmation of the image we may have of ourselves as 'ever-greens'. But as much as our environmental conscience can add to our sense of satisfaction and well-being, its greatest benefit lies in what it means for nature. An environmental conscience equips us to be advocates and protectors of the natural world, empathically attached to it and morally motivated to preserve its integrity and well-being.

Wanted urgently: people with environmental consciences

Humans are changing the conditions of life on Earth. This is something no other single species has ever done. What is more, we have managed to do it in 150 years, barely an 'eye-blink' in Earth-age terms (4.54 billion years). For the past 18,000 years, the Earth's climate has been relatively stable. But now the climate is warming and changing in other ways at an unprecedented and alarming rate. The reasons are clear. Human activities, mainly the burning of fossil fuels, the destruction of forests and the grazing of sheep and cattle, are overloading the Earth's atmosphere with carbon dioxide (CO_2) and other greenhouse gases. Along with water vapour, these gases act like a blanket, capturing and retaining the sun's heat. For thousands of years, the warmth of the blanket has remained relatively steady. This is because the Earth's oceans, land and plants have been able to absorb sufficient CO_2 to prevent it from accumulating in the atmosphere.

That's no longer the case. The proportion of CO_2 in the atmosphere is soaring, causing the planet to heat up. Consequently, summers across the globe are becoming hotter and droughts more frequent, intense and longer. Wildfires, such as those that ravaged south-eastern Australia in the summer of 2019 – 20 and the western states of the USA eight months later, are increasing in frequency and destructiveness. Cyclones (hurricanes or typhoons), which draw their energy from the warming oceans, are more intense and destructive. Glaciers are shrinking and with them the water security of millions of people. Continental ice sheets are melting, putting island nations and densely populated river deltas at imminent risk of inundation. Rising ocean temperatures are transforming marine ecologies, including those of coral reefs such as Australia's Great Barrier Reef, the world's biggest living organism. The patterns and paths of oceanic and atmospheric currents are changing and with them the climate of many regions.

Climate change is an existential crisis; it threatens the existence of our own and other species of animals and plants. It promises to disrupt the lives and livelihoods of people the world over. The day-to-day existence of millions is threatened as agricultural production is impacted and the oceans become less bountiful. Endemic diseases such as malaria and dengue fever are going to penetrate previously untouched populations. These are just some of the effects we know about, many because they are happening right now. Climate scientists are also deeply alarmed by what could happen if global warming exceeds 2 degrees Celsius. Some of the most recent climate change models indicate that the Earth is on track to reach that landmark by 2040, 10 years earlier than formerly expected, unless greenhouse gas emissions are radically reduced in the meantime[10]. The models are also suggesting that increases in the range of 2.7 – 6.2 degrees are real possibilities.

Climate change is worrying enough, but now we are facing a second existential crisis: loss of biodiversity, which may be even more serious. Biodiversity (from the two words 'biological' and 'diversity') refers to the variety of life (plants, animals, fungi and micro-organisms) that can be found on Earth, as well as the communities they form and the habitats in which they live. Human life is totally dependent on nature's biodiversity for oxygen, food, fibre and pharmaceuticals. And the devastating COVID-19 pandemic teaches us something else about biodiversity. Epidemic diseases like COVID-19, SARS, MERS and Ebola don't just happen. These diseases originate in animals, two-thirds in wildlife species such as bats and pangolins. The diseases spread to humans when contact is made with the animal hosts or carriers. Rarely, if ever, do animals engineer this contact. But humans do, by capturing and keeping the animals for food or other purposes, and by destroying habitat and thus forcing wild animals to encroach on human habitations.

According to the 2019 *Global Assessment Report on Biodiversity and Ecosystem Service*, the health of ecosystems is deteriorating more rapidly than at any other time in human history. Close to one million animal and plant species are threatened with extinction, many within decades. Ecosystems and wild populations are shrinking or vanishing. The web of life, of which we are all part and on which we are totally dependent, is getting smaller and increasingly frayed.

As with climate change, the biodiversity crisis is largely the result of human activities. Topping the list are unsustainable agricultural and ocean use practices followed by the direct destruction of plant and animal life, with the illicit poaching and trafficking of wild animals playing a big part. The list also includes practices responsible for climate change, pollution and the invasive spread of alien plant and animal species. These practices are the direct causes of the crisis but behind them are indirect causes, such as population growth and pressures, industrial, scientific and technological developments, materialistic life-styles, rampant consumerism (in well-off societies especially), and the lemming-like pursuit of wealth and economic growth.

But identifying the direct and indirect causes of the biodiversity crisis does not close the case. We need to probe deeper into human behaviour. The Intergovernmental Science-Policy Platform on Biodiversity and Ecosystem Services (IPBES) believes that the biodiversity crisis is really being driven by personal, social and political values[11]. The same is true of humanity's contribution to climate change. It is easy to identify the values of domination and exploitation in the human drivers of both climate change and biodiversity loss.

These are the values of industrial and economic development and of the modern urban lifestyle. They are values that push nature to the margins of day-to-day life and cause many of us to lose sight of our total dependence on it. In Stephen Kellert' words: 'We have separated ourselves from nature and degraded it in the dangerous delusion that we have become free of the constraints of the natural world and can aspire to transcend our biology and our natural origins'[12].

It is not that people are indifferent to the plight of nature or ignorant of the human contribution to it. According to Ipsos poll data, more than four in five people globally say issues such as pollution, degradation of nature, deforestation, overfishing and climate change currently pose a serious threat to health and well-being. Overall, people feel a strong responsibility to ensure that the current generation does not destroy the planet for following generations. Concern for the environment is growing, with Ipsos findings revealing a strong belief that the environment will be in a worse state 20 years from now than it is today. Concern is greater among older adults but is still widespread in younger people. Interestingly and perhaps surprisingly, Ipsos polling also indicates that, even during the massively disruptive COVID-19 pandemic, climate change remained a major concern in most people's minds.

The need for action is acknowledged, but the response has been slow, patchy and inconsistent. There are obvious structural or practical reasons. The transition from fossil fuel to renewable energy sources, for example, must deal with real and significant technical, commercial and social problems. But much of the resistance to effective action relating to the climate and biodiversity crises stems from choices guided by political ideology, economic self-interest, ignorance, apathy and downright foolishness. How else can we account for a former Prime Minister of Australia dismissing the warnings of climate science as 'crap', for example? Or climate change activism being attacked as a political conspiracy? Or corporations with interests in mining, energy production and urban development deliberately withholding or distorting the findings of unfavourable environmental impact assessments?[13] Or individuals mouthing pro-environment concerns and intentions but failing to act on them?

There is a deep cultural mind-set at work. Australian academic and social commentator, Robert Manne's forensic analysis of why the world has failed to address climate change unveils a host of obstructive actions[14]. His reflection on what needs to be done, politically, economically and otherwise led him to conclude:

> Yet, as many people now realise, something much more profound than all this [current approaches to climate change] is required: a re-imagining of the relations between humans and the Earth, a re-imagining that will be centred on a recognition of the dreadful and perhaps now irreversible damage that has been wrought to our common home by the hubristic idea at the very centre of the modern world—man's assertion of his mastery over nature.

Manne is correctly calling for a change in how we relate to nature. The change requires, he says, 'a moral shift no less deep than those that have already transformed humankind with regard to the ancient inequalities of race and gender'. To speak of a moral shift is to speak of values. Clearly, there must be a universal transformation in the way we value the natural world. Without it, action on behalf of the planet will never be wholehearted and successful. According to the great ecologist and ethicist, Aldo Leopold:

> There must be some force behind conservation more universal than profit. Less awkward than government,

less ephemeral than sport, something that reaches into all times and spaces…something that brackets everything from rivers to raindrops, from whales to hummingbirds, from land-estates to window boxes…I can see only one such force: a respect for land as an organism; a voluntary decency in land-use exercised by every citizen and every land-owner out of a sense of love for and obligation to that great biota[15].

By fostering an environmental conscience, nature connectedness cultivates just such a respect for nature. For that reason, facilitating nature connectedness is recognised as an environmental care and protection strategy that could be rolled out across communities large and small. It is a strategy that is supported by the 196-member countries of the United Nations sponsored Convention on Biological Diversity. In addition to endorsing the strategy, the report of the 2018 conference of the Convention calls for its urgent implementation, arguing that:

[Fostering the nature]…connection can start in the simplest of ways, beginning in childhood and renewing through all the stages of life. It can take many forms and occur in many ways. It requires places and spaces for people to connect with nature's richness and complexity from backyards to apartment rooftops, on city streets and rural roadways, on school grounds and in urban neighbourhoods, from wild protected areas to public urban spaces. Connecting with nature helps to bring us all peace and good health, and provides the foundation for resilient, healthy ecosystems to thrive and remain for generations to come[16].

The potential success of the strategy lies in its power to change people's environmental values and to strengthen their mental and emotional awareness of the natural world. In so doing, it creates a mind-set that takes full account of the rights and needs of nature. Such a mind-set consistently assesses proposed actions in terms of their likely environmental impact. Imagine how nature would benefit if decision-making at every level of society were to be based on such an assessment. Apart from increasing the pro-environment behaviour of individuals, it would strengthen community support for environmental protection initiatives launched by governments and corporations. A government-run recycling program, for example, is likely to be more successful in a community where most people are already motivated to get on board. As any smart politician will tell you, reforms succeed only when they accord with most people's desires and values.

The strategy would also reframe government and corporate policy and practices, making them far less vulnerable to opinionated ignorance, ideology, economic self-interest and the distorting (and sometimes corrupting) influence of money and power. It would make possible the broad consensus and co-operation that are needed if action to save planet Earth is to have any chance of success. 'We are all in this together' has been a popular mantra during the COVID-19 pandemic. We certainly need togetherness in dealing with the two environmental crises, especially the togetherness of people who are deeply connected with nature and guided by robust environmental consciences.

Fostering nature connectedness alone is not going to solve the planet's environmental problems or secure humanity's future. The problems are far too urgent and complex for that to be possible. But it deserves to be an integral part of the endeavour. Albert Einstein said that 'no problem can be solved by the same consciousness that caused it'. Nature connectedness changes the consciousness that governs our ways of relating to nature. An environmental conscience is a powerful expression of that change. It also enables us to work lovingly, respectfully and empathetically with nature, satisfying many of our basic needs while taking care of nature at the same time.

ACKNOWLEDGEMENTS

Researching and writing the book has been a long journey and I have been helped along the way by many people. It is impossible to acknowledge them all, but I am appreciative of every bit of assistance I have received. My special thanks go to Jane Tebbatt and my other bushwalking companions who provided the personal anecdotes and comments that I have recounted in the book.

Although responsibility for the content of the book is entirely mine, several people helped me with the writing. It would have been a less reader-friendly book without the extensive, patient and insightful editorial work of Wendy Moore and Margaret Higgins, and the helpful feedback from Jodi Griffiths, Kate Rotherham, Kirsten Mayer, Giselle Mawer, Jane Tebbatt, Professor Bill Boyd, Dr Rachel Yerbury, Dr Rebekah Potter and Tim Gibson. I am grateful to Anita Williams for the design of the one graphic in the book, *Tree of Green Activities*.

I could never have found the time needed to research and write the book without the unstinting support, patience and forbearance of my wife, Margaret. I am deeply conscious of how much time I spent in my study when we could have been sharing activities. The book must be for her.

NOTES

1. Introduction

1. *Conference of the Parties to the Convention on Biological Diversity, Fourteenth meeting*, Sharm El-Sheikh, Egypt, 17–29 November 2018, 7.

2. References to this research are provided in the endnotes to the chapters in Part 2 and in the following:

Capaldi, C., Passmore, H-A., Nisbet, E.K. et al., 2015, 'Flourishing in nature: A review of the benefits of connecting with nature and its application as a wellbeing intervention', *International Journal of Wellbeing*, 5 (4), 1–16. doi:10.5502/ijw.v5i4.1

Capaldi, C.A., Dopko, R.L. & Zelenski, J.M., 2014, 'The relationship between nature connectedness and happiness: A meta-analysis', *Frontiers in Psychology.* doi: 10.3389/fpsyg.2014.00976

McMahan, E.A. & Estes, D., 2015, 'The effect of contact with natural environments on positive and negative affect: A meta-analysis', *The Journal of Positive Psychology, 10* (6). doi.org/10.1080/17439760.2014.994224

Whitburn, J., Linklater, W. & Abrahamse, W., 2019, Meta-analysis of human connection to nature and proenvironmental behaviour', *Conservation Biology.* doi.org/10.1111/cobi.13381 Studies showing that nature connectedness influences pro-environmental behaviour by way of biocentric values are reported in

Martin, C. & Czellar, S., 2017, 'Where do biospheric values come from? A connectedness to nature perspective', *Journal of Experimental Psychology*, 52, 56–68._doi.org/10.1016/j.jenvp.2017.04.009

Much of the information about nature connectedness comes from studies undertaken to develop and test nature connectedness measures, for example:

Connectedness to Nature Scale. Mayer, F.S. & Frantz, C.M., 2004, 'The connectedness to nature scale: A measure of individuals' feeling in community with nature', *Journal of Environmental Psychology*, 24, 503–515. doi: 10.1016/j.jenvp.2004.10.001

The Nature Relatedness Scale. Nisbet, E.K., Zelenski, J.M. & and Murphy, S.A., 2009, 'The nature relatedness scale. Linking individuals' connection with nature to environmental concern and behavior', *Environment and Behavior*. 41, 715–740. doi: 10.1177/0013916508318748

3. Baxter, D.E. & Pelletier, L.G., 2019, 'Is nature relatedness a basic human psychological need? A critical examination of the extant literature', *Canadian Psychology*, 60, 21–34. http://dx.doi.org/10.1037/cap0000145

4. Husqvarna Group, 2013, *Global Green Space Report 2013: Exploring Our Relationship to Forests, Parks and Gardens around the Globe*. Available at http://greenspacereport.com

5. Louv, R., 2008, *Last Child in the Woods: Saving Our Children from Nature-deficit Disorder,* rev. ed., Chapel Hill, Algonquin Books of Chapel Hill.

6. Wilson borrowed the term, 'biophilia', from the psychoanalyst Erich Fromm who used it to mean a passionate love of life. Wilson gives the term a much broader and more complex meaning.

   Wilson, E.O., 1984, *Biophilia: The Human Bond with Other Species*, Cambridge, Mass, Harvard University Press.

7. Tang, I-C., Sullivan, W.C. & Chang, C-Y, 2015, 'Perceptual evaluation of natural landscapes: The role of individual connection to nature', *Environment and Behavior*, 47, 595–617. doi: 10.1177/0013916513520604

8. References to the relevant research can be found in the notes for chapters 7 and 8.

2. Getting started (For the first time or again)

1. The first 10 questions are based on the principles of biophilic design. Stewart-Pollack, J., 2006, 'Biophilic design for the

first optimum performance home', *Ultimate Home Design,* Issue 4, 36–41. Available at http://ultimatehomedesign.com/oph/uhd04gb02.pdf

These are guidelines that have been developed by architects committed to bringing natural and built environments together—to creating buildings and outdoor living spaces that incorporate as many of the beneficial attributes of natural environments as possible. Living in a built environment that reflects all the principles would be close to ideal as far as connecting with nature is concerned. I added those last two questions to cover important nature experiences that are not possible to have in even the best biophilically designed building or urban space.

2. 'Non-contemplation', 'contemplation', 'preparing', and 'action' are labels used by James Prochaska and Carlo DiClemente for the first four of the five stages people move through when adopting a new form of behaviour (The final stage is 'maintenance').

   Prochaska, J.O. & DiClemente, C.C., 1983, 'Stages and processes of self-change of smoking: Toward an integrative model of change', *Journal of Consulting and Clinical Psychology,* 51, 983–990. doi: 10.1037//0022-006X.51.3.390

3. Ware, B., 2012, *The Top Five Regrets of the Dying: A Life Transformed by the Dearly Departing,* Carlsbad, Ca., Hay House.

4. Lumber R., Richardson, M. & Sheffield, D., 2017, 'Beyond knowing nature: Contact, emotion, compassion, meaning, and beauty are pathways to nature connection', *PLoS ONE,* 12(5): e0177186. https://doi.org/10.1371/journal.pone.0177186

5. Lumber et al, 2017.

6. Hanson, R., 2013, *Hardwiring Happiness: The New Brain Science of Contentment, Calm, and Confidence,* New York, Harmony Books.

7. This is clear from the successful use of photos and videos to represent nature in countless studies. For example, see the notes for chapters 7 and 8.

8. The photo can be viewed at https://wildislandtas.com.au/products/peterdombrovskis-rockislandbend

9. Originally published in Oliver, M., 2006, *Thirst: Poems by Mary Oliver,* Boston, Beacon Press, 4.
    Reprints of the poem are published on numerous Internet sites. For example, https://medium.com/magazines-at-marquette/when-i-am-among-the-trees-musings-on-mary-oliver-bc992e1934b

10. There is an illustrated version of this post at www.ourgreengenes.wordpress.com. Go to the archive and click on Aug 2015.

3. Do it your way

1. White, M.P., Alcock, I., Grellie, J. et. al., 2019, 'Spending at least 120 minutes a week in nature is associated with good health and wellbeing', *Scientific Reports,* 9:7730. doi.org/10.1038/s41598-019-44097-3

2. Practical information about installing fire-pits and fire-bowls and the fun that you can have with them is available on my blog, www.ourgreengenes.com. Go to the archive link and select July 10, 2014, 'The campfire connection with nature' and also July 21, 2014, 'Sharing ideas for things to do around a campfire'.

3. The list of features is drawn largely from the findings of Twedt, E., Rainey, R.M. &_Proffitt, D.R., 2016, 'Designed natural spaces: Informal gardens are perceived to be more restorative than formal gardens', *Frontiers in Psychology*, 7. doi: 10.3389/fpsyg.2016.00088

4. Experiments conducted by the U.S. National Aeronautics and Space Administration (NASA) in the 1980s demonstrated that many indoor plants absorb volatile organic compounds and other toxins from the air. In confined spaces like space capsules, they can work as effective air cleaners. But there is no evidence that they have the capacity, except in very large numbers, to do the same in larger spaces with a lot of circulating air. See:

American Lung Association, 2018, *Getting into the Weeds: Do Houseplants Really Improve Air Quality?*. https://www.lung.org/about-us/blog/2017/02/do-houseplants-really-improve-air-quality.html

5. In compiling the list, I have drawn heavily on 'Kelly's' blog, *Being a Fun Mum*, specifically a post entitled, '100 ways to enjoy nature with kids'. Many of the items in her list are suitable for 'children' of all ages. https://www.beafunmum.com/2014/11/100-ways-to-be-a-fun-mum/

6. *Cloud Appreciation Society: Uniting cloud lovers around the world.* https://cloudappreciationsociety.org/

7. https://www.wildlifetrusts.org/about-us

8. Richardson, M., Cormack, A., McRobert, L. & Underhill, R., 2016, '30 Days Wild: Development and evaluation of a large-scale nature engagement campaign to improve well-being', *PloS ONE*, 11 (2): e0149777.doi:10.1371/journal.pone.0149777

4. Make it a family affair

1. Louv, R., 2008, *Last Child in the Woods: Saving Our Children from Nature-deficit Disorder,* rev. ed., Chapel Hill, Algonquin Books of Chapel Hill.

2. Based on data obtained using the *Connection to Nature Index* (NCI), a measure developed for children that mirrors the content and coverage of adult tests. The NCI consists of 16 statements including: 'Collecting rocks and shells is fun'; 'I feel sad when animals are hurt; 'Humans are part of the natural world'; 'My actions will make the world different'. Children respond to the items using the scale: 'strongly disagree', 'disagree', 'neither disagree nor agree', 'agree', 'strongly agree'. Hughes, J., Richardson, M. & Lumber, M., 2018, 'Evaluating connection to nature and the relationship with conservation in children', *Journal of Nature Conservation*, 45, 11–19. doi.org/10.1016/j.jnc-2018.07.004

Most children younger than seven are not ready to have their nature connectedness assessed, and certainly not by questionnaires calling for the kind of self-awareness and capacity for introspection little children do not have. Apart from that, few children before 6–7 years of age have all the learning and thinking capabilities nature connectedness requires. Some of these capabilities, such as curiosity and the capacity for wonder, appear early in life, but others, like seeing the world from the viewpoint of others, is still developing over middle childhood (5–9 years of age).

3. Hughes, et al., 2018.

4. Giusti, M., Svane, U., Raymond, C.M. & Beery, T.H., 2018, 'A framework to assess where and how children connect to nature', *Frontiers in Psychology*, 9:2283. doi:10.3389/fpsyg.2017.02283

5. Websites you locate should include:
'Mum's Grapevine'. https://mumsgrapevine.com.au/2016/05/19-diy-backyard-play-spaces/
Nature Play, WA. https://www.natureplaywa.org.au/resources/creating-a-child-friendly-backyard
Way, D. & Worrall, J., 2020, '14 easy ways to make your backyard more fun', *Parents*
https://www.parents.com/fun/activities/outdoor/make-your-backyard-more-fun/

6. Kohn, A., 1986/1992, *No Contest: The Case Against Competition*, Boston, Houghton Mifflin. For a brief statement of his case, see *The Case Against Competition*. https://www.alfiekohn.org/article/case-competition/?print-pdf

7. Donaldson, F.O., 1993, *Playing by Heart: The Vision and Practice of Belonging*, Deerfield Beach, FL., Health Communications Inc.

8. You will find a video showing how to improvise a fire bowl at this site: https://www.hometalk.com/18201283/portable-fire-pit?expand_all_questions=1

5. Turning to nature in difficult times

1. Louv, R., December 20, 2016, 'On the river: The restorative power of nature in difficult times', *Children & Nature Network*. https://www.childrenandnature.org/2016/12/20/on-the-river-the-restorative-power-of-nature-in-difficult-times-2/

2. Cowen, R., July 19, 2016, 'How to escape to the wild (and forget about modern life completely)', *The Telegraph*. https://www.telegraph.co.uk/men/the-filter/how-to-escape-to-the-wild-and-forget-about-modern-life-completel/ See also Rob Cowen, 2015, *Common Ground*, London, Penguin Random House.

3. Gonzalez, M.T., Hartig, T., Patil, G.G. et al., 2009, 'Horticulture in clinical depression: A prospective study', *Research and Theory for Nursing Practice.* 23 (4). doi: 10.1891/1541-6577.23.4.312
    Stuart-Smith, S., 2020, *The Well Gardened Mind: Rediscovering Nature in the Modern World*, London, HarperCollins.

4. Anne Halvorson, June 20, 2017, '3 ways gardening changed my outlook on grief'. https://www.taps.org/articles/2017/gardeningandgrief

5. Shawna Coronado, March 9, 2009, 'The healing benefits of gardening—how a garden saved my life'. Posted in Joe Lamp'l's blog, *Compost Confidential.* https://www.growingagreenerworld.com/the-healing-benefits-of-gardening-%E2%80%93-how-a-garden-saved-my-life/

6. Coronado, S., 2008, *Gardening Nude: A Common Sense Guide To Improving Your Health And Lifestyle By Increasing Exposure To Nature, Cultivating A Green Mindset, And Building A Strong Community*, The casual Gardener Co. The book may be out of print as it is no longer listed on Shawna Coronado's website. https://shawnacoronado.com/tag/gardening-nude/.

7. Kathryn Oda, December 6, 2017, 'How a dog helped me manage my anxiety and depression', *Huffington Post, Life*. https://www.huffpost.com/entry/how-a-dog-helped-me-manag_n_9301622

8. Sandy Fox, January 13, 2013, 'Life after loss, Maureen Hunter's story'. A post in *Surviving Grief: Death of a Child*. http://survivinggrief.blogspot.com.au/2013/01/life-after-loss-maureen-hunters-story.html (The post may have to be extracted from the archive.)

9. From an interview with John Bennett, http://bellingenwritersfestival.com.au/claire-dunn-interviewed-john-bennett/, about her book, Dunn, C., 2015, *My Year Without Matches: Escaping the City in Search of the Wild*, Collingwood, Vic., Nero.

10. The program is called: *Revolution School: Putting Education to the Test*. https://www.abc.net.au/tv/programs/revolution-school/

11. The findings of many of these studies have been pooled and analysed in a procedure called meta-analysis. Because the findings of meta-analyses are derived using data from many studies, they are more reliable. One of the strongest of these analyses is reported in:
Hattie, J., Marsh, H.W., Neill, J.T. & Richards, G.E., 1997, 'Adventure education and Outward Bound: Out-of-class experiences that make a lasting difference', *Review of Educational Research*, 67, 43–87. doi/10.3102/00346543067001043
The findings of this analysis along with others are helpfully summarised in:
Neill, J.T. & Richards, G.E., 1998, 'Does outdoor education *really* work? A summary of recent meta-analyses', *Australian Journal of Outdoor Education*, 39, 1–9.doi:10.1007/BF03400671
For a more recent review, see:
Bowen, D.J. & Neill, J.T., 2013, 'A meta-analysis of adventure therapy outcomes and moderators', *The Open Psychology Journal*, 6, 28–53. 10.2174/1874350120130802001

12. Erica Cirino, March 14, 2016, 'How collage made my life whole', *Centre for Humans and Nature*. https://www.humansandnature.org/how-collage-made-my-life-whole

13. Matthew Johnstone's story is told by Cathy Johnson in a June 20, 2014 broadcast: 'Happy snap your way to inner calm', *ABC Health and Well-being.*
    See also Matthew Johnston's books, e.g., Johnstone, M., 2013, *Capturing Mindfulness: A Guide to Becoming Present through Photography,* Sydney, Pan Macmillan Australia.
14. Dr Craig Hassed's teachings on mindfulness can be found on several YouTube videos and in
    Mc Kenzie, S. & Hassed, C., 2012, *Mindfulness for Life,* Wollombi, NSW, Exisle Publishing.

6. Caring for nature

1. Kellert, S.R., 2012, *Birthright: People and Nature in the Modern World,* New Haven and London, Yale University Press, x.
2. *The Sydney Morning Herald,* June 22, 2015.
3. Dubos, R., 1980, *Wooing the Earth: New Perspectives on Man's Use of Nature,* London, Althone.
4. The quote is from a *Sydney Morning Herald* article, October 8, 2008, 'Schoolboys help make Blacktown a leafy town'.
5. Quoted by Peter Meredith in the ABC Radio National program, *Ockham's Razor,* 16/5/1999. Peter Meredith is the author of *Myles and Milo,* Sydney, Allen and Unwin, 1999.
6. The links to these organisations are:
   https://conservationvolunteers.com.au/
   http://www.ecoshout.org.au/about-us.
   https://govolunteer.com.au/environment-conservation-volunteering/
7. Burroughs, J., 1908, *The Writings of John Burroughs XV Leaf and Tendril,* Boston and New York, Houghton Mifflin, 3.

7. Aesthetic pleasure, awe and wonder

1. The word 'aesthetic' comes from the Greek, *'aisthetikos',* which means 'sense perception'. This is interesting considering the point made later in the chapter that beauty is directly the

product of perception, i.e., of the brain's interpretation of information received via the senses.

2. Ward, K., 1996, *God, Chance and Necessity*, Oxford, Oneworld Publications, 50.

3. Orians, G.H., 2001, 'An evolutionary perspective on aesthetics', *Bulletin of Psychology and the Arts, Sample edition, Evolution, Creativity and Aesthetics.* Available at https://neuroaestheticsnet.files.wordpress.com/2020/09/ bulletin-psychology-and-the-arts-2001.2.1.pdf

4. An unimpeded view or prospect is one of three prominent concepts that have informed our understanding of the role of aesthetics in human survival. The other concepts are refuge and hazard. Prospect refers to the accessibility of information about an environment. Strong prospect enables the individual to evaluate the environment and to decide how to use it. Refuge refers to the degree to which an environment provides security. Hazard refers to the dangers the individual faces when moving through the environment.

   An early presentation of the prospect-refuge-hazard theory is in

   Appleton, J., 1975, *The Experience of Landscape*, New York, John Wiley & Sons.

   Examples of later writings on the subject are:

   Heerwagen, J.H. & Orians, G.H., 1993, 'Humans, habitats, and aesthetics'. In S.R. Kellert & E.O. Wilson (eds.), *The Biophilia Hypothesis*. Island Press, Washington, DC, 138–72.

   Stamps III, A.E., 2008, 'Some findings on prospect and refuge', *Perceptual and Motor Skills*, 106, 147–162. doi. org/10.2466/pms.106.1.147-162

5. The quote is from a transcript of the interview that was accessed at www.abc.net.au/talkingheads/txt/s1495890htm but is no longer available from that source.

6. Muir, J., 2008, *The Yosemite*, Charleston SC, BiblioLife, 149.

7. Carson, R., 1965, *The Sense of Wonder*, New York, Harper and Row, 88.

8. Carson, R., 1998, 'The real world around us', *Lost Words: The Discovered Writings of Rachel Carson*, Boston, Beacon, 160.

9. The Golden Ratio is a mathematical relationship (Phi = 1.618) that is aesthetically attractive. It is used by artists to bring harmony and good proportion to their compositions and is represented throughout nature. The spirals of snail and nautilus shells, for example, embody the ratio as does the spiral shape of stellar galaxies and cyclones. Your facial features are arranged according to the Golden Ratio. Our brains seem to be hardwired to prefer objects and images constructed according to the Golden Ratio.

10. A fractal is a pattern that is repeated on different scales. The overall branching pattern of a tree, for example, is repeated on the major limbs, the smaller branches and even the twigs.

11. Examples of articles reporting cross-cultural similarities in people's landscape preferences are

Kaplan, R. & Talbot, J.F., 1988, 'Ethnicity and preference for natural settings: A review and recent findings', *Landscape and Urban Planning,* 15, 107–117. /doi..org/10.1016/0169-2046(88)90019-9

Hull, R.B. & Revell, G.R.B., 1989, 'Cross-cultural comparisons of landscape scenic beauty evaluations: A case study in Bali', *Journal of Environmental Psychology*, 9, 177–191. doi.org/10.1016/S0272-4944(89)80033-7

Yang, B-E. & Brown, T.J., 1992, 'A cross-cultural comparison of preferences for landscape styles and landscape elements', *Environment and Behavior*, 24, 471–507. doi.org/10.1177/0013916592244003

Mustafa, K.B., 1994, *A Cross-cultural Comparison of Visual Landscape Preferences for the Natural Environment,* Fort Collins, Co., Colorado State University.

Petrova, E.G., Mironov, Y.V., Aoki, Y. et al., 2015, 'Comparing the visual perception and aesthetic evaluation of natural landscapes in Russia and Japan: Cultural and environmental factors', *Progress in Earth and Planetary Science*, 2,6. doi: 10.1186/s40645-015-0033-x

12. I have borrowed this term from Australian researcher, Dr Andrew Lothian, whose comprehensive review of what is known about scenic preferences is published in Lothian, A.,

2017, *The Science of Scenery: How We View Scenic Beauty, What It Is, Why We Love It, and How to Measure and Map It*, San Bernardino, California, CreateSpace Independent Publishing Platform.

13. Evidence of the two dimensions of aesthetic pleasure, pleasure and arousal, is reported in
Galindo, M.P.G. & Rodriguez, J.A.C., 2000, 'Environmental aesthetics and psychological wellbeing: Relationships between preference judgements for urban landscapes and other relevant affective responses', *Psychology in Spain*, 4, 13–27. http://www.psychologyinspain.com/content/full/2000/2.htm
Moreover, imaging studies of the brain's initial response to natural scenes and objects have identified a neural pathway comprised of cells that are highly receptive to natural opioids and therefore primed to generate feelings of pleasure.
Biederman, I. & Vessel, E.A., 2006, 'Perceptual pleasure and the brain', *American Scientist*, 94, 249–255. https://www.americanscientist.org/article/perceptual-pleasure-and-the-brain

14. 'Fascination' has a general and a psychological usage. More is said about the psychology of fascination in Chapter 8.

15. Csikszentmahali, M., 1992, *Flow: The Psychology of Happiness*, London, Rider, 107.

16. For direct evidence, see:
Laski, M., 1961, *Ecstasy: A Study of Some Secular and Religious Experiences*, London, The Cressett Press.
And for corroboration, see:
Chenoweth, R.E. & Gobster, P.H., 1990, 'The nature and ecology of aesthetic experiences in the landscape', *Landscape Journal*, 9, 1–8. doi: 10.3368/lj.9.1.1

17. Zhang, J.W., Piff, P.K., Iyer, R. et al., 2014, 'An occasion for unselfing: Beautiful nature leads to prosociality', *Journal of Environmental Psychology*, 37, 61–72.
doi.org/10.1016/j.jenvp.2013.11.008

18. Bryant F.B. & Veroff, J., 2006, *Savoring: A New Model of Positive Experience*, NY, Psychology Press.

19. The unexpected does not always give rise to amazement, of course. If someone comes up behind you and says, 'Boo!', for example, you are much more likely to be startled than amazed. Likewise, your response to finding that your car won't start or your favourite TV show has been cancelled is going to be surprise (along with anger and frustration perhaps) rather than amazement.

20. Keltner, D. & Haidt, J., 2003, 'Approaching awe, a moral, spiritual and aesthetic emotion', *Cognition and Emotion*, 17, 297–314, doi: 10.1080/02699930244000318, 297

21. Gibbard, M., 1985. *Prayer and Contemplation*, Oxford, Mowbray, 106–107.

22. The 'cosmic sense' is the awareness of the universe's fundamental unity and our place in that unity. This is a key concept in much of Pierre Teilhard de Chardin's writings. A geologist more famous for his contribution to natural theology, he believed that the cosmic sense must have been born as soon as humans found themselves facing the forest, the sea, the stars.

23. This section draws on the work of the Greater Good Science Centre at the University of California, Berkeley. Professor Dacher Keltner, the director of the Centre, has pioneered the study of awe. More information about the Greater Good Science Centre can be found at https://ggsc.berkeley.edu/who_we_are/about

24. A Dutch study, for example, found that people who watched awe-inspiring videos estimated their physical body size to be smaller than those who watched funny or neutral videos.
van Elk, M., Karinen, A., Specker, E. et al., 2016, 'Standing in awe: The effects of awe on body perception and the relation with absorption', *Collabra*, 2(1), 4. doi: http://doi.org/10.1525/collabra.36

25. Findings from a 2013 study co-authored by APS Fellow Michelle 'Lani' Shiota (Arizona State University), Keltner, and Belinda Campos.

26. Guan, F., Xiang, Y., Chen, O. et al., 2018, 'Neural basis of dispositional awe', *Frontiers of Behavioral Neuroscience*, 12, 1–7. doi: 10.3389/fnbeh.2018.00209

27. Stellar, J.E., Gordon, A., Anderson, C.L. et al., 2017, 'Awe and humility', *Journal of Personality and Social Psychology.* Advance online publication. http://dx.doi.org/10.1037/pspi0000109

28. Piff, P.K., Dietze, P., Feinberg, M. et al., 2015, 'Awe, the small self, and prosocial behavior', *Journal of Personality and Social Psychology,* 108, 883–899. doi: 10.1037/pspi0000018

29. Rudd, M., Aaker, J. & Vohs, K., 2012, 'Awe expands people's perception of time, alters decision making, and enhances well-being', *Psychological Science,* 23, 1130–1136. doi:10.1177/0956797612438731

30. https://www.goodreads.com/quotes/4097-wonder-is-the-beginning-of-wisdom 6/8/18

31. Walt Streightiff, *Goodreads* 26/7/2018.

32. Carson, R., 1965, *The Sense of Wonder: A Celebration of Nature for Parents and Children,* New York, Harper Row.

33. Fuller, R.C., 2006, 'Wonder and the religious sensibility: A study in religion and emotions', *The Journal of Religion,* 86, 364–384, 370. doi:10.1086/503693

34. Weinstein, N., Przybylski, A.K. & Ryan, R.M., 2009, 'Can nature make us more caring? Effects of immersion in nature on intrinsic aspirations and generosity', *Personality and Social Psychology Bulletin,* 35: 10, 315–1329. doi: 10.1177/0146167209341649

Rudd, M., Vohs, K. & Aaker, J., 2012, 'Awe expands people's perception of time, alters decision making, and enhances well-being', *Psychological Science,* 23, 1130–1136. doi:10.1177/0956797612438731

Zhang, J.W., Piff, P.K., Iyer, R. et al., 2014, 'An occasion for unselfing: Beautiful nature leads to prosociality', *Journal of Environmental Psychology,* 37, 61–72. doi.org/10.1016/j.jenvp.2013.11.008

Piff, P.K., Dietze, P., Feinberg, M. et al., 2015, 'Sublime sociality: How awe promotes prosocial behavior through the small self', *Journal of Personality and Social Psychology* 108, 883–899.doi.org/10.1037/pspi0000018

Zelenski, J.M., Dopko, R.L. & Capaldi, C.A., 2015, 'Cooperation is in our nature: Nature exposure may promote cooperative and environmentally sustainable behaviour', *Journal of Environmental Psychology*, 42, 24–31. doi. org/10.1016/j.jenvp.2015.01.005

Joye, Y. & Bolderdijk, J.W., 2015, 'An exploratory study into the effects of extraordinary nature on emotions, mood, and prosociality', *Frontiers of Psychology*, 28. doi.org/10.3389/ fpsyg.2014.01577

8. Relaxation, restoration and tranquillity

1. Findings from two surveys are mentioned in Campaign to Protect Rural England, 2005, *Mapping Tranquillity: Defining and Assessing a Valuable Resource.* Available at https:// www.cpre.org.uk/wp-content/uploads/2019/11/mapping_ tranquillity.pdf

2. Beatley, T., 2009, 'Biophilic urbanism: Inviting nature back into our communities and into our lives', *William and Mary Environmental Law and Policy Review,* 34:1, 209. Available at http://scholarship.law.wm.edu/wmelpr/vol34/iss1/6

3. Tsunetsugu, Y., Park, B. & Myazaki, Y., 2010, Trends in research related to 'Shinrin-yoku (taking in the forest atmosphere or forest bathing) in Japan', *Environmental Health and Preventive Medicine*, 15, 27–37. doi 10.1007/s 12199-009-0091/z

   Hansen, M.M., Jones, R. & Tocc K., 2017, 'Shinrin-yoku (forest bathing) and nature therapy: A state-of-the-art review', *International Journal of Environmental Research and Public Health*, 14, 851. doi:10.3390/ijerph14080851

4. Benson, H., 1975, *The Relaxation Response*, New York, William Morrow.

5. Ulrich, R.S., Simons, R.F., Losito, B.D. et al., 1991, 'Stress recovery during exposure to natural and urban environments', *Journal of Environmental Psychology*, 11, 201–230, 203. doi.org/10.1016/S0272-4944(05)80184-7

6. Gould van Praag, C.D., Garfinkel, S.N., Sparasci, O. et al., 2017, 'Mind-wandering and alterations to default mode network connectivity when listening to naturalistic versus artificial sounds', *Scientific Reports*, 7:45273. doi:10.1038/srep45273

7. Ulrich R.S. & Simons, R.F., 1986, 'Recovery from stress during exposure to everyday outdoor environments'. In J. Wineman, R. Barne & C. Zimring (eds.), *Proceedings of the Seventeenth Annual Conference of the Environmental Design Research Association*, Washington, D.C.: EDRA, 115–122.

8. Lubick, N., 2013, 'Green fix', *New Scientist*, June 15, 42–44.

9. Craig, A., Torpy, F., Brennan, J. & Burchett, M.D., 2010, 'The positive effects of office plants', *Nursery Paper #6*, Nursery and Garden Industry Australia. Available at http://www.ngia.com.au/files/nurserypapers/NGIA_NP_2010-06.pdf

10. Lohr, V., 2010, 'What are the benefits of plants indoors and why do we respond so positively to them?', *Acta Horticulturae*, 881, 675–682. An author's text version of this article is available at http://public.wsu.edu/~lohr/pub/2010LohrBenefitsPltsIndoors.pdf

11. An example is located at https://www.youtube.com/watch?v=c2NmyoXBXmE

12. Professor Frances Kuo and colleagues at the University of Illinois have taken advantage of a naturally occurring experimental situation to study the effects of natural features on individual behaviour and community life in an inner-city housing estate. Their investigation of the link between DAF, restoration and anti-social behaviour is reported in:
Kuo, F.E. & Sullivan, W., 2001, 'Aggression and violence in the inner city: Impacts of environment via mental fatigue', *Environment and Behavior*, 33, 543–571.
doi/10.1177/00139160121973124

13. Taylor, A.F. & Kuo, F.E., 2009, 'Children with attention deficits concentrate better after a walk in the park', *Journal of Attention Disorders*, 12, 402–409.
doi/abs/10.1177/1087054708323000

14. Examples of the evidence can be found in Hartig, T., Mang, M. & Evans, G.W., 1991, 'Restorative effects of natural environment experience', *Environment and Behavior,* 23, 3–26.
doi/10.1177/0013916591231001
For more recent studies, see:
Hartig, T., Evans, G.W., Jamnser, L.D. et al., 2003, 'Tracking restoration in natural and urban field settings', *Journal of Environmental Psychology*, 23, 109–123.
doi.org/10.1016/S0272-4944(02)00109-3
Berto, R., 2005, 'Exposure to restorative environments helps restore attentional capacity', *Journal of Environmental Psychology*, 25, 249–259. doi.org/10.1016/j.jenvp.2005.07.001
Berman, M.G., Jonides, J. & Kaplan, S., 2008, 'The cognitive benefits of interacting with nature', *Psychological Science*, 19, 12, 1207–1212. doi: 10.1111/j.1467-9280.2008.02225.x

15. The Kaplans' work is comprehensively described in
Kaplan, R. & Kaplan, S., 1989, *The Experience of Nature: A Psychological Perspective.* Cambridge, Cambridge University Press.
Kaplan, S., 1995, 'The restorative benefits of nature: toward an integrative framework', *Journal of Environmental Psychology,* 15, 169–182. doi.org/10.1016/0272-4944(95)90001-2

16. Craig, et al., 2010.

17. Relevant experimental studies are reported in
Staats, H., Kieviet, A. & Hartig, T., 2003. 'Where to recover from attentional fatigue: An expectancy-value analysis of environmental preference', *Journal of Environmental Psychology,* 23, 147–157. doi: 10.1016/S0272-4944(02)00112-3
Hartig, T., 2004. 'Restorative environments'. In C. Spielberger (ed.), *Encyclopedia of Applied Psychology. Vol. 3*, San Diego, Academic Press, 273–279.

18. Taylor, A.F., Kuo, F.E. & Sullivan, W.C., 2001, 'Coping with ADD: The surprising connection to green play settings', *Environment and Behavior*, 33, 54–77.
doi/10.1177/00139160121972864

Kuo, F.E. & Taylor, A.F., 2004, 'A potential natural treatment for Attention-deficit/Hyperactivity Disorder: Evidence from a national study', *American Journal of Public Health*, 94, 1580–1586. doi: 10.2105/ajph.94.9.1580

19. Evidence comes from several studies, including:
Berto, R., Baroni, M.R., Zainaghi, A. & Bettella, S., 2010, 'An exploratory study of the effect of high and low fascination environments on attentional fatigue', *Journal of Environmental Psychology*, 30, 494–500. doi: 10 .1016/j. jenvp. 2009.12.002
Kjellgren, A. & Buhrkall, H., 2010, 'A comparison of the restorative effect of a natural environment with that of a simulated natural environment', *Journal of Environmental Psychology*, 30, 464–472. doi: 10.1016/j.jenvp.2010.01.011
Gamble, K.R. & Howard, J.H., 2014, 'Not just scenery: Viewing nature pictures improves executive attention in older adults', *Experimental Aging Research*, 40, 513–530. doi: 10.1080/0361073X.2014.956618
McAllister, E., Bhullar, N. & Schutte, N.S., 2017, 'Into the woods or a stroll in the park: How virtual contact with nature impacts positive and negative affect', *International Journal of Environmental Research and Public Health*, 14, 786. doi:10.3390/ijerph14070786

20. McMahan, E.A., & Estes, D., 2015, 'The effect of contact with natural environments on positive and negative affect: A meta-analysis', *The Journal of Positive Psychology*, 10 (6). http://dx.doi.org/10.1080/17439760.2014.994224

21. Collard, F. & Margulies, D.S., 2011, 'The subject at rest: Novel conceptualizations of the self and brain from cognitive neurosciences study of the resting state', *Subjectivity (Special Issue of Neuroscience and Subjectivity)*, 4, 227–257. doi:10.1057/sub.2011.11

22. See previous note.

23. Mooneyham, B. & Schooler, J., 2013, 'The costs and benefits of mind-wandering: A review', *Canadian Journal of Experimental Psychology*, 67 (1), 11–18. doi:1037/a0031569

24. Marcus Tullius Cicero, *De Nature Deorum* (1, 20).

25. Quotes are from MacFarlane, R., Haggett, C., Fuller et al., 2004. *Tranquillity Mapping: Developing a Robust Methodology for Planning Support*, Report to the Campaign to Protect Rural England, Countryside Agency, North East Assembly, Northumberland Strategic Partnership, Northumberland National Park Authority and Durham County Council, Centre for Environmental & Spatial Analysis, Northumbria University.

26. Eliovson, S., 1971, *Gardening the Japanese Way*, London, George C. Harrop.

27. *CPRE, How We Mapped Tranquillity*. Available at http://www.cpre.org.uk/what-we-do/countryside/tranquil-places/in-depth/item/1688-how-we-mapped-tranquillity
Watts, G.R., Pheasant, R.J. & Horoshenkow, K.R., 2011, 'Predicting perceived tranquillity in urban parks and open spaces', *Environment and Planning B: Planning and Design*, 38, 585–594. doi:org/10.1068/b36131
Pheasant, R.J., Horoshenkow, K.R. & Watts, G.R., 2010, 'Tranquillity rating prediction tool (TRAPT)', *Acoustic Bulletin*, 35 (6), 18–24.

28. Herzog, T.R. & Bosley, P.J., 1992, 'Tranquillity and preference as affective qualities of natural environments', *Journal of Environmental Psychology*, 12, 115–127.

29. Tranquillity has been defined as a combination of aesthetic pleasure and fascination. See
Herzog T.R. & Chernick, K.K., 2000, 'Tranquillity and danger in urban and natural settings', *Journal of Environmental Psychology*, 20, 29–39.doi: 10.1006/jevp.1999.0151 and Chapter 5 for an explanation of 'soft fascination'.

30. For a review of research indicating that 'the primary reasons for visiting natural environments include the escape from the stress of urban areas and the attainment of tranquillity and solitude', see:
Mace, B.L., Bell, P.A. & Loomes, R.J., 1999, 'Aesthetic, affective and cognitive effects of noise on natural landscape assessment', *Society and Natural Resources*, 12, 225–242. doi/abs/10.1080/089419299279713

31. For a research study showing that total aloneness is not necessary for a sense of solitude to be enjoyed, see:
Hollenhorst, S., Frank, E.(3rd) & Watson, A., 1994, 'The capacity to be alone: Wilderness solitude and the growth of the self'. In J.C. Hendee & V.G. Martin (eds.) *International Wilderness Allocation and Research*, Ft Collins, CO, International Wilderness Leadership (WILD) Foundation, 234–239.

32. Quoted in Fredrickson, L.M. & Anderson, D.H.,1999, 'A qualitative exploration of the wilderness experience', *Journal of Environmental Psychology*, 19, 21–39. doi.org/10.1006/jevp.1998.0110

33. Winton, T. (Writer) & Woldendorp, R. (Photographer), 1999, *Down to Earth: Australian Landscapes*, Fremantle, Australia, Fremantle Arts Centre Press.

9. Connections

1. Fredrickson, L.M. & Anderson, D.H.,1999, 'A qualitative exploration of the wilderness experience', *Journal of Environmental Psychology*, 19, 21–39. doi.org/10.1006/jevp.1998.0110

2. Fredrickson & Anderson, 1999, 31.

3. Fredrickson & Anderson, 1999, 32.

4. For an analysis of the contribution of solitude to social relationships, see:
Buckholz, E., 1997, *The Call of Solitude: Alone Time in a World of Attachment*, New York, Touchstone.

5. Fredrickson & Anderson, 1999, 30.

6. Joseph Campbell, famous for his commentaries on the place of myths legends in the human experience, describes the archetypal hero's journey in Campbell, J. & Moyers, B., 1988, *The Power of Myth*, New York, Doubleday.

7. For further evidence that women benefit from outdoor physical challenges, see:
McDermott, L., 2004, 'Exploring intersections of physicality and female-only canoeing experiences', *Leisure Studies*, 23, 283–301. doi: 10.1080/0261436042000253039

8. Chester, Q., 1998, *The Wild Calling: Confessions of a Hit-and-miss Adventurer*, Sydney, New Holland, 37.

9. Cumes, D., 1998, *Inner Passages, Outer Journeys: Wilderness Healing and the Discovery of Self*, St Paul, Minn, Llewellyn Publications.
An unpublished revision of the book can be downloaded from https://www.yumpu.com/en/document/read/10925096/inner-passages-outer-journeys-revised-david-cumes/103

10. Cumes, 1998, 37.

11. Cumes, 1998, 37.

12. Cumes, 1998, 34.

13. Other accounts of re-entry depression can be found in
Greenway, R., 1993, 'On crossing and not crossing the wilderness boundary'. In J.C. Hendee & V.G. Martin (eds.), *International Wilderness Allocation, Management, and Research*, Tromso, Norway, International Wilderness Leadership Foundation, 205–216.
Kaplan, R. & Kaplan, S., 1989, *The Experience of Nature: A Psychological Perspective*. Cambridge, Cambridge University Press.

14. The term, 'primary relationship' is used in
Ewert, A. & Heywood, J., 1991, 'Group development in natural environments', *Environment and Behavior*, 23, 592–615.

15. Chester, 1998, 35.

16. Kimball, R.O. & Bacon, S.B., 1993, 'The wilderness challenge model'. In M.A. Gass (ed.), *Adventure Therapy: Therapeutic Applications of Adventure Programming*. Dubuque, IA, Kendall/Hunt Publishing Company. 11–41.

17. Gass, M.A., 1995, 'Adventure family therapy: An innovative approach answering the question of lasting change with adjudicated youth?' *Monograph on Youth in the 1990s*, 4, 103–117.
Hopkins, D. & Putnam, R., 1993, *Personal Growth Through Adventure*. London: David Fulton Publishers.
Walsh, V. & Golins, G., 1976. *The Exploration of the Outward Bound Process*. Denver: Colorado Outward Bound School.

18. Chapman, S., McPhee, P. & Proudman, B., 1995, 'What is experiential education?' In K. Warren, M. Sakofs, & J.S. Hunt, Jr. (eds.), *The Theory of Experiential Education*. Boulder, CO: Association for Experiential Education. 235–247.
Witman, J.P., 1995, 'Characteristics of adventure programs valued by adolescents in treatment', *Monograph on Youth in the 1990s*, 4, 127–135.

19. Donaldson, F.O., 1993, *Playing by Heart: The Vision and Practice of Belonging*, Deerfield Beach, FL., Health Communications Inc.

20. Quoted by Donaldson, 1993, 39.

21. Teasdale, W., 2003, *Bede Griffiths: An Introduction to His Interspiritual Thought*, New York, Woodstock, VT, Skylights Path Publishing, 38–39.

22. Butler, D., 1991, *The Barefoot Bush Walker*. Sydney, Australian Broadcasting Corporation, 45.

23. McCoy, M., 2003, 'Home Ground'. In M. Tredinnik (ed.), *A Place on Earth: An Anthology of Nature Writing from Australia and North America*, Sydney, University of New South Wales Press, 176–180, 180.

24. The two kinds of transcendent experiences are described in Williams, K. & Harvey, D., 2001, 'Transcendent experience in forest environments', *Journal of Environmental Psychology*, 21, 249–260, 249.

25. Some of the enduring effects of connecting with nature have been tracked by Stephen Kellert. He also warns that a commitment to the welfare of the environment needs to be regularly renewed to ensure that action follows. See:
Kellert, S.R., 1998, *A National Study of Outdoor Wilderness Experience*. Available at www.childrenandnature.org/uploads/kellert.complete.text.pdf

10. A healthier you

1. World Health Organisation 1947, *World Health Organisation: Constitution*, Geneva, World Health Organisation.

2. The following are technically sound reviews of the evidence:

Nadha Hassen, N., 2016, *The Influence of Green Space on Mental Health | Wellesley Junior Fellowship Report*, Wellesley Institute.
Twohig-Bennett, C. & Jones, A., 2018, 'The health benefits of the great outdoors: A systematic review and meta-analysis of greenspace exposure and health outcomes', *Environmental Research*, 166, 628–637. doi: 10.1016/j.envres.2018.06.030 *Urban green spaces and health.* Copenhagen: WHO Regional Office for Europe, 2016.
Capaldi, C., Passmore, H-A., Nisbet, E.K. et al., 2015, 'Flourishing in nature: A review of the benefits of connecting with nature and its application as a wellbeing intervention', *International Journal of Wellbeing*, 5(4), 1–16. doi:10.5502/ijw.v5i4.1
Capaldi, C.A., Dopko, R.L. & Zelenski, J.M., 2014, 'The relationship between nature connectedness and happiness: A meta-analysis', *Frontiers in Psychology.* doi: 10.3389/fpsyg.2014.00976
McMahan, E.A., & Estes, D., 2015, 'The effect of contact with natural environments on positive and negative affect: A meta-analysis', *The Journal of Positive Psychology,* 10 (6). doi.org/10.1080/17439760.2014.994224

3. An example of such a study is:
Crouse, D.L., Pinault L., Balram, A. et al., 2017, 'Urban greenness and mortality in Canada's largest cities: A national cohort study', *The Lancet Planetary Health,* 1 (7) E289-E297. doi.org/10.1016/S2542-5196(17)30118-3

4. Office of National Statistics, 2018, *Surveys using our four personal well-being questions: A guide to what surveys include our four ONS personal well-being questions*, ONS, London. https://www.ons.gov.uk/peoplepopulationandcommunity/wellbeing/methodologies/surveysusingthe4officefornationalstatisticspersonalwellbeingquestions

5. Bratman, G.N., Gross, J.J., Kahn P.H. et al., 2019, 'Nature and mental health: An ecosystem service perspective', *Science Advances,* 5 (7). doi: 10.1126/sciadv.aax0903

6. Capaldi, et al., 2014 and Capaldi et al., 2015.

7. Fredrickson, B.L., 2013, 'Chapter one—positive emotions broaden and build', *Advances in Experimental Social Psychology*, 47, 1–53. https://doi.org/10.1016/B978-0-12-407236-7.00001-2

8. See Chapter 2, note 6.

9. Evidence is provided in Part 2, especially chapters 7 and 8.

10. For references, see the relevant notes in Chapter 8.

11. One of the first people to observe the connection between resilience and health through scientific eyes was a medical sociologist, Aaron Antonovsky. By studying the health of women Holocaust survivors about 20 years after their horrendous experiences, he found that while most of the women had been damaged, a minority (29 percent) was in sound mental and physical health. He observed that the healthy survivors exhibited an approach to life that made them more resilient to, or better able to deal with, the unimaginable stress of their incarceration and its aftermath. He referred to this health-promoting (or salutogenic) orientation or approach to life as a strong 'sense of coherence'. See:

Antonovsky, A., 1987, *Unraveling the Mystery of Health: How People Manage Stress and Stay Well*, San Francisco, Jossey Bass.

Suzanne Kobasa and Suzanne Ouellette have observed much the same kind of resilience and its positive consequences for health in different groups of people including highly pressured corporate executives. See:

Madi, S.R. & Kobasa, S.C., 1984, *The Hardy Executive: Health under Stress*, Homewood, Ill, Dow Jones-Irwin.

Oulette, S.C., 1993, 'Inquiries into hardiness'. In L. Goldberger and S. Breznitz (eds) *Handbook of Stress: Theoretical and Clinical Aspects 2ⁿᵈ ed.*, New York, Free Press.

Madi, S.R., 2005, 'On hardiness and other pathways to resilience', *American Psychologist*, 60, 261–262. doi: 10.1037/0003-066X.60.3.261

12. Bartone, P.T., Valdes, J.J. & Sandvik, A., 2016, 'Psychological hardiness predicts cardiovascular health', *Psychology, Health and Medicine*, Sep., 21(6),743–749. doi: 10.1080/13548506.2015.1120323

Bartone, P.T., Spinosa, T. & Robb, J., 2009, 'Psychological hardiness is related to high-density lipoprotein (HDL) cholesterol levels'. Paper presented at the Association for Psychological Science Convention, San Francisco CA, 24 May 2009. doi: 10.1080/13548506.2015.1120323

Dolbier, C.L., Cocke, R.R., Lieferman, J.A. et al., 2001, 'Differences in functional immune responses of high vs low hardy healthy individuals', *Journal of Behavioral Medicine*, 24, 219–229. doi.org/10.1023/A:1010762606006

13. Both characteristics are implicit in Antonovsky's account of 'sense of coherence' and Kobasa's concept of 'hardiness' and have been isolated in psychometric analyses of a test that measures psychological hardiness. See:

Sinclair, R.R. & Tetrick, L.E., 2000, 'Implications of item wording for hardiness structure, relation with neuroticism, and stress buffering', *Journal of Research in Personality*, 34, 1–25. doi: 10.1006/jrpe.1999.2265

Hystad, S.W., Eid, J., Johnson, B.H. et al., 2009, 'Psychometric properties of the revised Norwegian Dispositional Resilience (hardiness) Scale', *Scandinavian Journal of Psychology*, 51, 237–245. doi: 10.1111/j.1467-9450.2009.00759

The characteristics also feature very prominently in the following analysis of personality traits that can be linked to well-being and health. See:

Gezondheidsraad. Health Council of the Netherlands, 2004, *Nature and Health: The Influence of Nature on Social, Psychological and Physical Well-being*. The Hague, Health Council of the Netherlands and RMNO, publication no. 2004/09E. Available at http://www.gezondheidsraad.nl/en/publications/environmental-health/nature-and-health-influence-nature-social-psychological-and-physic

14. The concept of being one's own hero by embarking on a hero's journey is discussed in Chapter 9.

15. See Chapter 5, note 11.

16. House, J.S, Landis, K.R. & Umberson, D., 1988, 'Social relationships and health', *Science*, 241, 540–545, 541. doi.org/10.1126/science.3399889

17. Berkman, L.F., Glass, T., Brissette, I. & Seeman, T.E., 2000, 'From social integration to health. Durkheim in the new millennium', *Social Science and Medicine*, 51, 843–857. doi: 10.1016/s0277-9536(00)00065-4
Holt-Lunstad, J., Smith, T.B. & Layton, J.B., 2010, 'Social relationships and mortality risk: A meta-analytic review', *PloS Medicine*, 7,7, doi:10.1371/journal.pmed.1000316

18. Penninx, B.W.J.H., Tilburg, T.G., Kriegsman, D.M.W. et al., 1997, 'Effects of social support and personal coping resources on mortality in older age. The Longitudinal Aging Study Amsterdam', *American Journal of Epidemiology*, 146, 509–510.
doi: 10.1093/oxfordjournals.aje.a009305

19. Kuo, F.E., Sullivan, W.C., Coley, R.L. & Brunson, L., 1997, 'Fertile ground for community: inner-city neighborhood common spaces', *American Journal of Community Psychology*, 26, 823–851. doi: 10.1023/A:1022294028903

20. Bartolomei, L., Corkery, L., Judd, B. & Thompson, S., 2003, *A Bountiful Harvest: Community Gardens and Neighbourhood Renewal*, Sydney, NSW Department of Housing and the University of New South Wales, Faculty of the Built Environment, School of Social Work.
Kingsley, J., Townsend, M. & Henderson-Wilson, C., 2009, 'Cultivating health and well-being: Members' perceptions of the health benefits of a Port Melbourne community garden', *Leisure Studies*, 28, 207–219. doi.org/10.1080/02614360902769894

21. Maslow, A. H., 1964, *Religions, Values, and Peak Experiences*. London, Penguin Books Limited.

22. The term 'self-actualisation' was first coined by Abraham Maslow.
Maslow, A.H., 1943, 'A theory of human motivation', *Psychological Review,* 50 (4): 370–396. https://doi.org/10.1037/h0054346

23. Canby, H.S., 1937, *The Works of Thoreau*, Cambridge, Mass., Houghton Mifflin Co.

24. See note 2.

25. The connection between air pollution and respiratory and cardiovascular disease is well established. Less broadly recognised are the alarming effects of air pollution on the central nervous system in adults as well as children. In adults, ambient pollution is associated with stroke and depression. In children, the effects include cognitive impairment and other forms of long-term brain damage. See:
Calderón-Garcidueñas, L., Calderón-Garcidueñas, A., Torres-Jardón, R. et al., 2015, 'Air pollution and your brain: What do you need to know right now', *Primary Health Care Research & Development*, 16(4):329–345. doi: 10.1017/S146342361400036X

26. Pino, O. & La Ragione, F., 2013, 'There's something in the air: Empirical evidence for the effects of negative air ions (NAI) on psychophysiological state and performance', *Research in Psychology and Behavioral Sciences,* 1(4), 48–53. doi:10.12691/rpbs-1-4-1

27. Jiang, S., Ma, A. & Ramachandran, S., 2018, 'Negative air ions and their effects on human health and air quality improvement', *International Journal of Molecular Sciences*, 19, 2966. doi:10.3390/ijms19102966

28. Li, Qing, 2010, 'Effect of forest bathing trips on human immune function', *Environmental Health and Preventive Medicine*, 15, 9–17. doi 10.1007/s12199-008-0068-3.

29. Lynch, S.V., Wood, R.A., Boushey, H. et al., 2014, 'Effects of early-life exposure to allergens and bacteria on recurrent wheeze and atopy in urban children', *Journal of Allergy and Clinical Immunology*, 134, 593–601. doi: 10.1016/j.jaci.2014.04.018

30. Rook, G.A., 2013, 'Regulation of the immune system by biodiversity from the natural environment: An ecosystem service essential to health', *Proceedings of the National Academy of Sciences, USA*, 110(46), 18360–7. doi: 10.1073/pnas.1313731110

31. Kuo, M., 2015, 'How might contact with nature promote health? Promising mechanisms and a possible central pathway', *Frontiers in Psychology*, 6. doi: 10.3389/fpsyg.2015.01093

32. *Urban green spaces and health.* Copenhagen: WHO Regional Office for Europe, 2016.

33. Astell-Burt, T., Feng, X. & Kolt, T.G.S., 2013, 'Does access to neighbourhood green space promote a healthy duration of sleep? Novel findings from a cross-sectional study of 259,319 Australians', *British Medical Journal Open*, 3.e003094. doi:10.1136/bmjopen-2013-003094

34. Grigsby-Toussaint, D.S., Turi, K.N., Krupta, M. et al., 2015. 'Sleep insufficiency and the natural environment: Results from the US Behavioral Risk Factor Surveillance System Survey', *Preventive Medicine*, 78–84. doi: 10.1016/j.ypmed.2015.07.011

35. *Urban green spaces and health,* 2016.

36. Abraham, A., Sommerhalder, K. & Abel, T. 2010, 'Landscape and well-being: A scoping study on the health-promoting impact of outdoor environments', *International Journal of Public Health*, 55, 59–69. doi.10.1007/s00038-009-0069-z

37 Gladwell, V.F., Brown, D.K., Wood, C. et al., 2013, 'The great outdoors: How a green exercise environment can benefit all', *Extreme Physiology & Medicine*, 2, 3. doi: 10.1186/2046-7648-2-3

38. The psychological factors influencing exercise adoption are still being investigated, but the theories that are proving to be productive all say in one way or another that people choose actions according to the value (or pay-off) that performing the action is expected to deliver. A prominent example of such a theory is provided in
Bandura, A., 1986, *Social Foundations of Thought and Actions: A Social-cognitive Theory*, Englewood Cliffs, N.J., Prentice–Hall.
As this theory would predict, monetary incentives significantly increase participation in gym-based exercise programs. Charness, G.B. & Gneezy, U., 2008, 'Incentives to exercise'. Available at http://escholarship.org/uc/item/3tc3j5x7

39. Wilson, E.O., 1993, 'Biophilia and the Conservation Ethic'. In S.R. Kellert & E.O. Wilson (eds), *The Biophilia Hypothesis*, Washington DC, Island Press, 31–41.

40. Pretty, J., Angus, C., Bain, M. et al., 2009, *Nature, Childhood, Health and Life Pathways*, Interdisciplinary Centre for Environment and Society Occasional Paper 2009-2, University of Essex.

11. A precious legacy (To share with the children in your life)

1. Wilson, E.O., 1984, *Biophilia: The Human Bond with Other Species*, Cambridge, Mass, Harvard University Press.

2. These words are said at the end of the documentary, which can be viewed at https://www.youtube.com/watch?v=4tGBlP8pYxM

3. For articles reporting the findings of large-scale studies or reviews of the evidence, see:

Engemanna, K., Bøcker Pedersen, C.A., Tsirogiannisf, C. et al., 2019, 'Residential green space in childhood is associated with lower risk of psychiatric disorders from adolescence into adulthood', *Proceedings of the National; Academy of Sciences*, 116 (11), 5188–5193. https://doi.org/10.1073/pnas.1807504116

Kuo, M., Barnes, M. & Jordan, C., 2019, 'Do experiences with nature effect learning? Evidence of a cause-and-effect relationship', *Frontiers of Psychology*.10 (Article 305), 1–9. doi: 10.3389/fpsyg.2019.00305

Kuo, M., Browning, M.H.E.M., Sachdeva, S. et al., 2018, 'Might school performance grow on trees? Examining the link between 'greenness' and academic achievement in urban, high-poverty schools', *Frontiers of Psychology*. 9, 1669. doi: 10.3389/fpsyg.2018.01669

Muñoz, S., 2009, *Children in the Outdoors: A Literature Review*, Forres, Sustainable Development Research Centre. https://www.ltl.org.uk/wp-content/uploads/2019/02/children-in-the-outdoors.pdf

Planet Ark, 2011, *Climbing Trees: Getting Aussie Kids Back Outdoors.* http://treeday.planetark.org/documents/doc-534-climbing-trees-research-report-2011-07-13-final.pdf

Planet Ark, 2012, *Planting Trees: Just What the Doctor Ordered.* http://treeday.planetark.org/document/doc-812-planting-trees-report-2012-06-25-final.pdf

Wing Tuen, V.L., Tuen Yee, T.T., Wen-Chi P. et al., 2019, 'How is environmental greenness related to students' academic performance in English and Mathematics?', *Landscape and Urban Planning*, 181, 118–124. https://doi.org/10.1016/j.landurbplan.2018.09.021

Wooley, H., Pattacini, L & Somerset-Ward, A., 2009, *Children and the Natural Environment: Experiences, Influences and Interventions - Summary*. Natural England Commissioned Reports, Number 026. https://helenwoolley.wordpress.com/2014/05/27/housing-and-greenspace-children-and-the-natural-environment/

4. Louv, R., 2008, *Last Child in the Woods: Saving Our Children from Nature-deficit Disorder*, rev. ed., Chapel Hill, Algonquin Books of Chapel Hill.

5. A major source of the relevant research is the Child Study Centre at the University of Virginia. See, for example:

    DeLoache, J.S., Bloom-Pickard, M., & LoBue, V., 2010, 'Babies and bears: Human infants' interest in non-human animals'. In P. McCardle, S. McCune, J.A. Griffen, J.A. & V. Malhomes, (eds.). *How Animals Affect Us: Examining the Influence of Human-animal Interaction on Child Development and Human Health.* Washington, DC: NIH.

    Rakison, D.H., 2003, 'Parts, motion, and the development of the animate-inanimate distinction in infancy'. In D.H. Rakison & L.M. Oakes (eds.), *Early Category and Concept Development*, New York: Oxford University Press.

6. Sebba, R., 1991, 'The landscapes of childhood: The reflections of childhood's environment in adult memories and in children's attitudes', *Environment and Behavior*, 23, 395–422. https://doi.org/10.1177/0013916591234001

7. Cunningham, C. & Jones M., 2006, *Middle Childhood and the Built Environment: A Submission to the Parliamentary Committee on Children and Young People*. Chris Cunningham, Margaret Jones and the NAPCAN Foundation, 8. https://www.parliament.nsw.gov.au/ladocs/submissions/44768/ SUBMISSION%20NO29%20NAPCAN.pdf

8. Winton, T. (Writer) & Woldendorp, R. (Photographer), 1999, *Down to Earth: Australian Landscapes*, Fremantle, Australia, Fremantle Arts Centre Press, *xvii*.

9. One of the requirements for the Duke of Edinburgh Award, for example, is an 'adventurous journey' (trek, canoe trip etc) undertaken as an independent venture by candidates for the award.
There are many such programs in the United States of America, and they have emerged in other countries as well. *Operation Flinders* is an Australian example. An account of the rationale underpinning these programs is contained in Wilson, S.J. & Lipsey, M.W., 2000, 'Wilderness challenge programs for delinquent youth: A meta-analysis of outcome evaluations', *Evaluation and Program Planning*, 23, 1–12. doi.org/10.1016/S0149-7189(99)00040-3

10. Ungar, M., 2009, 'Overprotective parenting: Helping parents provide children the right amount of risk and responsibility', *The American Journal of Family Therapy*, 37 (3). doi. org/10.1080/01926180802534247

11. For overviews of the importance of unstructured play for children's well-being and development, see:
Ginsburg, K.R., 2007, 'The importance of play in promoting healthy child development and maintaining strong parent-child bonds', *Pediatrics*, 119, 183–191. doi: 10.1542/ peds.2006-2697
Burdette, H.L. & Whitaker, R.C., 2005, 'Resurrecting free play in young children: Looking beyond fitness and fatness to attention, affiliation and affect', *Archives of Pediatric and Adolescent Medicine*, 159, 46–50. doi:10.1001/archpedi.159.1.46

12. Gray, P., 2011, 'The decline of play and the rise of psychopathology in children and adolescents', *American*

Journal of Play, 3, 443–463. http://www.journalofplay.org/ issues/3/4/article/decline-play-and-rise-psychopathology-children-and-adolescents

13. Brown, S. & Vaughan, C., 2009, *Play: How it Shapes the Brain, Opens the Imagination and Invigorates the Soul,* Penguin, New York.

14. Rossmanith, A., 1997, *When Will the Children Play: Finding Time for Childhood,* Melbourne, Mandarin, 13.

12. An environmental conscience

1. These statements are drawn from the Connectedness to Nature Scale. Mayer, F.S. & Frantz, C.M., 2004, 'The Connectedness to Nature Scale: A measure of individuals' feeling in community with nature', *Journal of Environmental Psychology*, 24, 503–515. doi: 10.1016/j.jenvp.2004.10.001

2. These statements are drawn from the New Ecological Paradigm (NEP) Scale. Dunlap, R.E. Van Liere, K. D. Mertig, A.G. et al., 2000, 'Measuring endorsement of the new ecological paradigm: A revised NEP scale', *Journal of Social Issues*, 56, 425–442. Available at https://www.researchgate. net/publication/279892834_Measuring_Endorsement_of_ the_New_Ecological_Paradigm_A_Revised_NEP_Scale

3. These statements and the ones immediately following are taken from the Dispositional Empathy with Nature Scale. Tam, K., 2013, 'Dispositional empathy with nature', *Journal of Environmental Psychology*. 35, 92–104. doi: 10.1016/j. jenvp.2013.05.004

4. Studies linking empathy and pro-environmental behaviour include:
Schultz, W., 2000, 'New environmental theories: Empathizing with nature: The effects of perspective taking on concern for environmental issues', *Journal of Social Issues*, 56, 391–406. doi: 10.1111/0022-4537.00174
Jaime De Berenguer, J., 2010, 'The effect of empathy in environmental moral reasoning', *Environment and Behavior,* 42,110–134. doi: 10.1177/0013916508325892
Tam, 2013.

5. See Chapter 7 notes for references.

6. Whitburn, J., Linklater, W. & Abrahamse, W., 2019, 'Meta-analysis of human connection to nature and proenvironmental behaviour', *Conservation Biology.* doi.org/10.1111/cobi.13381

7. Schultz, P.W. & Zelezny, L., 1999, 'Values as predictors of environmental attitudes: Evidence for consistency across 14 countries', *Journal of Environmental Psychology*, 19, 255–265. doi.org/10.1006/jevp.1999.0129

    Davis, J.L., Le, B. & Coy, A.E., 2011, 'Building a model of commitment to the natural environment to predict ecological behavior and willingness to sacrifice', *Journal of Environmental Psychology*, 31, 257–265. doi.org/10.1016/j.jenvp.2011.01.004

    Martin, C. & Czellar, S., 2017, 'Where do biospheric values come from? A connectedness to nature perspective', *Journal of Experimental Psychology*, 52, 56–68._doi.org/10.1016/j.jenvp.2017.04.009

    Balundė, A., Perlaviciute, G. & Steg, L., 2019, 'The relationship between people's environmental considerations and pro-environmental behavior in Lithuania', *Frontiers of Psychology*, 15. doi.org/10.3389/fpsyg.2019.02319

    Mackay, C.M.L & Schmitt, M.T., 2019, 'Do people who feel connected to nature do more to protect it? A meta-analysis', *Journal of Environmental Psychology*, 65. doi.org/10.1016/j.jenvp.2019.101323

    Alcock, I., White, M.P., Pahl, S. et al., 2020, 'Associations between pro-environmental behaviour and neighbourhood nature, nature visit frequency and nature appreciation: Evidence from a nationally representative survey in England', *Environment International*, 136.doi.org/10.1016/j.envint.2019.105441

8. Lavelle, M.J., Rau, H. & Fahy, F., 2015, 'Different shades of green? Unpacking habitual and occasional pro-environmental behavior', *Global Environmental Change*, 368–378. doi.org/10.1016/j.gloenvcha.2015.09.021

9. Kellert, S.R., 2012, *Birthright: People and nature in the modern world*, New Haven, Yale University Press.

10. Gergis, J., 2020, 'Witnessing the unthinkable', *The Monthly*, July, 3–14.

11. IPBES, 2019, *Summary for policymakers of the global assessment report on biodiversity and ecosystem services of the Intergovernmental Science-Policy Platform on Biodiversity and Ecosystem Services*. IPBES secretariat, Bonn, Germany.

12. Kellert, 2012, 187.

13. Driscoll, D.A. Garrard, G.E., Kusmanoff, A.M. et al., 2020, 'Consequences of information suppression in ecological and conservation sciences', *Conservation Letters* 2020;e12757. doi: 10.1111/conl.12757

14. Manne, R., 2015, 'Diabolical: Why have we failed to address climate change?', *The Monthly*, 2015 Summer edition. Available at: www.themonthly.com.au/issue/2015/december/1448888400/robert-manne/diabolical

15. These musings are from notes for lectures given by Leopold in the 1940s.

16. *Conference of the Parties to the Convention on Biological Diversity*, Fourteenth meeting, Sharm El-Sheikh, Egypt, 17–29 November 2018, 7.

INDEX